Bloodbath - 18th Street Gang Story

Los Angeles Gang Stories, Volume 1

Tribhuvan and Tribhuvan Singh Shekhawat

Published by Tribhuvan Singh Shekhawat, 2023.

This is a work of fiction. Similarities to real people, places, or events are entirely coincidental.

BLOODBATH - 18TH STREET GANG STORY

First edition. October 29, 2023.

Copyright © 2023 Tribhuvan and Tribhuvan Singh Shekhawat.

ISBN: 979-8223310839

Written by Tribhuvan and Tribhuvan Singh Shekhawat.

Dedicated to my family, school and college friends and the TV Show on History TV Gangland, which covered many Gangs like 18 and MS-13, and this book details a fictional outlook on the life of Bullet David Lopez and his friends, in the end David dies due to an illness, surviving many Gang Wars and Raids from the Police and Other Police Forces.

Bloodbath – an 18th Street Gang story

Background –

The 18th Street Gang was formed in 1950s by Mexican Youth who came to Los Angeles for Protection, only to evolve into a large gang and they function like a Fortune – 500 by having branches called sets or cliques, Los Angeles also called The City of Angels is where they have at least 16 different groups of the same gang, most of them are into Extortions, Distribution of Narcotics, Blackmailing, Car Thefts and even Racial Assaults of Koreans, Blacks and many other groups, this gang has members in America, Mexico, El Salvador, Honduras, Guatemala and Spain, their crimes all together include the following –

1. Drug Trafficking
2. Arms Trafficking
3. Human Trafficking
4. Extortion
5. Blackmailing
6. Murder – For – Hire
7. Auto Thefts
8. Intimidation

One Story of them was famous was called the Columbia Little Psychos story which I heard, 18th Street Gang comes under Mexican Mafia, the story is of a successful ring established by one Juan Romero aka Termite and Francisco Martinez aka Puppet which came crashing down after Martinez House was raided and all the cash was taken away from them under the raid performed by FBI, it was set during late 1990s and early 2000s, Martinez put out a hit or a contract for the murder of Termite, Romero survived and turned himself to the police and gave away information which shut down and got more than 20 members arrested under various charges, Termite is said to have moved away, 18th Street Gang is said to have a mural in the West Lake area of Los Angeles and it has never been painted over even by MS – 13 who are sworn enemies, the mural is said to have the names of atleast multiple

successful names from 18th Street and people from their areas who found success in Business and Acting as well, Termite has his name written there as well, I watched Gangland, which is a documentary covering the fascinating yet deadly stories about various gangs of the United States of America which had Aryan Brotherhood, Mara Salvatrucha 13, Chinese Tongs of San Francisco, Los Zetas Cartel, Barrio Azteca, Vice Lords, Mexican Mafia & Nuestra Familia, Bloods & Crips, Almighty Latin Kings & Queens Nations and even Aryan Circle and mentioned various names like Tom Metzger, Mark Gaspard aka Cowboy, Luis Felipe aka King Blood, Raymond Washington & Stanley Williams aka Tookey, Raymond Chow, Juan Romero aka Termite and Francisco Martinez aka Puppet with Antonio Riojnas among more, I understand many of them would not like being named out and many people will be upset too with this book but I wish to do my best to make sure nobody is hurt plus all characters and incidents mentioned here will be fictional and will have 0 resemblence with any of the above mentioned people, so sit back and enjoy the ride.

Meet Tribhuvan Singh Shekhawat –

Born on September 1st of 2003, Shekhawat is a New Writer on the block, he is a student of Manipal University Jaipur and graduated from Saint Xaviers School Jaipur batch 2022, and lives with his parents, two house keepers, one Golden Labrador Retriever and his Older Brother who is older by four whole years, Shekhawat is the author to Dennis Miller an MMA Story.

Tribhuvan Singh Shekhawat is currently a Bachelor of Computer Application and has one book under his name, he is keen on books about Fighting Sports, Action – Adventure, Romance and Drama Comedy usually and plans to extend his domain too, he is also keen on seeing other countries and learning about them, he has shown interest in Northern American Countries (Canada, America, Mexico, Iceland, Greenland), Caucuses (Russian Republics, Turkic Countries and Azerbaijan), Eastern World (South Korea, Republic of China, Japanese Republic and Mongolia) as well as Nordic Nations (Sweden, Denmark, Finland, Norway and Germany), he is fascinated by Indian, Celtic, Viking, Korean and Slavic Culture and Religions as well as Red American Tribals and their stories too, often listening to podcasts like Survive The Jive, Joe Rogan Expirence etc.

Displayed an interest in Dogs and had owned a German Shephard named Bruno who died after 10 years and a Golden Labrador Retriever named Misthibai or Misthi who is as of now 3 years old, he also likes all types of Bears & Gorillas plus Capybaras and Deers too, he also likes myth creatures like Elves, Dwarves, Giants etc too.

Shekhawat inspiration is The World of Mixed Martial Arts aka MMA paticulary the UFC, Choices Stories you Play by Pixelberry and The Legend of Biker Clubs, and fascination with States of Iowa, Kansas, Arkansas, Mississippi, Mississouri, Colorado and Montana with Idaho and Wyoming is also here, writing gang novels about gangs of Los Angeles and Texas was a wish he always had which is an interesting thing given he comes from a very peaceful home and has nothing special in him except writing books.

Protagonist –

David Lopez aka Bullet is the Protagonist who is a Mexican – American with slightly Reddish – Brown Hair, many Hmongs,

Latinos and Pacific Islanders have similar traits of Lighter Hair and Eye Colours, he is a member of a set in West Lake called West Lake Homies which was created in 2003, been a member of this since 1998, present day is 1999 to 2009, a span of about 10 years or a decade, he is 24 and will age till 34, eventually becoming a member, distribution head, collector, dealer and eventually a shot caller, and eill develop a knack for killing people, losing both his parents in a freak car crash, with his older brother, his cousin Conejo (Rabbit)

recruited him into becoming an 18th Streeter which his family was a part of, he lives initially in Los Angeles and later moves to Fresno, Dallas and Longmont, Fresno is also California, Dallas is in Texas and Longmont is Colorado, Snowfall on FX is a big inspiration in the making of this with Gangland Documentaries as well as Tax Collector, Harsh Times, End of Watch & Street Kings all of which are directed by David Ayer of Hollywood, he is American, let us not confuse him for a South Indian fellow here, the movies were tragic, violent and about drug gangs and warfares between the gangs, most emotional being Harsh Times, End of Watch and Tax Collector, with actors like Christian Bale, Shia Lebouf, Bobby Soto, George Lopez, Jake Gyllanhall and rising UFC Fighter and a Taekwondo + Brazilian Jiu-Jitsu Practitioner Brian Ortega in one cameo as well, and yes the gangs mentioned in here are –

1. 18th Street
2. Surenos (F)
3. MS13
4. Mexican Mafia (F)
5. Bloods
6. Crips
7. Yakuza (F)
8. Triads (F)
9. Aryan Brotherhood (F)

10. Nazi Low Riders
11. Public Enemy Number 1 (F)
12. White Pride
13. Latin Kings
14. Sinaloa Cartel
15. Snakehead
16. Armenian Power (F)
17. Albanian Mafia (F)
18. Aryan Circle
19. Asian Boyz
20. Avenues
21. Logan Heights Gang
22. Playboys-13
23. Florencia-13
24. Azure-13
25. Tiny Rascalz (F)
26. Vice Lords
27. Black Guirella Family
28. Israeli Mafia

And now, let the story begin, after about introducing the author, the character and the gangs, plus the backstories, members of Youth Groups, Law Enforcment, Armed Groups, Smuggling Groups and Bounty Hunters will also be mentioned in here, the time is set in between late 1990s and 2000s, so sit back and enjoy hard.

Season 1, Episode 1-2, California knows how to party –

David Lopez is now a member of 18th Street, born to Construction Workers, Lopez worked at a Theater and a Shopping Mall, but he earned a knack for being violent, beating up on anyone who didn't pay for tickets or was caught stealing, he was eventually under his uncle's care after both his parents died in a Car Crash with his 2 Older Brother and Younger Sister, leaving him and his Younger Brother and Sister named Javier and Rosemary behind, and wanting a better future, Javier and Rosemary parted ways into Dallas and Houston, living with their other Aunties and Uncles, cousin Conejo came back from prison after serving a year on some felony charges, and now he joined 18th Streeters, his family was with them too, and now, David was told about the gang's allies and enemies –

David's room had the list of allies on the left hand side which was –

1. Mexican Mafia & Surenos
2. Armenian Power
3. Inagawa-Kai Yakuza
4. 14K Triads
5. Albanian Mafia
6. Aryan Brotherhood
7. Armenian Power
8. Public Enemy Number 1
9. Fullerton Boys (Korean Gang)
10. Greek Mafia

David's room had the list of enemies on the right hand side which was –

1. MS13
2. Playboys13
3. Florencia13
4. Azura13
5. Bloods
6. Crips

7. Vice Lords
8. Tiny Rascalz
9. Avenues
10. Logan Heights
11. White Pride
12. Snakehead
13. Latin Kings
14. Sinaloa Cartel
15. Nazi Low Riders
16. Israeli Mafia
17. Black Dragons
18. Aryan Circle
19. Born to Kill
20. Asian Boyz

And now, we had disputes over Drug Wars, Contracts and Personal Differences between Individual Gang Members too, and now, we had learnt that members of MS13 are coming here and we went down, now this isn't the Loco West Side, they are Hoover MS and they started shooting down, killing a few members, and now, we had to take revenge and we meet up with the guy who grows and sells weed to us, Bryce James aka Weeder and he mentioned MS13 nonsense and wanted help too, and we agreed to do so, and now, well we realized what had happened one of our members Oscar Ramirez was at a party where a Crip, a MS13 & Asian Boy grouped and began touching a White Blonde Girl, her boyfriend another White Blonde Guy and Oscar came by, the two are in Irish Mob, not a Gang but a Militia instead of Mercenaries and Police Officers, and now the girl pushed the crip and punched him down, he shoot her down, she was pregnant and shoot the boyfriend too, killing both, and Oscar shoot and killed the Crip and Asian Boy, and he was attacked by MS13 Member, only for another MS13 Member to break it up, Crips started shooting, Jamie who stopped Alex from killing Oscar got a heart attack and passed there, and Oscar stabbed Alex, and Alex survived, he was arrested for Sexual Assault, Club Manager responded and mentioned the attacks caused by Crips and MS13 Members, many Crips and MS members are against and dislike sexual assaults but they happen, we also had a few creeps here too, but I am against them and would kill as many as I can, Sexual Offenders, Animal Attackers and anyone who harassed old people and im Game with them actually, anyways and now, we had a run in with members of LA County Sheriff Department and they mentioned members of another clique called Eagles Street, have done some unthinkable things and during a raid, a gunfight happened between MS13 & Sheriff + causing deaths of almost about at least 19 officers and 19 MS Member, 1 cop and member survived, La Eme members were being killed down one after another and a new cop was in town, named James Lincoln Abraham and he wanted that power and he contacted members of Nuestra Familia and Nortenoes, and began working, like he claims we are violent but he keeps and now, he is on a payroll, from White Pride Gangs and member and he is a White Supremacist, but he can be proud of who he is and he can celebrate it, but he cannot attack Non White People and White People who disagree with him, but anyways, that rumor was disproven, he isnt racist or anything, he has friends there too and now, we had a call, Crips and ABZ and MS13 are planning on attacking someone and a break-in happened, and shot caller Armando Cortez called in, his mother and grandmother were killed, he stepped in to stop too, his best friends, another friend, mother and grandmother, kidnapped his daughter and sister away too, his female relatives got gunned down, and now, he wants revenge, and he called West Lake Locos and now, we took up arms, Korea Town members, Community Members mentioned where many members lived and we went in there, there was about 6 of us, and we had pictures clicked where they took his daughter into, they were planning to kill her or sell her out, his wife and sons were also shot and killed, man lost everything, 18th members have committed the same crimes too many times, especially Mexico & Triangle which comprises of Honduras, El Salvador & Guatemala where criminals and corruption made it unlivable there only, causing many to go abroad to America, Mexico, Canada and even Europe and Central Asia, some went to India too, Mumbai, Ajmer, Jaipur, Pune, Ahmedabad, New Delhi and Bangalore are some of the best places too, Bihar and UP are like Gangster's Paradise, and now, we drove to MS Territory, there are many areas in Los Angeles, this was near Koreatown and Chinatown, somewhere in between and now, we got to meet the locals and members of the Irish Militia, who paid us a lot of money about 10K to take them all out, we recognized the shooters, and there was the list of people involved into this –

A. MS 13 Members –

1. Xavier Carlos Rodriguez
2. Brendon Paz
3. Oscar Lopez
4. George Mendez

A. Asian Boy –

1. Cesar In
2. John Vanna
3. Damian Johns
4. Matt Zhang

A. Crips –

1. Jamal Knight

2. Tyrone Smith
3. Jordan Knight
4. Latrelle Jones

And now, we needed to go to Black Areas, Asian Areas and Salvadoran Areas for that, we started with The Crips Jason and Jordan were Somalian Immigrants, Somalis are said to have immigrated around 1800s or so, Chinese and Indians are said to have started Immigration too, I am not sure about it.

And we arrived somewhere at the Hoover Crips areas, and now, we found out there was a party happening there and we crashed it all, Silencers were placed on the guns, and we began moving, there were 6 of us, I with Armando were there and we had Xavier, Herman, Jason and Angel with us, and we got out, here you go, meet the gang first –

1. Armando is the oldest member in here at 34, he runs the gang and smuggling and family businesses too, he does IT Work as well, just became a Widower, brother is in jail with La Eme aka Mexican Mafia
2. Herman is half Indian and half Mexican, his parents died due to Illnesses and his brother is also a gang member but moved away to Texas and Kansas later, he is in love with the sister of Xavier named Carla, not a gang member
3. Jason is another member, he is born to a Hmong Dad and a Samoan Mom, he is having Red Hair and Blue Eyes, a lot of us have them too, partially due to Spanish and English Heritage or just we have the same pigmentation too, dude has a Japanese Girl named Jenny it's a White Name not

Japanese but that is her name

4. Xavier is a member who loves to kill actually and isnt like anyone else around in here, Gangs here do all kinds of stuff together, not just Crimes and Terrorism or Smuggling but also Businesses and all too, he is a Human Calculator actually, loves a Chinese named Marie Zhang Yung, Triad Members sister, we have ties with them too, would marry her soon enough

5. Angel is another member, quiet guy and driver, his sister is Fernanda and she is my girlfriend, and his girlfriend is Ishika, Herman's sister, he is a calm killer and seller too, increases price but saved many from over dosing out as well too, good hearted dude actually

6. Jamie is another member, he is on the run, and he killed members of Bloods, Snakehead and Arabic Armed Groups too, he is a known killer and he is older too, his wife died due to Cancer but left two kids in his name, he had four but the other two died away too, killed by a Crip even though they were friendly to him

7. Felipe is a Samoan – Mexican Man, who dates a nurse named Maya, he is not into Drugs or anything, but still fights for us and attends meetings and stuff, handles packaging and warehousing instead and does well too, good guy actually

Felipe and Maya are out now, but they have heard and Felipe wants blood too and so does Maya.

And now, we got blood ready, and we heard of a party happening and our Samoan friends mentioned it, there are about 6 guys outside on the front lawn, drinking, smoking, partying and taking energy drinks too, we sold out Energy Drinks in back markets with food and clothes too, and like yes and now, back to the mission, we entered a housing project, and with silencers placed on them, we attacked and shot down one member, and he couldn't make noises, and now, after that, and we shot down another member, and realized two of them went inside the house for more beer or bathroom, we killed all four men, and went inside, shooting down the wife and the brother of them all, and now, Armando saw Skull and Korn, kidnapping both of them, Skull and Korn meant unarmed and hurt, we just killed both, and realized MS members raped and killed his daughter and disposed off and crip members sounded happy about it, and we called Yakuza and Triads, we are in league with many clans and some we aren't in touch with is another thing, and now we contacted and heard that their friends have the same issues and we agreed to take out members of MS13 and Asian Boyz and now, Snakehead attacked my girlfriend and she sprayed and shot down one of them, and now Snakehead doesn't have enough members here, they are about to do some stuff, and now they started shooting down and Maya and Felipe somehow talked them out of there, being a medic, he was not respected around either, and now, ladies are dating each other's brothers or gang members are dating each other's sisters both work here, Fernanda and Ishika run a Scamming Scheme around, looting from other ethnic groups too and running honest business, and The Knights renamed their clique as Crip Knights and now, they send more drive-by shootings, and now, Armando realized his son is alive and send him to a relative in Sinaloa, an older aunt and her son, and now, we began working on revenge planning and now, we looked at the new drug crew, like we all have other jobs too and we still fight each other too, and now, we needed to take them all out one after another.

A. MS 13 Members –

1. Xavier Carlos Rodriguez
2. Brendon Paz
3. Oscar Lopez

4. George Mendez

A. Asian Boy –

1. Cesar In
2. John Vanna
3. Damian Johns
4. Matt Zhang

A. Crips –

1. Jamal Knight
2. Tyrone Smith – Knight
3. Jordan Knight
4. Latrelle Jones – Knight

14K Triads brought down payment and told us what is needed to be done, Knights are meant to be taken out, meanwhile Knights attacked and came to our doorstep, killing many members but somehow Mexicans attacked them, and Jamal escaped, Jordan was captured by the cops with Tyrone and Latrelle too escaped down the lane and Armando attacked Latrelle down and tried beating him up, and both with Tyrone ended up in a jail cell, and now Ty and Lat attacked Armando, and he was sent to the hospital and now, we had to take the war to the next level now, and we needed to backup, and now, things were getting sour, when one of our truck employees was killed and steam rolled down, and now, Armando was released and now, Crips, Snakehead, Asian Boys and MS Members teamed up, and we needed to level up the playing field too, and we got help from Surenos, Rascals, Bloods and Irish Militias, and now, we got into a position, and we were attacked by MS 13 members, and now, Armando decided to call a meeting and we agreed to make up a few plans, for us, Knights were the latest, they didn't have enough members, as many members are leaving for better work, many committed suicide and died in car crashes and many shifted to Nigeria and Algeria for Foreign Working Conditions too and now, we began working down on something, and now, Knights and Armando's Rodriguez Family went to Warfare, and now, we began getting deals, and we worked in metal industry, made handguns and bullets and grenades now, and now, Irish Militia reported another incident, killing 3 of the 5 crips and selling the other two away to of course the family of the girl and the girl killed both of them, and now, Militia was something people feared, Crips wanted a War and were bonding black people to join them, and Bloods and Lords attacked us and Avenues, killing a leader and we sat down together and began working out the differences and got together to band up on them, gaining allies from Samoan and Tongan Smugglers and Militias too, and now the war was on, Samoans began joining in Mass and Filipinos too.

And now, war time was on, and now, we began shooting down on them, and began selling LSD and Weed, and began protecting ourselves from the cops and the racist people.

Avoiding fights one after another, and now we all decided to play cards and organize a gambling den, where winners bet on MMA like Iceman and Rampage and Fedor etc. or Boxing as Wladimir Klitschko or Football etc. and even on Reality Shows and Political Elections among more things, and now, we had less shootouts happening and whatnot and now, and now, we needed to work, now with many of us having White or Chinese Wives and Girlfriends and many of our females dating or being married to Chinese and Whites, relations are strengthened to a level, Knights have a Larger

Enemy, getting Drugs from Mexicans, we don't want hard drugs and stuff on our areas, we don't want that smoke, money is something too, and now, we heard of that stuff, and Crips, Asian Boys, Snakehead and MS 13 Members attacked Irish Militia and many of them got killed and mauled by the bears and dogs they own, I mean a Crip tried stabbed a Pitbull who bit down his fingers, alerting other dogs and the Gate Keeper to start shooting at them all and now, the war was on, and now, with that, we began handling the crips, and now we needed to get rid of them, they attacked and killed another one of our members, killed a Samoan for being with us, killed his entire family, and was killed by the police, and now, we called out and agreed to land in a deadly blow to these guys and I looked at the list again.

A. MS 13 Members –

1. Xavier Carlos Rodriguez
2. Brendon Paz
3. Oscar Lopez
4. George Mendez

A. Asian Boy –

1. Cesar In
2. John Vanna
3. Damian Johns
4. Matt Zhang

A. Crips –

1. Jamal Knight
2. Tyrone Smith – Knight

3. Jordan Knight
4. Latrelle Jones – Knight

And now, Jordan Knight and his girlfriend turned Wife Owens was targeted, a Puerto Rican – Black and now, we came across her, and now she killed my cousin sister, payback time, I went in with a silencer on, and shoot her down in the shoulder and neck and walked away, Jordan Knight went in to check on her, and Armando shoot him down, and killed him, no data could back up who killed them, Bloods and MS 13 are the big targets with White Supremacists too, and now, a War was on, Latrella attacked Bloods, actually Jordan Knight survived and was kidnapped down by members of another Surenos gangsters, for killing a gangsters daughter and now, we escaped and a police surveillance cam can catch us, turns out we killed a black lady who worked for them as Owens or Lara Owens was never there and was seen in our regions, Lara killed a member by shooting him and his mom and wife on the heads and just running away.

Season 1, Episode 3-4, Jordan Knight –

And now, we found out, Surenos kidnapped him under orders from The Mexican Mafia, and now, we told the Crips, if we kidnapped Jordan, he would have been dead or treated fairly, something they lacked, they had skinned and killed a bunch of Mexican Workers and Mexican Children too, and they killed the son of a La Eme Member, he worked with Armando's older brother and sister in law Alexa Rodriguez and mother in law Janna Cortez, and now we orders, find and kill the ones responsible, Armando mentioned he had a heart attack and passed away, on the arms of his prison roommate and Aryan Brotherhood Member named Ripper aka Hunter Jackson, who released is coming to work with us, his girlfriend had 4 children and he raises them away from here at a farm in Rural California, he is a Hindu and Neopagan, he is not Racist or anything, he has a disliking for many groups and that is true too, and now he got here and joined in by Association, being friends and stuff, they had fights and arguments too, but they had support, and now, Jordan was sold into a Human Trafficking, we wore masks and were unrecognizable, somehow Knight escaped and Armando and Ripper saw him run away somewhere else and he escaped causing Owens and the Brothers to be happy he has escaped away from custody of the gangsters via Police and Mob intervention, Red Feathers MC Member Magnus freed him actually buying him down, and turning them to Cops, Crips attacked his family too, and he had to pay his grandsons' ransom, he is on his last days he claims, Harley Ares Fitzgerald and his club took many crips out too, many crips are having wars on other crip sets over Human Trafficking too, and now, we needed to edge them all out, Jordan Knight is still alive and Jordan & Latrelle w/ Owens are now at War with us, after we killed another member of theirs prior.

1. MS 13 Members –

    a. Xavier Carlos Rodriguez
    b. Brendon Paz
    c. Oscar Lopez
    d. George Mendez

1. Asian Boy –

    a. Cesar In
    b. John Vanna
    c. Damian Johns
    d. Matt Zhang

1. Crips –

    a. Jamal Knight
    b. Tyrone Smith – Knight

   c. Jordan Knight

   d. Latrelle Jones – Knight

   1. Snakehead –

   a. Xing Jaa

   b. Lang Zu

   c. Wang Li

   d. Jimmy Chan

And now, Jamal knocked on our doors and killed a drug dealer and collected away our cash, killing his wife and newborn too, and now we have no proof against him, and now, we had plans too and now MS 13 and AB and Snakehead Members also started wars, and Snakehead and MS 13 members attacking us, we packed our guns, and opened up shops with White or Red American Employees and began shooting their members not dead but by Tasers, and capturing them and letting them know, the consequences and telling them about Yakuza and 14K Triad Members with us and now, many Snakehead Members changed sets and ran out and now we painted down ABZ, MSX3 and Crips all over, Bloods are 18th went to a war and now, we went to Bloods Projects and loading silencers and blasters, and we hid inside, and now we went out, one after another began killing Blood Members after Blood Members, here is how it happened, remembered the gang –

   1. Armando is the oldest member in here at 34, he runs the gang and smuggling and family businesses too, he does IT Work as well, just became a Widower, brother is in jail with La Eme aka Mexican Mafia

   2. Herman is half Indian and half Mexican, his parents died due to Illnesses and his brother is also a gang member but moved away to Texas and Kansas later, he is in love with

the sister of Xavier named Carla, not a gang member

3. Jason is another member, he is born to a Hmong Dad and a Samoan Mom, he is having Red Hair and Blue Eyes, a lot of us have them too, partially due to Spanish and English Heritage or just we have the same pigmentation too, dude has a Japanese Girl named Jenny it's a White Name not Japanese but that is her name

4. Xavier is a member who loves to kill actually and isnt like anyone else around in here, Gangs here do all kinds of stuff together, not just Crimes and Terrorism or Smuggling but also Businesses and all too, he is a Human Calculator actually, loves a Chinese named Marie Zhang Yung, Triad Members sister, we have ties with them too, would marry her soon enough

5. Angel is another member, quiet guy and driver, his sister is Fernanda and she is my girlfriend, and his girlfriend is Ishika, Herman's sister, he is a calm killer and seller too, increases price but saved many from over dosing out as well too, good hearted dude actually

6. Jamie is another member, he is on the run, and he killed members of Bloods, Snakehead and Arabic Armed Groups too, he is a known killer and he is older too, his wife died due to Cancer but left two kids in his name, he had four but the other two died away too, killed by a Crip even though they were friendly to him

7. Felipe is a Samoan – Mexican Man, who dates a nurse named Maya, he is not into Drugs or anything, but still fights for us and attends meetings and stuff, handles packaging and warehousing instead and does well too, good guy actually

8. Ripper Jackson – Father of 4, Neopagan + Hindu, Red Haired and Green Eyed, he is a Sniper Member for Aryan

Brotherhood and now an MMA Fighter, Biker Club Member, Professional Wrestler, Super-Model and Fighting Coach as well as a Farmer, Businessman and resumed his Medical as well being a Heart Doctor with his wife, Jessica Lindsey Jackson something, his children are Wrestlers and doing Family Businesses with School like Astrid 11, Thora 12, Freya 13 and Asalaug 14 and his sons Thor 8, Magnus 8, Ragnar 9 and Donald 9, dude is 34 and his wife is like 32, he is in the towers nearby

And now, he sniped down a Blood Member, and now, we went inside with the Van, kidnapping down a Bloods Member and making him drive inside, and now he told everyone he may do another trip for personal stuff, lost his family in a Road Rage Brawl, and now, as everyone went inside, we shot him, as he stepped outside, no blood on the van and we got out, and hid, this was a mansion or something, like a small house at the outskirts, and we realized, they made a 70 year old grandmother do it, Ripper's Auntie, Herman was the friend who passed away, Herman Gomez Cortez, he worked here as well, and now, we made her leave and got inside, she was forced to do the dealings and now, Ripper's brother, sister in law, nephews and nieces (Alexander 36, Boudicca 40, Ceaser 16, Augustus 15, Bellatrix 14 and Daphne 13 + twin sisters named as Lagartha 12 and Harley 12) and now, with her husband and brothers passing, she remains and wants her last days in peace, we killed more and more bloods, one after another, Ripper sniped 3 bloods at his rooftop, and now, there were 4 men chilling, Ripper shot one of them, and everyone was shocked, Ripper hid himself, and he sniped another member of the bloods head and chest shots, and he shot a man in his neck, and the 4th man spotted him, Armando shoot him dead, falling from the roof to the dog house, where he was not bitten or anything, the dog was a small one and the dogs climbed him up, he was rude too, and the nicest blood member was Shawn and well we got him to pack and leave Cali with his family, he was well a FBI Informant, and Granny cut the wires and made him leave, a blood member mistakenly shot him instead and now, Granny took a shotgun and told everyone to calm down, knowing the plan, crips began shooting, bloods were killed and Ripper sniped the tires down, allowing AB Members, Outlaw Bikers and Local Rednecks with Irish Militia to shoot them all dead one after another, and Sheriff was coming after the shootings, and everyone ran down, nobody spoke a word, and with a bunch of lies, Sheriff was told into leaving down.

And now, we decided to chill, Ripper and Armando went away and now, Jamie, Angel, Xavier, Herman and Jason got into my car and took off, going away and taking a drift into Los Angeles and now driving West Lake, Pico Union, Chinatown, Koreatown, Hollywood Hills and having fun around in town, picking up Latinas, Asians and Samoans too and now Jordan Knight showed up, and started shooting, in Koreatown, a Korean shot him, in the neck, angrily he killed a Korean family of 4, and stole a car, when cops came by, he drove over a bunch of puppies and a white teenage dog walker, 26 year old Emily Johnson, her boyfriend White Boy Rick 24 is a Skater Boy, she was pregnant with his 2nd child, he drove over him, their son Bo and 2 World War II Veterans and bunch of people, and started shooting more and more people, and Latrelle came by, Owens did too, and now, realising so many dead bodies are around, Felipe and Maya knocked him out and took him into a Van, and drove him off, and he jumped out as they took a break and hitch hiked himself away, before being chased by Magnus and Harley and Other Bikers, and now Latrelle and Owens stayed away too, and now we began chasing away too, he got out, and with a hostage, Ripper's aunt, his cousin is Bentley, Magnus Parker

Gunderson aka Packer, been using Magnus again nowadays that was in-fact his real name, also he changes his name after a while, Icelandic – American Biker, Bentley aka Cumin James McCauley is Ripper's 2nd cousin and he shot the aunt, and Ripper shoot him but he escaped, running over Rip's Nephews and Nieces and shooting his Sister in law as well, a Crip killed his cousin, Cops shoot out killed many Crips and riots began, Latinos and Blacks and Koreans began attacking down on each other and mayhem happened.

And now, bad blood is happening once again, and now Jordan got killed, Triad Member Manny Zhang Lin shot him to death and took advantage, he was caught in the tapes, but he mentioned how Jordan killed his grandmother, mother, sister and daughter, four murders in his family, he and his two sons wanted the murder, and he well walked away, it was in his house, he shot him with a registered gun, and survived, Jordan Knight's family made him an enemy, we brought him here to 18th, send his kids to uncle in Kyrgyzstan Bishkek to study and stuff, and from there to Vietnam and now, we began working, and now I woke up, we were baked, Jordan Knight was seen trying to meet his Korean Ex, she is dating an Indian dude, and a War begins and now, we escaped, and we opened up Identity Thefts, Illegal Racing & Gambling Schemes, and now, we began making money but added Bootlegging and Rumrunning too, and now, we made a good operation without Human Trafficking, Extortion, Blackmail and Narcotics Involvement and Knights are looking when someone dropped dead, a child of ours, and now we wanted revenge and Latrelle and Armando had a confrontation, Maya killed Owens out of anger, she broke into the house to kill Mexicans, Maya and Felipe killed her only, that is what we thought, Owens has been kidnapped and kept there for a few days, Jordan and Latrelle now trust us to be the kidnappers and open warfare is happening, realising she can speak we kept her there with food, water and television, she wanted

Maya dead too, and now we remembered the brothers too, Tyrone is running around, running jeep over puppies, children, disabled veterans and many more female bikers too, dude tried killing Parker's Daughter and got beaten up for it, and no, Bloods pulled him out, the Female Bikers pulled away, they avoid Blacks and Arabs to a level, parker isnt racist but his children usually prefer white and red tribals for company and Indians too, and anyways now, Tyrone killed some members grandmother and tried forcing himself causing Owens to disown him, Jamal and Latrelle and Jordan do not want him around either, but that was proven false he wanted the watch, she headbutted him, stabbed him in the neck, collapsed via heart attack before Tyrone ran out, and now, he flipped over a bunch of people, Jordan and Tyrone on the run and Owens kidnapped down, Latrelle and Jamal began making deals with different group of people one after another and now,

Snakehead Members killed an 18th Streeter from another Clique and now, 4 wars are upon us, recruiting happened, and we now had Surenos behind us and we wailed at other gangs, and now I travelled with a bunch of Surenos smaller groups and we went to a Bloods Neighborhood, about like 20 of us went there, Silencers and Blasters were there, Police cannot enter the neighborhood without consent and stuff, only for MS13 members to be there.

MS 13 Members –

a. Xavier Carlos Rodriguez
b. Brendon Paz
c. Oscar Lopez
d. George Mendez

Paz and Mendez began shooting Bloods, 3 sets were partying when members from Surenos, Latin Kings, MS – 13, Sinaloa Cartel and

18th Streeters and began shooting down and one of our members Jessy Quick got down and shoot down and killed a member, we drove past and Blood Members shot into his directing killing a car driver, his wife and sister, and grandmother got killed too, Quick killed both the children, and moved out, got into the car, drove away, and we did commit down a drive-by shooting, my grandmother passed away, I am the last of my family and I need to get in line, and now, I tackled down a Blood, allowing a Sureno to shoot him thrice in the guts down and a member behind me and now, we escaped, Jessy and Us left and a shootout happened between Latinos, Blacks and The Cops where Cops ended up killing many from both sides and lost many of their own too, we went in there undetected and got out quickly too, and now, Mexican Mafia Tax Collectors named Michael Lopez and Ivan Hernandez aka Caleb and Denny came by, and began telling us what to do, and now, we needed to have a major leader killed, Owens suffered memory loss, Jamal and Tyrone went into Prison and Latrelle and Jordan came back and made deals with Guerilla Family and that did not work out, and they attacked Maya and Felipe, Owens couldn't be found and a Festival was hosted, and the two celebrated their marriage happening, and we visited Tyrone and Jamal and demanded to end the war to which both refused down and ABZ and MS and SH members were already coming in, and we meet Snakehead Members – Xing Jaa, Lang Zu, Wang Li and Jimmy Chan and now, they told us to check our surroundings and shot and killed a member of Crips hiding and ended the war revealing they were never there to attack or pickup females, they have females and they wanted revenge on Crips and MS 13 Members and even ABZ and now we formed an Alliance, War b/w Triads, Yakuza and Snakehead was also over too, and now, Jamal and Tyrone ordered a hit from their prison cell, but anyways, we organized a festival at our homeland, I mean our homes and began working on a housewarming party and we found out Owens was at their basement and we did the famous thing, she lost all of her memory and now, we gave her food and stuff, Jamal and Tyrone may come back after us.

And now, well Jamal and Tyrone killed Eme Members with NF Members and now, Armando's Brother was sent to Colorado Supermax something and now, well the party happened and we had a good time too, I loved every single bit of it all actually, it is 1998 and now, we had chilled bears and a fun time, and now, we needed to do something against some people and now, we begin, Hermanos (Spanish for Brothers) organized a Party and rolled into a Bowling Park, and Knights started firing again, and now, we escaped, a few non-gangster friends got clipped and killed and our party was cancelled as another shootout, Jordan and Latrelle came out and Armando swore killing them all, they killed his son too, his last family, he survived and Armando swore revenge now, having nothing left to live for now, swore revenge, Jamal realized they killed the wrong man, as their family was killed by MS13 members and they targeted the wrong person, Snakehead agreed to help in, but many sets are still against us and now, we still fight them and now, we began taking out food and cheering up Armando, who is too upset but not bitter, and now, well a Crip attacked us, shooting him in the shoulder instead and now, we escaped and he was shot dead, menace of Latino and Black Gangs has increased more and often now, and we needed to deal with them too, and now, Jamal, Jordan, Tyrone and Latrelle with Owens who isnt on sight, her husband name was Greg Jackson, he was mixed race with African, Indigenous and Latino Ancestry, he and her sons passed away, the daughters ran away, she like Armando is the last one, she is also at odds with her family, turns out she isnt a Knight, she just works for them, and they ratted her out and she wants revenge, Armando and his wife were close friends, and they weren't boyfriend and girlfriend.

And now, Owens was sent out, surviving and revealing she was never their sister and sent to another state, Owens survived, and now, well we had to deal with the brothers Jamal, Latrelle, Tyrone & Jordan Knights, and Snakehead formed a partnership around with us and we formulated down a plan to take down the Knight Brothers just as that when Asian Boyz and MS 13 members attacked us all down, and remember their names too

MS 13 Members –

    a. Xavier Carlos Rodriguez
    b. Brendon Paz
    c. Oscar Lopez
    d. George Mendez

Asian Boy –

    a. Cesar In
    b. John Vanna
    c. Damian Johns
    d. Matt Zhang

Cesar In and John Vanna attacked our gang and began shooting killing a few of our members and Snakehead chased them down, killing some of their too, shooting at the back seats while wearing masks and running off too and now we began working down on some of these issues and began formulating down a plan against the groups to kill away as many members as we can because they don't like us and we called Irish Mob, Yakuza ad Triads for help down the lane and that was enough said and done and I played out a song by David Bowie called h=Heroes=s and we began working down on that one, Brown Bears & Red Feathers Members were attacked into a shootout too, and now things got ugly, their new leader, Bottles aka Bjorn Hermanson was a Mercenary, MMA Star, Professional Wrestler and a Street Fighter too, dude is a successful businessman, and they killed his son, a 10 year old boy, he has 2 sons and 2 daughters at 33, marrying at 23, but a mutual divorce happened as Karen married Gareth James another RFMC Member who with her died, Bjorn married Lagartha Sigmarson (Featherwoods MC President) and had 3 children more, and now, with that both want revenge, recruitment happened and now, the sister Owens escaped, and died in a Car Crash, she was killed by the police, after she shot and killed ½ of a Patrol Car, another officer shoot her dead down and we all remained inside, except some of the Unarmed Members and now we helped her out and put her in City Morgue where Tyrone, Jamal and Jordan found out about it and began a shooting spree down too, killing members after members and their family members too and we needed to deal with that, Jordan Knight killed more people and now, Warzone was On, Snakehead pulled out due to some personal issues and now they are out of drug and weapons business and now, we had 2 gangs at 1 go and now we were battle born too.

And now, we began working on our schemes, Felipe and His Wife moved out, Owens got killed lol, and now, we had to seal all the deals with Knights after all, and now shit got serious, and Knights made a deal with Black Guerilla Family and now, they killed one of our members down.

Season 1, Chapter 5 & 6, Knights Vendetta –

And we made a plan, that is to take out one of the Knight Brothers, Shawn Knight got out of prison, and now he was running the show with Daniel Knight, another mob boss and now things were getting out of hand, and now, we got word that Snakehead Members had a giant shootout and that left many dead as a 6-way shootout happened.

1. Los Angeles Police + SWAT Teams
2. Snakeheads
3. Ku Klux Klan
4. Sheriff Department
5. MS 13 Members
6. Mexican Mafia + Sinaloa Cartel

And that resulted in disbanding of Snakehead Chapters as they all died, I mean Cartel brought Grenade and Rocket Launchers and Sheriff and Cops shot each other down and dead instead too, and now all of that happened and many people died, and now, Snakehead Members came here and joined 18th Street Gang instead and now, we have numbers and diversity too, and now with that, Jamal and Tyrone Knight began sending people after us and began a streak of killing and now, we got into a fight with some Brown Bears MC Members and now well we challenged them to a 4 vs 4, got beaten up quick, Romero retired and leads a chapter in Tijuana with Rana, now it is George Pettis aka Phenomenal One, dude thinks he is AJ Styles, I am a MMA Fan, he watches PFLMMA and Bellator MMA a lot, I am a One Championship and UFC fan, and now, we began laying grounds against Knight Brothers and revenge happened too, we attacked a Red Feather Member and he brought a giant beardog, now I made a mistake, head butting him, Ken the owner wanted to apologize, and we made a scene, he beat me and Jose up, and Jose tried shooting, the dog started playing with him, causing me to tell him to not shoot, he cocked the gun, dog bit the hand, with that Shawn and Daniel killed some more of our members and attacked Felipe and Maya, where both of them began shooting, killing Latrelle Knight, causing Shawn to kill both of them and their children, and now it was time for revenge and payback, Latrelle the Asshole is still alive, unfortunately and we kidnapped him, we took him to our room, he escaped and ran off, and contacted Shawn & Daniel Knight who came to his rescue too, they have cousins in other states, some of the most crazy motherfuckers and bastards for sure, and these guys have a long story of Murder, Trafficking, Extortion and Smuggling too, working on making illegal energy drinks and selling them on the black market, stole from us and now, we are ready, Felipe and Maya and the entire family was buried down and good people were taken away, Lat and Tyrone will come back again for sure now, and we began shooting down, attacked MS 13 members down too, and now, Felipe and Maya died Jordan Knight killed them and now we are ready to take Jordan Knight out only, and now, we began smuggling in Phenethyl & Heroine plus Energy Drinks and sold them underground and ran clinics too, and now with that we began working on taking Knight Family out and now, it was us vs them again, and now Snakehead came back to help us all out and we formulated a plan to kill Jordan Knight, Felipe kids were killed too, Jordan really had zero fear of people and now, we wanted to put the fear of god in that man again and we began working on it, and now, we needed to find out more about that man and his dealing partners, and we approached down one gang he worked down with which was Vietnamese and told them we will do work better and at a lower price and they cut ties with Knights and began working for us and we sold them drugs and now, Knights lost a source or stream of income and money down the lane, we chilling with stuff and doing what we do the best and now, we had a meeting and I checked the deck again.

1. Armando is the oldest member in here at 34, he runs the gang and smuggling and family businesses too, he does IT Work as well, just became a Widower, brother is in jail with La Eme aka Mexican Mafia

2. Herman is half Indian and half Mexican, his parents died due to Illnesses and his brother is also a gang member but moved away to Texas and Kansas later, he is in love with the sister of Xavier named Carla, not a gang member

3. Jason is another member, he is born to a Hmong Dad and a Samoan Mom, he is having Red Hair and Blue Eyes, a lot of us have them too, partially due to Spanish and English Heritage or just we have the same pigmentation too, dude has a Japanese Girl named Jenny it's a White Name not Japanese but that is her name

4. Xavier is a member who loves to kill actually and isnt like anyone else around in here, Gangs here do all kinds of stuff together, not just Crimes and Terrorism or Smuggling but also Businesses and all too, he is a Human Calculator actually, loves a Chinese named Marie Zhang Yung, Triad Members sister, we have ties with them too, would marry her soon enough

5. Angel is another member, quiet guy and driver, his sister is Fernanda and she is my girlfriend, and his girlfriend is Ishika, Herman's sister, he is a calm killer and seller too, increases price but saved many from over dosing out as well too, good hearted dude actually

6. Jamie is another member, he is on the run, and he killed members of Bloods, Snakehead and Arabic Armed

Groups too, he is a known killer and he is older too, his wife died due to Cancer but left two kids in his name, he had four but the other two died away too, killed by a Crip even though they were friendly to him

7. Felipe is a Samoan – Mexican Man, who dates a nurse named Maya, he is not into Drugs or anything, but still fights for us and attends meetings and stuff, handles packaging and warehousing instead and does well too, good guy actually

And with Felipe Gone and Maya dead too, we wanted revenge and nothing more than that, and now, plotting was going on too well, we wanted to have a little focus first on Knights and now, the ladies walked in, as I stated Jenny sees Jason, Ishika sees Angel, Herman and Carla together, Xavier and Marie together and I am with Tracy I remember now, AGC Andy is so good, I mean I forget peoples name like Andy Cox makes amazing videos no denying and now, we began looking out and now Latrelle, Jordan, Tyrone and Jamal Knight have declared down a War, killing a pregnant Hispanic Women and her Children, while making the man watch it all happen, killing him too, people are dangerous nowadays.

And now, we needed to do something about that, and we need to plan it all down big enough to make a ruckus and a message has to be send down, we are not letting the Knights take our business away, when a MS member killed their wives, in laws, kids and parents down and this is where Race Wars started down, and we did not kill any innocent black here, and now, with the Yakuza we began drug distribution center, now we turned towards underground markets, buying from super markets and selling them at a little premium, and now, we began selling away sting and monster cans in secret and it was unlicensed down and now, we had parties, and we stalked Jordan Knight planning our first kill, and that was where we are jumped again.

MS 13 Members –

   a. Xavier Carlos Rodriguez
   b. Brendon Paz
   c. Oscar Lopez
   d. George Mendez

Asian Boy –

   a. Cesar In
   b. John Vanna
   c. Damian Johns
   d. Matt Zhang

And now, we heard that John Vanna attacked and send his best shooters, killing the girls, Tracy survived, the wives and kids were killed and now, we had a suicide too, and now revenge was needed and we began to formulate a plan, and we called in Tongan Gangsters too who too have faced losses from the likes of MS Members and together we banded together and began working together, Tongans kidnapped and tortured a MS Member who wont speak up, we had to beat him down and he got shoot up, he was a child killer and he murdered Aaron's kid, Aaron leads Tongan Crips and he isnt too happy about that either, causing him to unload the clips on him and now, ABZ and MS and Bloods under Knights called Knight Bloods and now, we began dealing Cocaine and Weapons, and made fortune, keeping the cops away, we saved a few druggies from overdosing down, and now, we needed to stay away from many things, and now, we recruited Marlon Vasquez, Ecuadorian Immigrant with Korean Heritage too, mom and dad died and siblings too, took him in, he was a crazy kid at 14, and now I and Tracy are like Parents Marlon became a pickpocket and now he began dealing with issues here and there and now, well we needed to do some to Jordan Knight and he went into Knight area, with a pocket knife, stabbed an innocent girl and killed her down, and began searching down for one of the Knights, killing their 6 year old nephew too, and now, Jordon Knight attacked him and he shoot Jordan Knight three times in the ribcage and stomach, and he was hospitalized and he escaped down, and now, we felt bad too and now, we found out where Knight was and pulled the plug, no we didn't pull it, he did make it, he lost his memories and went into asylum, and now, Jordan came out one day and began looking for Marlon Vasquez and Tracy shoot him in his knee, and I shot him in the head, we kidnapped him and took him secluded and had him killed there, and now one of the four knights was dead, their other two died due to Cancer and Car Accidents, leaving Tyrone, Jamal and Latrelle Knight to take care of the business.

Season 1, Chapter 7, Gang Politics

And now, Latrelle and Jamal and Tyrone are mad at us all too

MS 13 Members –

1. Xavier Carlos Rodriguez
2. Brendon Paz
3. Oscar Lopez
4. George Mendez

Asian Boy –

1. Cesar In
2. John Vanna
3. Damian Johns
4. Matt Zhang

Asian Boy began shooting down and killed some people too, and in the massacre, Tracy survived and killed JK or Jordan Knight for what he did, they and MS raped and molested and killed our nieces, wives, mothers, sisters, daughters and girlfriends down and with that, they cannot get away with that one, and now, we began shooting down, and now we needed to take out one more, and Matt Zhang and his 5 friends were arrested by the police, it was our house and we had guns with numbers on them, police did not arrest anyone, 2 cops killed 4 AB Members down too, and now, we got a call, members of Sinaloa Cartel showed up, this branch isnt selling weapons or drugs or anything but run a logistics and armed contractorship, and now, they told us they wanted to recruit and they recruited Marlon among others and now we began learning their ways of fighting and training ourselves down and began working up, and now, we used the strategic assault at an MS – 13 Party, sneaking up from behind and doing a shootout with silencers, shooting down the teenagers one by one, shooting them all down, and killing an adult member down too, and now It was all up on a hill with water tower, and nobody realized 6 bodies were lying on one side, and there were like 8 more on the outside, Sinaloa Cartel and 18th Street Gang together killed MS 13 members, writing 18 all over them as 666, XV3, XVIII or 18th and now, we were ready for their attacks and they came in, and I shoot down 2 of their own members and killed them, when from behind Tracy stabbed a member in his eye when Jason, Herman and Xavier came in, Xavier got married to his girlfriend, Marie and Janie got hurt, been in ICU for Months now, and Ishika is going good, leaving with Angel somewhere in Texas, she is a doctor, joining a local clique but transfer did not work, and now the ladies are busy too and now she got to stay here for a month but Ishika and Angel may go away at any point and now, sadly they were attacked by MS-13 Members and Ishika is in a Coma, Angel is somewhat on a Wheelchair too, and now revenge is going to happen, Justin Gaethje beat Dustin Poirer, Bobby Green beat Tony Ferguson, Derrick Lewis and Kevin Holland won their fights at @UFC291 and Danny Sabatello lost but he will get Magomed back in a rematch @bellatorxrizin2 and Kyoji Hariguchi is fighting for Bellator MMA Flyweights or 125 pounds Championship and I hope he wins this, Justin Gaethje and Colby Covington are getting their 3rd Title Shots, both men better win, Sean Strickland & Stipe Miocic can always have rematches, Jon is 35 and Stipe is 37, both are at the end of their careers in Mixed Martial Arts, ironically Steve Borden aka Sting is jumping and doing outside dives at 64, he is a Childhood Hero of mine too, Wolfpack Sting was awesome too.

Latrelle Knight and MARA-13 Members began another attack, ambushing the house party and killing 13 members, how did they do it, they snuck inside, shooting people with silencers, now people here are drunk too, shooting drunk members down and ran off, Mara – 13 and Knights and now, we began to know of their plots and Asian Boyz attacked my house, Tracy and I shoot down 1 guy, and we found out there will be 4 more inside and 1 outside, I strangled a guy down, and Tracy told me a guy coming our side, we have stun guns too, Tracy called the police, we are at an apartment outside the hood, and Tracy grabbed the man down and chocked him out, when I held the other two at gunpoint and told them to kneel down, and the police showed up and took everyone in, and now Asian Boyz did not realize they had Informants and Federal Agents in there too, and now, we went back home, Marlon came bruised and bloodied, and now, Latrelle Knight was coming in with 3 goons, when Rednecks began firing shots at The Knight goons, they raped someone's older daughter down and pimped her, she was killed, Knights kidnapped the underaged girls too, usually

Rednecks, and Trevor, Mitchell and James didn't back off, I handed Marlon a Gun, shooting Latrelle Knight on the face, and I got another Gun, shooting a second goon down, when Marlon fired another shot, and I shot and killed the 3rd goon, there were 6 of them, the other 2 came inside, when Mitchell and James got them, Trevor was crying when his daughter is dead, he has 4 daughters now, they killed the oldest 2 and his wife, he is only 34 though.

And now, Marlon took him to his room, he is in Peckerwoods Group but he is neither a Racist, Criminal or a Bodybuilding Jerk or anything, he has friends in a Biker Club too, and losing everything but he has his daughters, one of them bit Jordan's arm and fingers when he killed the mother and ran off, and the police came by, Knights have been kidnapping and pimping girls below 20 and selling to big elites, many of them were arrested down and imprisoned, many would die in there only and now, and now, Mara 13 members are also here, they engaged down into a war with other 18th Cliques too now, and we needed to take out someone, Tracy mentioned fending off MS13 members, Knight Brothers Mother and Father and other siblings, Jordan and Tyrone are Brothers the rest are cousins they have a brother named Shawn who is married to Shannon, she is also black, but she likes Hispanic Culture, they died many years ago, mother is alive, father and Shawn died in a Car Crash, my parents car, Shannon died in a Heart Attack, John is going to a College, and mother Delilah and father Samuels were the family, Samuels left Stealing decades ago, Delilah doesn't believe in revenge, knowing her sons failed her by Child Prostitution but I believe she would not be okay but I heard a word she passed away too when she got hit by a car and shoot in the back of her head by a member of 18th not our clique we renamed ourselves again as Red Locos now.

MS 13 Members –

1. Xavier Carlos Rodriguez
2. Brendon Paz
3. Oscar Lopez
4. George Mendez

Asian Boy –

1. Cesar In
2. John Vanna
3. Damian Johns
4. Matt Zhang

Damian Johns is our next target and TRG aka Tiny Rascals Gangster attacked and killed Damian and his entire family (Parents, Siblings, Kids) his wife survived but a MS member killed her down, Matt Zhang and John lost their girlfriends and children already, Cesar In and his wife lead the group, and now we need to kill his wife and sister and get to him, and first we came across Matt Zhang and his 3sons, and Xavier shoot all of them in broad daylight and ran off, he was a mask, a hyena mask and ran off, and now, it made highlights, and we hid him away and stashed his clothes elsewhere, and now, John and Ceaser remain, Snakehead attacked and killed everyone, Cesar lost his wife, mother and sister now, and John barely survived, Snakehead Members left the city now, and we got to do something up, it was not going well enough and now we needed a break and went to a Football and a Baseball stadium for fun, and now, we like football like that is a blast, we had Avenues, Nazi Low Riders, Hoovers, Yakuza, Samoans and many more in there, there were Armed Groups, Biker Clubs, MMA Fighters, Mercenary Contractors and Military Veterans on one side, and there were us criminals and robbers on the other side and now, Avenues mentioned Knights and I told them about it, they killed their mother and sisters down, and we told them to deal with the Knights and they are Bloods and they had rolling 20s and other bloods come in and start shooting down, and now we jumped and a shooting happened again, Koreans ambushed them with Japanese and Mexicans and killed many behind and sped off when cops came and cops were gunned down too, and killed many of the bloods, and now a group of raids happened, like many of Surenos attacked and killed Blood Members and bombed their tat shops down too,

and now, Bloods and 18th clashed down daily and we attacked Bloods too, and we are rallying away on working for smaller gangs and avoiding police raids and all, checking each other's phones to make sure nobody is a rat or a snake either, and now, we were attacked down and many gunned down by Bloods and Asian Boyz and now, we needed to get revenge and end them all, leaving MS13 behind and we called Avenues Leader/Shot-Caller Rolly Alvarez and he got his homeboys in a war with MS13 Members and now,

Avenues & 18 started selling cocaine and 38th and MS bonded up now besides that, Latrelle and Jordan are dead, leaving Tyrone and Jamal are the ones alive, and now with that happening and now, we got down and begin thinking ways to get on the inside members when Mexican Mafia send in member Rafael Velasquez and John Vasquez and they joined in on our operations too, Marlon and Xavier checked down on Angle and Ishika with Tracy and Marie there too, and an Earthquake happened, the building collapsed and a thunder strike put down another nail in the coffin too, and Tracy was the survivor and now with everyone else gone or thought to be gone, I got Ishika, Angel, Marlon, Marie etc to leave the city away as Raf and John ordered us to, and now, SWAT Teams raided our homes, we don't keep drugs or unregistered weapons at home and got away with them, Koreans and Mexicans are at a War,

Avenues and Border Brothers raided down a Korean Grocery Store and now Rooftop Koreans are back and they were shooting down people, and they killed 3 of our own members too and now, we needed to end Asian Boyz, John and Raf agreed, and we ambushed and killed Cesar In and sent a message, Mexican Mafia and Surenos broke down and killed many members and we all made an escape, and now, War was Over, Jamal and Tyrone are still around.

MS 13 Members –

1. Xavier Carlos Rodriguez
2. Brendon Paz
3. Oscar Lopez
4. George Mendez

Asian Boy –

1. Cesar In
2. John Vanna
3. Damian Johns
4. Matt Zhang

Damian and Cesar are dead, Matt and John survived and went into prison where greenlight killed Matt and John died fighting TRG Members and TRG made ties with Mexican Mafia, Raf and John aren't bad people, they seem pretty cool for 30 year olds actually and now, we began It all with MS13 but Raf and John took us to a basketball courthouse and had a meeting and now, we had a meeting with Surenos who were at a Race War with Pacific Islanders and Eastern Asians and now, there were about 4000 Surenos when Police Officers called for backup and someone threw a bomb and we open fired, the police killed 4 gangsters and ran off, when SWAT Teams, ATF, FBI, ICE, HSI, DEA, LAPD and Sheriff Department came by and a full blown war happened, after killing a few we all from Red Locos escaped Raf and John too were saved, and now, an all out riot had happened, and now we had 50 Northerners coming in with ABZ and the shootout happened and we all escaped when a crackdown happened and now, with that, we shifted underground, fearing the clique may disband now, we began working with Sinaloa, Raf and John were wanted by the police and we took them away from Los Angeles under Fake Passports and now, we stayed cool for weeks and now, with Tyrone and Jamal sending goons here for Angel and Xavier, Angel killed Jamal out of anger and Tyrone was captured by the police and taken into custody and now, we learnt Avenues wiped down remaining Knight Bloods and took their children and sold them too, they run Human Trafficking too, and Tracy and I got married and one year had passed, she is my best friend too, and Tyrone came back with MS Members, joining MS13 and now on a revenge path, and now, he broke in and killed everyone, Tracy survived, Angel and Ishika and everyone else died, I became Shot Caller, killing Tyrone there only, and his MS 13 Friends, it was my house, another self defense situation and now,

I got them out, and got 18th Street Members to leave Organized Crime, Violence and Narcotics behind and sent most of them to School, College and Offices, Marlon and I formed a way to defeat down MS 13 Members too, and now, Los Avenues attacked us down, Los Conejo and El Rincon attacked and killed more of our members, and we formed a Hit Squad for this purpose down, and now, we tore down Asian Boyz and Knights and concentrated down on MS13 Members and started to target them all down, and called a peace via Mexican Mafia.

Season 1, Chapters 8 – 9, MS vs 18th –
And now, with that, we needed to rid down MS – 13 Members down and now, we began working on the members and starting down a new chapter, Tracy and I had twins Maverick and Goose

from Top Gun and now we had the list below and did a plan to fight the MS13.

MS 13 Members –

1. Xavier Carlos Rodriguez
2. Brendon Paz
3. Oscar Lopez
4. George Mendez

Mendez was spotted and now we agreed on there, when other leaders of 18th Street Gang and Members of Los Avenues El Rincon and Conejo came by, being members of Mexican Mafia with Rafael and John, and they took us to the summit, now in Los Angeles, we had Hispanic, African, Caucasian, Eastern Asian, Southeast Asian, Pacific Islanders, Native Americans and Middle Easterners and there was an all out War, Caucasian or White Gangs don't do much anything, Latin Kings and Nortenos want to fight too, and an all out war was happening down the lane, and now, Marlon and I represented with Tracy staying behind, everyone was dead, and El Rincon and Conejo joined in, Avenues & 18th Street were both now friends, we funded Food Businesses and turned an eye down.

And now, we began working on it, and now, we saw MS-13 Members and a large Police Squad came down, as members from the Los Angeles Police Department, Orange County Sheriff Department, Bureau of Alcohol, Tobacco and Firearms, Drug Enforcement Agency, SWAT Teams and Many More came in and began shooting down, and many members were killed down, one of the EMEs was a Snitch, and now, we all were taken, lack of evidence, got us out, and now, there must have been 100s of Snitches, Rats and Insiders for them and now, we focused down on MS13 and now, Mendez attacked us all, killing the grandmother of Rincon and Conejo, and now, we wanted revenge, their kids were killed down too, and we got ready for a War, and now, I was playing down some songs in my playlist.

[Verse 1]
I got a long way to go
And a long memory
I been searching for an answer
Always just out of reach
Blood on the floor
Sirens repeat
I been searching for the courage
To face my enemies
When they turn down the lights
[Chorus]
I hear my battle symphony[1]
All the world in front of me[2]
If my armor breaks[3]
I'll fuse it back together[4]
Battle symphony
Please just don't give up on me
And my eyes are wide awake
[Bridge]
For my battle symphony
For my battle symphony
[Verse 2]

---

1.   https://genius.com/11571844/Linkin-park-battle-symphony/I-hear-my-battle-symphony-all-the-world-in-front-of-me

2.   https://genius.com/11571844/Linkin-park-battle-symphony/I-hear-my-battle-symphony-all-the-world-in-front-of-me

3.   https://genius.com/11848682/Linkin-park-battle-symphony/If-my-armor-breaks-ill-fuse-it-back-together

4.   https://genius.com/11848682/Linkin-park-battle-symphony/If-my-armor-breaks-ill-fuse-it-back-together

They say that I don't belong
Say that I should retreat
That I'm marching to the rhythm
Of a lonesome defeat
But the sound of your voice
Puts the pain in reverse
No surrender, no illusions
And for better or worse
When they turn down the lights
[Chorus]
I hear my battle symphony
All the world in front of me
If my armor breaks[5]
I'll fuse it back together[6]
Battle symphony
Please just don't give up on me
And my eyes are wide awake
[Bridge]
If I fall, get knocked down
Pick myself up off the ground
If I fall, get knocked down
Pick myself up off the ground
When they turn down the lights
[Chorus]
I hear my battle symphony
All the world in front of me
If my armor breaks[7]
I'll fuse it back together[8]

5.　　　https://genius.com/11848682/Linkin-park-battle-symphony/If-my-armor-breaks-ill-fuse-it-back-together

6.　　　https://genius.com/11848682/Linkin-park-battle-symphony/If-my-armor-breaks-ill-fuse-it-back-together

Battle symphony
Please just don't give up on me
And my eyes are wide awake
For my battle symphony
For my battle symphony

Linkin Park was a great band and now, George Mendez is going for a Land Grab, when we covered down our Tattoos and went into a Cassata and attacked and killed 3 members down, with Silencer Guns, killing George's Family, newest member Alexander Rodriguez slaughtered everyone down and we went away, before anyone noticed it, and the drug stashes were gone, and George attacked the Bikers, Peckerwoods, Rednecks, Cowboys and Bouncers nearby and now, someone ended up dead, and now, they found out we killed them when one member who had cameras installed showed the footage and Lopes now called in for a War, with Crackdown on LA Gangs in full swings happening, many members of Avenues, Border Brothers, MS13, 38th St, 18th St, Eme, AB, Sinaloa Cartel, Latin Kings, AC, Nazi LR, PEN1 DS, and many more were behind bars now, and now, George Mendez was lured into the shadows under the cloak of nightfall and now, Rincon and Conejo were there waiting for him and now, with a massive earthquake happening and houses being thrown down, many of us took shelter in warehouses and trucks down the lane, and now, we did do Home Invasions, and took over various Cassitas for housing and now, MS13 Members attacked again and George Mendez is a target now, Gregory Mendoza is a new member for

7.   https://genius.com/11848682/Linkin-park-battle-symphony/If-my-armor-breaks-ill-fuse-it-back-together

8.   https://genius.com/11848682/Linkin-park-battle-symphony/If-my-armor-breaks-ill-fuse-it-back-together

us and he mentioned about MS13 Members in Arizona, Texas and New York, and how terror of MS works.

And now, Gregory Mendoza was initiated, George got Tracy, Maverick and Goose kidnapped but in his gang they had an 18th, Marlon had a cousin Jessy and he and Tracy worked in when Rafael got EME Members to release her, and taking advantage, Mendez was drugged and killed by Jessy, who deserted and joined 18th Street Gang, and with Mendoza getting Mendez killed, we moved past ahead too and Oscar Lopes is next in line for sure, Brendon Paz got his Gang Members to come down to our area and started firing, killing a gang affiliate and his son, and now, War was on, they killed down the wife too and the daughter, leaving behind 1 son and we got him into my house, and now Brendon Paz and Oscar Lopes starting a fight, Jamal and Tyrone survived is what they claimed but Hermanos we had them killed and now, I had a meeting with Gangmates.

Jessy – "we need to take out Brendon Paz and Oscar Lopes, they have a warehouse, we are in Pico Union and they have 1 – 10 freeway, we need to throw them off guard and maybe get Avenues help "

Conejo – "Avenues and 38th St are beefing now, and we wont have help, besides Avenues got 800 – 900 members and we have more than a thousand or let us say 1200 "

John – "Rincon, Jessy, Marlon and David w/ Tracy go there and scout out the area with the troopers, loyalty will be decided, and now let us get it done "

Raf – "We want Lopes or Paz dead, it is bad if neither dies and even better if both men die, if they are unavailable, kill whosoever we can, avoid the police "

Rincon – "David what do you say? Will Tracy do this? She would be a good doctor soon enough "

I said "We will get Business done, after this no more drugs, let us be a street gang but no killings, Jessy better stay behind and we get gear, masks and armor, silencers and big guns, handguns and knives, at midnight, we go to their hangout, scope in, scope out, kill everyone, take a member down, take drugs, weapons, contraband, money, whatever else we can get and then we bounce, see if they have our missing friends and family members too "

Conejo – "Good thinking and let us go get it done "

We Spent Time dressing in Armors/Vests, Masks, Black Cloths, Masks, Handguns and Rifles down, Knives in and we started doing this, and now, we saw Paz and Lopes leave, 5 members, 2 outside and 3 inside, 1 has his girlfriend watching too, and now we got out, and walked up to them, White Boy and his girlfriend kissing are our Irish Friends from Irish Armed Group, they and their friend Freddy, is an Avenue and they moved out, claiming to buy coffee, and we moved in, and I held a member down at Gunpoint, and two more were had Guns aimed at them, and the women at the counter was having Conejo who winked, the women left and Conejo killed a member, freed someone from the other room, and told a member to get his clothes, after the victim who the clothes, Conejo shot the man dead, John and Raf killed the two men and I pulled the trigger too, like we will tell you how this all happened, Irish Mafia has ties with MS13 for a while now, and their members were there and an Avenue discussing outside, Conejo told them to leave, and we got in, and did the job, and well we send them a message, walking in and yes, they do Child Prostitution and I got the children to go with Conejo in his Van, we washed some of their Cocaine down, and now, Brendon Paz and Oscar Lopez with 6 more had a shootout with Crash Officers, 4 Officers and 8 MS-13/MSX3 Members and Crash Officers killed Brendon Paz and Oscar Lopes, and finally after that, we had one member remaining and he would recruit more members, but clashes and raids got many to leave, turn against, change gangs or become inactive, and now, Xavier Carlos Rodriguez or XCR began forming a new plan, and now, he formulated a plan against us, and got CRASH & SWAT Teams to after us, most of buried in Drugs and Weapons and Contraband we had in Maya's grave and escaped down, and no arrest was made down, and Tracy is alive, but my kids Maverick and Goose are not dead, living with Tracy and her sisters, I lied to everyone, told John and Raf, a Car Crash, and now, with that Tracy was seeing a man named James, a Peckerwood, he died from a heart attack, and now I met a girl called Camilla, she is an Individual, has no Gang Affiliation, Murder For Hire and Thefts Queen, and Camilla is of Mexican, Red Indian and Scottish Origin, I too have White Genetics in me, Irish are tough bastards not going to lie, Scottish and Icelandic Dudes even stronger, no denying of that one, whether Danish, Swedish, Icelandic or Norwegian, Nordic and Gaelic are strong, and yes Xavier Carlos Rodriguez is an extorter, blackmailer and racketeer and now, he engaged into a final shootout, taking out some LAPD Members down and calling out all of us to which we answered down, we opened up legit shops and began transporting goods down, as well as food deliveries too, and now, we answered it all down to the battle call, John and Raf called in a meeting with me, Conejo and Rincon.

Season 1, Chapter 10, Ending of Year 1 –

Marlon, Jessy and Camilla got the shops started and trucking too and now afterwards, we meet up, Cigarettes, Alcohol, Marijana, Subways and Burgers with Pizzas were all up for display down the lane, and now CRASH Officer Lincoln Smith, Wayne Wilkerson & Mary Mavericks, were appointed down, and they did monitor us all, and Mary and Wayne were also eyeing down

Camilla, and there was something there too, John and Raf with Conejo and Rincon moved down to the area, and had a meeting.

Raf – "Xavier Carlos is the end of it all, new gangs will keep coming up, brought and sold a gift to many rivals, we see if anyone accepts it down, and now, MSX3 will keep coming from the locked down cells of El Salvador, Guatemala, Mexico and Honduras to New York, everyone takes orders from The Big Homies down in San Salvador Prisons and they will never end this War down, next in the next century and I found it dumb, sick of this whole Gang-Life, we are not Gangsters, selling dope and killing people, fucking Mara Salvatrucha 13 Members and fucking Nortenos, remembered the assaults in Prisons, Nuestra Familia has issues, I was innocent and got out, never filed anything against Wayne, Mary and Smith, Lincoln is a good guy to be honest and let us see what happens"

John – "Carnal we have to take care of this deal, Yakuza and Kkangpae, The Japanese and The Koreans coming back, they aren't the ones we worked with, different clans, gangs, or groups, they will have instigated down a Race Riot between us Latinos, Aztec Blood Brothers, The Fucking Russians and Eastern European Bullshit is also coming here, like Europe is not even a country, White People are usually Europeans, Central Asians, Middle Eastern and Many More Parts, most of them are either Junkies or Macho Gangsters, The Wrestling Nordic and Aryan Brotherhood, sorry about the language" Freddy with Irish Mob Members Fiona and Aiofe (Aiofe sounds feminine, this dude is a Bomber and a Killer, reformed tbh) and Camilla came in, a packet of drugs came in, Kkangpae and Yakuza were outside, a member of EME killed a Yakuza Son (a Gangster's Son) and the Cocaine Packet had a smoke, and now, Yakuza and Kkangpae attacked, killed a Korean Gangster too, and now, our members got killed, we had no idea where it came from, message was in an Eastern Language, and I stepped up and began looking outside, and firing happened, it was Wayne, Mary and Lincoln.

I yelled and spoke – "there is no drugs in here, we are smoking Marijuana and Drinking Alcohol, what nonsense is this, where is your warrant?" and Wayne yelled back "we didn't do this, meet Police Captain Jonathan Doherty and Allen Jenkins (Punkish Criminal, officially called Punk Baron, not related to Punks of Iowa City, 3rd Generation kicking asses already, I know they wrote the wrong dates on purpose to fool us all, Damon Maxwell III is a good guy tbh, and MMA came in the 1980s-1990s, before that Mixed Rules Fights or MRFs used to happen) and Camilla and Aiofe and Fiona escaped, Freddy got arrested with a bag of cocaine in there, he pled guilty and took rehab center, 6 months of prison.

And now, we were there, and now, and now we had SWAT & CRASH Teams to care about, and with that Xavier Carlos Rodriguez is a man to worry about too.

And now, we went to a local baseball group, and Bloods & Crips and Latin Kings had a shootout and got some members killed, Bloods and Crips kill each other more then we and MS, Yakuza and Triads, White Knights and Aryan Circle, and now they also have many rappers or singers etc, with that Freddy, Aiofe and Fiona came by and we went to local nightclub and had fun, and now, Xavier Carlos Rodriguez goons were there and Fiona and Aiofe attacked them down and Bouncers stepped up and we came down, and now, Kkangpae Members killed them all and vanished, and now we met members of Yakuza & Kkangpae Members in a meetup and now, we are working with them for shipment of various stuff, not drugs but some weapons and shipping goods too, and now they had a War with Nortenos and teamed up with Mexican Mafia aka EME Members and now, Xavier Carlos killed down many members from our side, and now, we began cleaning out people and now, for those unaware, he had a go fund me scam lol.

Now the go fund me is a website used for fund raising and that is where people raise money for various events usually medical, charity and human rights purposes, and now, we had Carlos Xavier alive and running around, MSX3 members have been arrested, taking advantage of Illegal Immigrants, many decided to shelter them, one businessman poisoned 4 members and threw them away outside, and now, began working downtown, selling the shop to his son – in – law's friend, a Redneck (an Outlaw Biker, clean record, no drugs) and went away, and now, many Koreans shifted there, and they started rooftop shooting again and began killing many more members, plus 38th and Avenues attacks increased and Kkangpae took over, weakening down MSX3.

And now, Kkangpae and Yakuza members we met, they retired actually, working on Sports Teams and Businesses now, Xavier Carlos and his Squad, went into a Bloods area, and staged a shootout, luring police and crash officers, and got Bloods killed, getting Surenos and doing Murders, and escaping, only one member died, and now, Crackdown on Bloods happened, and now, Bloods Members were attacked and killed down too, and now, we needed to go with the flow, when we got a call from Russia, Solntskaya Bravta & Kkangpae are working with The Yakuza Clans and they need us to do their dirty work as Albanians, Israelis, Ukrainians and Nuestra Familia made their own blocks and now, there was something and now, sides have been chosen, Albanians and Mexicans had a major fight in Prison Yard, John and Rafael retired from Mexican Mafia, they started their own business, the only way out is death and they can be killed if that happened, but those two are staying out of trouble instead, Conejo and Rincon and Camille began shipping with me, and now, Koreans and Russians came in with Big Cars and Awesome Suits too, and I was like who are they, Russians and Irish made peace too, and they mentioned Xavier Carlos killed 2 members and their entire families under the influence of the Albanians and they brokered a peace with EME Members and expect us to take Carlos and his men out asap.

Russian Mob shipped us 2000 Kilos of Cocaine and said that 1 Kilo should be sold at 300 – 600 Dollars and We said we will do it but we don't want Drugs afterwards, and they agreed, and we called in the members of Los Angeles Crime Family, Aryan Brotherhood, Texas Syndicate, Dead Man Incorporated, Texas Mexican Mafia and Vietnamese Mafia and got them to buy it at 2x the price, walking to their houses and shipping them down and the cash flow kicked in, we brought better houses, we got members of Russian and Korean Mobs to come and we sold Contraband, ran Nightclubs and sold Energy Drinks and Alcohol underground, dealing with The Major Players, their members do not touch Prison and now, we needed to get it under Government Crackdown, many Members of Street Gangs, White Supremacist Groups, Political Activists, Contract Killers and more were gunned down, even those with no evidence against them and reformed, their families got gunned down, and we remembered the Police Officers and their tactics, Fiona and Aiofe got Russian and Koreans to work at their Shopping Malls stalls now, Russians brought the whole mall and had so much money in their bank accounts, the richest clans actually and the closest ones too, like they were inactive actually, had so much Cocaine, Heroine and Meth, they sold it now, Kkangpae and Solntskaya Bravta made an alliance and brought off everyone and now members of Solntskaya Bravta & Kkangpae showed up.

Kkangpae Council –

1. Chan Jung Song (Weird Name) (Head)
2. Sung Junkook (Weird Name) (Second)
3. Chen Jin Jung (Weird Name) (Smuggling)
4. Kim Chen Quin (Weird Name) (Trafficking)

5. Lee Sung Jung (Weird Name) (Warehousing)

Russian Mobsters had send their own men down too and Koreans are different from The Yakuza Members and Triad Members too.

Solntskaya Bravta Council –

1. Anatoly Drago (he should have been Ivan Drago) (Head)
2. Aleksander Pavlovich (Sergei Pavlovich Fan) (Second)
3. Vladimir Malakyan (Smuggling)
4. Yuri Oleinik (Trafficking)
5. Sergei Popov (Warehousing)

Surenos Council –

1. John Castro (Head)
2. Rafael Alvarez (Second)
3. John Calsada (Smuggling)
4. David Lopez (Trafficking)
5. Camille Lopez (Warehousing)

Irish Mob –

1. Vincent McMahon (Head)
2. Fiona McCauley (Second)
3. Aiofe Grotto (Smuggling)
4. Vance Macdonald (Trafficking)
5. Archer Johns (Warehousing)

Warehousing meant our Legitimate Businesses and Employment too, and now, Carlos Xavier got Albanians, Israelis and Romanians on his side too, and drive for revenge was something too, and now Irish Mob will deal some Meth and Coke too, but mostly protection and distribution, they usually run Grocery, Liquor, Warehousing and Trucks only.

And now, we all began working down on this, and we came across members of 38th Street, Israeli Mob, Aryan Circle and many more gangs, ms13 isnt done, and neither are Bloods when new leaders rise in, and now, we needed to be dealing with the following new board of Bloods – 13 Alliance membership now the 4 J and Williams Family –

1. Javier Rodriguez
2. Jose Silva Calsada
3. Javi Romero Rodriguez
4. Jair Garcia
5. Mansa Williams
6. Henry Williams
7. Gino John Willliams
8. Jermiah Williams

Williams are the successors of Knight Brothers and J4s replaced down Xavier Carlos and Javi and Javier are his Blood Cousin Brothers, allowing his younger brother and sister in law to be killed the two turned on him, and the parents died and grandparents too, and now, the savages are coming, Xavier Carlos broke into our warehouse, killing Marlon and Jessy down, we saved them, he killed many of our staff members and a cop too, and now, with the members holding a funeral, we called Bravta and Kkangpae in and to discuss the things and flow of events for retaliation too.

Kkangpae and Bravta unanimously agreed and signed the Death Warrant, and now, he killed his own friends and family here too, who pleaded for his life, leaving one, who got killed in a Car Crash too, and now, we needed to do something to him and this is the council –

Solntskaya Bravta Council –

1. Anatoly Drago (he should have been Ivan Drago) (Head)
2. Aleksander Pavlovich (Sergei Pavlovich Fan) (Second)
3. Vladimir Malakyan (Smuggling)
4. Yuri Oleinik (Trafficking)
5. Sergei Popov (Warehousing)

Surenos Council –

1. John Castro (Head)
2. Rafael Alvarez (Second)
3. John Calsada (Smuggling)
4. David Lopez (Trafficking)
5. Camille Lopez (Warehousing)

Irish Mob –

1. Vincent McMahon (Head)
2. Fiona McCauley (Second)
3. Aiofe Grotto (Smuggling)
4. Vance Macdonald (Trafficking)
5. Archer Johns (Warehousing)

Kkangpae Council –

1. Chan Jung Song (Weird Name) (Head)

2. Sung Junkook (Weird Name) (Second)
3. Chen Jin Jung (Weird Name) (Smuggling)
4. Kim Chen Quin (Weird Name) (Trafficking)
5. Lee Sung Jung (Weird Name) (Warehousing)

And now, well all 20 members vote down, and are barely here, never here, are captured and released, why are they captured, searched and released?

Answer – The Council Members aren't found with Drugs, Weapons, Counterfeit Items, Stolen Goods or with Excessive Clothes, members wear Casual T-Shirts and Jeans, and drive without drinking anything but Sodas, if there is no Gun, there is no Cocaine, there is no Fake Currency or Passports, why keep them in a Prison, released and we found a way, rounding Junkies, giving them fixes and making them do work at our businesses too, giving us protection, we had send some Junkies to Rehab Centers, adopting unusual and maybe destructive policies, we do not want Over Doses and Deaths happening to keep it all quiet, Xavier

Carlos rallied down Avenues, MSX3 and 38th Streeters as well as Crips and attacked our warehousing, killing Koreans, Russians and Mexicans, many of them being family members with zero ties to our businesses, and Kkangpae and Irish Mob took the matters on their own hands and Aryan Brotherhood Members joined our council too.

Solntskaya Bravta Council –

1. Anatoly Drago (he should have been Ivan Drago) (Head)
2. Aleksander Pavlovich (Sergei Pavlovich Fan) (Second)
3. Vladimir Malakyan (Smuggling)
4. Yuri Oleinik (Trafficking)
5. Sergei Popov (Warehousing)

Surenos Council –

1. John Castro (Head)
2. Rafael Alvarez (Second)
3. John Calsada (Smuggling)
4. David Lopez (Trafficking)
5. Camille Lopez (Warehousing)

Irish Mob –

1. Vincent McMahon (Head)
2. Fiona McCauley (Second)
3. Aiofe Grotto (Smuggling)
4. Vance Macdonald (Trafficking)
5. Archer Johns (Warehousing)

Kkangpae Council –

1. Chan Jung Song (Weird Name) (Head)
2. Sung Junkook (Weird Name) (Second)
3. Chen Jin Jung (Weird Name) (Smuggling)
4. Kim Chen Quin (Weird Name) (Trafficking)
5. Lee Sung Jung (Weird Name) (Warehousing)

Aryan Brotherhood Council –

1. Jerry Manson (Head)
2. Phil McCall (Second)
3. Arthur Bennington (Smuggling)
4. Jamie Price (Trafficking)
5. Ian Jameson (Warehousing)

And now, we found Xavier Carlos and in a Barn, in the Jungles, Lee Sung Jung found him and his coalition and pretending to be their friend, drugged Carlos and put sleeping pills in their Alcohol and Sodas, killing many members and Police Raids happened, everyone died in the raids, since no Weapons were found, the Special Forces Leaders, the Assholes were suspended and fired from duty, and a new chapter awaited us all, Camille and I married and had a daughter Rose and a twin James, I want them to be Doctors or Lawyers not Druggies or anything.

Lincoln Smith, Wayne Wilkerson & Mary Mavericks were all fired down, and we paid them to become Smugglers, they all unanimously agreed to our terms and conditions, and unaware, we never called the cops, Williams Family called them and they knew the sabotage, and also how the department has Corrupt, Cowardly and Communist Cops who don't do anything and many who are not interested in taking cases, better paychecks too happened and now the Syndicate increased and we got into Legitimate Jobs too, using our skills to make Martial Arts Dojos, MMA Fights, Private Security Contractorship as well as Nightclub Professional Wrestling.

Season 2, Episodes 1 to 3, Williams declare Warfare –

And now, it has been one year, the council members are friends with each other and moreover, Mexican Mafia is at War with Black Guerilla Family, DC Blacks & Black Disciples in a Black Coalition.

Williams engaged into a Bloody Shootout and had one of our residents and retired gang member and friend killed, and now that was a blow, and now, we needed to keep it done, and we called in for revenge, Bravta and Kkangpae called in Ukrainians, Romanians & Albanians with Israelis and Greeks showed up and attacked with

Weapons and a bloody shootout happened with us all here, and we were angry at that too, and shootout killed many here and took away everything down the lane too, and now, we supplied the chains and emptied the warehouse, and now, Coalition was first to get rid of as the Super Surenos would race a Race War or a Gang War, we got a drug meeting between Crips and Avenues, Crip Homie was eye balling a Mexican Girl, we had the girl killed and Marlon escaped, and Avenues killed the Crips, signaling down a Crip vs Avenue Warfare and now, toppled it down, okay not really, Avenues don't deal with Blacks or Asians, and now, we needed to spot an ambush, and now, we went into Williams Household, where they kept White Girls, Blonde hair and Blue eyes, they kept them as house slaves and some Korean Girls too, Hmong Girls too have Blonde and Red Hair plus Blue and Green Eyes, anyways Korean Dudes entered the household, killed a few gunmen, opened the cages and called the police, 4 Brothers went to Prison for Human Trafficking, Physical Abuse & Drugs Possessions.

1. Javier Rodriguez
2. Jose Silva Calsada
3. Javi Romero Rodriguez
4. Jair Garcia
5. Mansa Williams
6. Henry Williams
7. Gino John Willliams
8. Jermiah Williams

File Time begins here, we will talk about the Brothers and the Gangsters of Super Surenos, and how to deal with them actually, a little background check should be done, and here is the real story behind it all.

Jermiah Williams and Mansa are born to Nigerian – Jamaican Immigrant Parents, their family was not Criminals but Assassins and Contract Killers as well as Arms Dealers, both parents died naturally and the four brothers and some cousins took over, Jamaican Posse cracked in, Police disbanded them and they joined Crips and one went over to The Bloods Gang, leaving for Crips Hustle, and killing Asians and Slavic Gangsters and rooting their money for hustle, earning wrath of many gangs.

Ukrainians Mafia created The Slavic Alliance, and we told them, Jermiah will be handed or killed if they stop the fight.

The Group joined our side and we got into this, and now Albanians and Russians got into a group of Vans and now, we stepped outside a meeting Black Coalition, and shooters started shooting when we used better guns and shoot down dozens of people and police officers too, this was at some highway, and now we disposed down a lot of gang members while being mysterious and now, a lot of dissention has happened, we got more cops on the payroll and now, turned many policeman against each other, also many cops like sleeping with hookers, and now, well we got the cops to perform a crackdown on MS-13 instead, 18th's mortal rivals and now, things were far from over.

Gino Williams is out on bail, he was never that bad to anyone, but he came and killed someone's mother, a member of Kkangpae, his sister and friend too, Kkangpae issued a hit, and we are meant to take him out, flush him out basically, and Kkangpae brought out Dope Fiends, sending most of them to rehab, Kkangpae don't want attention, and they are doing things differently, Protection was given here, Extortion does not happen anymore, Contraband selling is more common, selling things at Market Price + 500$ for keeping it quiet, and now Underground Shops are a new idea too.

Gambling and Fixing Horse Races, we brought the horses and feed them, no horses got killed here, and we opened up community centers, police is off us too now.

The Council meet up and discussed down to do what with who, and now, we came up with something to do.

1. Take William Brothers out one by one with their top leadership
2. Take out Super Surenos cliques too
3. Get into Nightclubs, Restaurants and Legal Business
4. Avoid Legal Trouble too

And now, with that thing going around, we needed to do something, and now, Jermiah and Gino were going down and we decided to watch Irishman down too.

Solntskaya Bravta Council –

1. Anatoly Drago (he should have been Ivan Drago) (Head)
2. Aleksander Pavlovich (Sergei Pavlovich Fan) (Second)
3. Vladimir Malakyan (Smuggling)
4. Yuri Oleinik (Trafficking)
5. Sergei Popov (Warehousing)

Surenos Council –

1. John Castro (Head)

2. Rafael Alvarez (Second)
3. John Calsada (Smuggling)
4. David Lopez (Trafficking)
5. Camille Lopez (Warehousing)

Irish Mob –

1. Vincent McMahon (Head)
2. Fiona McCauley (Second)
3. Aiofe Grotto (Smuggling)
4. Vance Macdonald (Trafficking)
5. Archer Johns (Warehousing)

Kkangpae Council –

1. Chan Jung Song (Weird Name) (Head)
2. Sung Junkook (Weird Name) (Second)
3. Chen Jin Jung (Weird Name) (Smuggling)
4. Kim Chen Quin (Weird Name) (Trafficking)
5. Lee Sung Jung (Weird Name) (Warehousing)

Aryan Brotherhood Council –

1. Jerry Manson (Head)
2. Phil McCall (Second)
3. Arthur Bennington (Smuggling)
4. Jamie Price (Trafficking)
5. Ian Jameson (Warehousing)

Jerry and Chan Jung got along, talking about Race, Religion, Politics and Pop Culture, Smack was liked by both sides, Aryan Brotherhood is no longer dope or weapons, buying warehouses and keeping the muscles but they got into BJJ, MMA and Muay Thai.

Many Gangsters do Security, Military, Professional Fighting as well as Contract Killer jobs, but avoiding trouble now, and keeping away from people, Ian is also friends with Chan, and now, they also do Surfing, Skating, Bike Riding and Trekking too.

Brothers in Prison also do not fight but Read Books, Excersize and Carpentry too, like many members do Construction Working too, Judo is what they do in their free time too, Gino Williams attacked Kkangpae shops, killing 3 members, Chan lost his mind, and now, we are looking for him everywhere when Garcia attacked Russians, major mistake is what he made, when he gunned entire Russian Families down for his pettiness and which is messed up, and we decided to take Garcia out too.

Garcia family was not killed, Avenues killed them in a shootout, and now, Russians beat down his brothers and nephews and took them in, and mentioned how Garcia killed their families, Garcia staged a shootout and lost some family, except his family was never there but he saw a clip of Police Officers raiding his household and shooting, killing his grandmother, girlfriend and best friend.

And now, Super Surenos may fall down too, they are a few cliques left and right being led by Some Surenos, payment to Mexican Mafia goes regularly.

And now, we needed to take out members from Super – Surenos and Black Coalition down too, and now Gino and Jermiah Williams, and I played Zombies by The Cranberries.

[Verse 1]
Another head hangs lowly[9]
Child is slowly taken[10]
And the violence caused such silence

---

9.   https://genius.com/1321114/The-cranberries-zombie/Another-head-hangs-lowly-child-is-slowly-taken

Who are we mistaken?
[Pre-Chorus]
But you see, it's not me, it's not my family[11]
In your head, in your head, they are fightin'
With their tanks and their bombs and their bombs and their guns[12]
In your head, in your head, they are cryin'
[Chorus]
In your head, in your head[13]
Zombie, zombie, zombie-ie-ie[14]
What's in your head, in your head?[15]
Zombie, zombie, zombie-ie-ie-ie, oh[16]
[Post-Chorus]
Du, du, du, du

---

10.   https://genius.com/1321114/The-cranberries-zombie/Another-head-hangs-lowly-child-is-slowly-taken

11.   https://genius.com/8560359/The-cranberries-zombie/But-you-see-its-not-me-its-not-my-family

12.   https://genius.com/13579206/The-cranberries-zombie/With-their-tanks-and-their-bombs-and-their-bombs-and-their-guns

13.   https://genius.com/4074082/The-cranberries-zombie/In-your-head-in-your-head-zombie-zombie-zombie-ie-ie-whats-in-your-head-in-your-head-zombie-zombie-zombie-ie-ie-ie-oh

14.   https://genius.com/4074082/The-cranberries-zombie/In-your-head-in-your-head-zombie-zombie-zombie-ie-ie-whats-in-your-head-in-your-head-zombie-zombie-zombie-ie-ie-ie-oh

15.   https://genius.com/4074082/The-cranberries-zombie/In-your-head-in-your-head-zombie-zombie-zombie-ie-ie-whats-in-your-head-in-your-head-zombie-zombie-zombie-ie-ie-ie-oh

16.   https://genius.com/4074082/The-cranberries-zombie/In-your-head-in-your-head-zombie-zombie-zombie-ie-ie-whats-in-your-head-in-your-head-zombie-zombie-zombie-ie-ie-ie-oh

Du, du, du, du
Du, du, du, du
Du, du, du, du
[Verse 2]
Another mother's breakin'[17]
Heart is takin' over[18]
When the violence causes silence
We must be mistaken
[Pre-Chorus]
It's the same old theme, since 1916[19]
In your head, in your head, they're still fightin'[20]
With their tanks and their bombs and their bombs and their guns
In your head, in your head, they are dyin'
[Chorus]
In your head, in your head[21]
Zombie, zombie, zombie-ie-ie[22]
What's in your head, in your head?[23]

---

17.   https://genius.com/4275235/The-cranberries-zombie/Another-mothers-breakin-heart-is-takin-over

18.   https://genius.com/4275235/The-cranberries-zombie/Another-mothers-breakin-heart-is-takin-over

19.   https://genius.com/1320574/The-cranberries-zombie/Its-the-same-old-theme-since-1916-in-your-head-in-your-head-theyre-still-fightin

20.   https://genius.com/1320574/The-cranberries-zombie/Its-the-same-old-theme-since-1916-in-your-head-in-your-head-theyre-still-fightin

21.   https://genius.com/4074082/The-cranberries-zombie/In-your-head-in-your-head-zombie-zombie-zombie-ie-ie-whats-in-your-head-in-your-head-zombie-zombie-zombie-ie-ie-ie-oh

22.   https://genius.com/4074082/The-cranberries-zombie/In-your-head-in-your-head-zombie-zombie-zombie-ie-ie-whats-in-your-head-in-your-head-zombie-zombie-zombie-ie-ie-ie-oh

Zombie, zombie, zombie-ie-ie-ie, oh-oh-oh-oh-oh-oh-oh, eh-eh-oh, ra-ra[24]

[Instrumental Outro]

And now, Garcia was found, and not killed, Gino and Jermiah were found too, and unfortunately it was neither of them, but work of Jamal Williams and Jose Rodriguez who led the groups, and against each other too.

And now, we played choices and Council came by, and now Garcia and Williams Brothers were tough and resilient too.

And we played Zombie by The Cranberries again.

---

23.   https://genius.com/4074082/The-cranberries-zombie/In-your-head-in-your-head-zombie-zombie-zombie-ie-ie-whats-in-your-head-in-your-head-zombie-zombie-zombie-ie-ie-ie-oh

24.   https://genius.com/4074082/The-cranberries-zombie/In-your-head-in-your-head-zombie-zombie-zombie-ie-ie-whats-in-your-head-in-your-head-zombie-zombie-zombie-ie-ie-ie-oh

[Verse 1]
Another head hangs lowly[25]
Child is slowly taken[26]
And the violence caused such silence
Who are we mistaken?
[Pre-Chorus]
But you see, it's not me, it's not my family[27]
In your head, in your head, they are fightin'
With their tanks and their bombs and their bombs and their guns[28]
In your head, in your head, they are cryin'
[Chorus]
In your head, in your head[29]
Zombie, zombie, zombie-ie-ie[30]
What's in your head, in your head?[31]

---

25.   https://genius.com/1321114/The-cranberries-zombie/Another-head-hangs-lowly-child-is-slowly-taken

26.   https://genius.com/1321114/The-cranberries-zombie/Another-head-hangs-lowly-child-is-slowly-taken

27.   https://genius.com/8560359/The-cranberries-zombie/But-you-see-its-not-me-its-not-my-family

28.   https://genius.com/13579206/The-cranberries-zombie/With-their-tanks-and-their-bombs-and-their-bombs-and-their-guns

29.   https://genius.com/4074082/The-cranberries-zombie/In-your-head-in-your-head-zombie-zombie-zombie-ie-ie-whats-in-your-head-in-your-head-zombie-zombie-zombie-ie-ie-ie-oh

30.   https://genius.com/4074082/The-cranberries-zombie/In-your-head-in-your-head-zombie-zombie-zombie-ie-ie-whats-in-your-head-in-your-head-zombie-zombie-zombie-ie-ie-ie-oh

31.   https://genius.com/4074082/The-cranberries-zombie/In-your-head-in-your-head-zombie-zombie-zombie-ie-ie-whats-in-your-head-in-your-head-zombie-zombie-zombie-ie-ie-ie-oh

Zombie, zombie, zombie-ie-ie-ie, oh[32]
[Post-Chorus]
Du, du, du, du
Du, du, du, du
Du, du, du, du
Du, du, du, du
[Verse 2]
Another mother's breakin'[33]
Heart is takin' over[34]
When the violence causes silence
We must be mistaken
[Pre-Chorus]
It's the same old theme, since 1916[35]
In your head, in your head, they're still fightin'[36]
With their tanks and their bombs and their bombs and their
guns
In your head, in your head, they are dyin'
[Chorus]
In your head, in your head[37]
Zombie, zombie, zombie-ie-ie[38]
What's in your head, in your head?[39]

---

32.   https://genius.com/4074082/The-cranberries-zombie/In-your-head-in-your-head-zombie-zombie-zombie-ie-ie-whats-in-your-head-in-your-head-zombie-zombie-zombie-ie-ie-ie-oh

33.   https://genius.com/4275235/The-cranberries-zombie/Another-mothers-breakin-heart-is-takin-over

34.   https://genius.com/4275235/The-cranberries-zombie/Another-mothers-breakin-heart-is-takin-over

35.   https://genius.com/1320574/The-cranberries-zombie/Its-the-same-old-theme-since-1916-in-your-head-in-your-head-theyre-still-fightin

36.   https://genius.com/1320574/The-cranberries-zombie/Its-the-same-old-theme-since-1916-in-your-head-in-your-head-theyre-still-fightin

Zombie, zombie, zombie-ie-ie-ie, oh-oh-oh-oh-oh-oh-oh, eh-eh-oh, ra-ra[40]

[Instrumental Outro]

And we made our list of enemies again, Super Surenos and Black Coalition attacked us all again, council called u7s all in, and demanded we kill Garcia, Gino and Jermiah, because they killed them under someone else's orders and now with that thing happening around at us, we got into the fighting mood.

1. Capital Cities – Safe & Sound
2. Hand of Blood – Bullet for my Valentine
3. Bored to Death – Blink 182
4. Adventure – Angels & Airwaves
5. Million Pictures – Simple Plan
6. Thing of Beauty – Danger Twins
7. All the Same – Sick Puppies
8. Miami 2 Ibiza – Swedish House Mafia
9. Hello – Mallory Knox
10. High Hopes – Panic at the Disco

Our Top Ten.

---

37.   https://genius.com/4074082/The-cranberries-zombie/In-your-head-in-your-head-zombie-zombie-zombie-ie-ie-whats-in-your-head-in-your-head-zombie-zombie-zombie-ie-ie-ie-oh

38.   https://genius.com/4074082/The-cranberries-zombie/In-your-head-in-your-head-zombie-zombie-zombie-ie-ie-whats-in-your-head-in-your-head-zombie-zombie-zombie-ie-ie-ie-oh

39.   https://genius.com/4074082/The-cranberries-zombie/In-your-head-in-your-head-zombie-zombie-zombie-ie-ie-whats-in-your-head-in-your-head-zombie-zombie-zombie-ie-ie-ie-oh

40.   https://genius.com/4074082/The-cranberries-zombie/In-your-head-in-your-head-zombie-zombie-zombie-ie-ie-whats-in-your-head-in-your-head-zombie-zombie-zombie-ie-ie-ie-oh

Season 2, Chapter 4, The Hit –

And now, The Cops on our Payroll and the Cops we hired all ended up dead, Wayne and The Lady and the other guy, Camille was also wounded, and now, our buildings were burnt alive, a Government Crackdown happened too, and now we began looking around when a drive by happened and a bombing happened, Jermiah and Gino were captured and Black Coalition and many more began rebelling and looting, Kkangpae Council now had a hard time, Rooftop Koreans began shooting harder and more people began falling, a Police Officer came to our house, and took Marlon & Jessy in for questioning while Camille and Lincoln Smith, Wayne Wilkerson & Mary Mavericks survived down the lane as Camille saved them all, Hector Garcia was an assassin hired and we gave them the official list –

1. Javier Rodriguez
2. Jose Silva Calsada
3. Javi Romero Rodriguez
4. Jair Garcia
5. Mansa Williams
6. Henry Williams
7. Gino John Willliams
8. Jermiah Williams

Taking them all out one at a time was better and now, Mansa and Henry broke into our territory and shoot down an innocent old lady, and shot down a Korean Gangsters and now Kkangpae declared War, Kkangpae send in Cars, kidnapping and torturing down Williams Goons and killing them all off, they were not killed but beaten down and thrown at somewhere, with two options – Death or Running Away and now, with that Mansa and Henry bombed a Car, nearly killing Marlon and Jessy, and now, we were ready to go to War, Aryan Brotherhood members were killed while sleeping, and now, Williams was pulling the strings, together with Asian, Mexican, White and Native American Inmates, a Race War happened, where many Black Inmates got shanked, Williams wanted to rid them so he can keep his money with him, Mansa Williams is the ring leader, losing his wife and raising 2 sons alone, 1 of them committed suicide in academic pressure, his wife's sister and brother in law took his other son, he lost his daughters too, Jair Garcia had them killed actually, Super Surenos & Black Coalition have no honor in them.

And now, the council stepped up, the council of California or Californian Council is ready to talk to us all, and now, AB and Kkangpae Members were having a disagreement but got settled quickly, a Peckerwood and a Kkangpae Member got into a dispute which John settled easily, we are like The Five Families of New York or NY (Gambino, Lucchese, Bonano, Colombo and Genevese) which operate in all five boroughs of New York (Staten Islands, Brooklyn, Manhattan, The Bronx & Queens) and now, the commence happened down the lane.

Solntskaya Bravta Council –

1. Anatoly Drago (he should have been Ivan Drago) (Head)
2. Aleksander Pavlovich (Sergei Pavlovich Fan) (Second)
3. Vladimir Malakyan (Smuggling)
4. Yuri Oleinik (Trafficking)
5. Sergei Popov (Warehousing)

Surenos Council –

1. John Castro (Head)

2. Rafael Alvarez (Second)
3. John Calsada (Smuggling)
4. David Lopez (Trafficking)
5. Camille Lopez (Warehousing)

Irish Mob –

1. Vincent McMahon (Head)
2. Fiona McCauley (Second)
3. Aiofe Grotto (Smuggling)
4. Vance Macdonald (Trafficking)
5. Archer Johns (Warehousing)

Kkangpae Council –

1. Chan Jung Song (Weird Name) (Head)
2. Sung Junkook (Weird Name) (Second)
3. Chen Jin Jung (Weird Name) (Smuggling)
4. Kim Chen Quin (Weird Name) (Trafficking)
5. Lee Sung Jung (Weird Name) (Warehousing)

Aryan Brotherhood Council –

1. Jerry Manson (Head)
2. Phil McCall (Second)
3. Arthur Bennington (Smuggling)
4. Jamie Price (Trafficking)
5. Ian Jameson (Warehousing)

Ian and Jamie spoke "Garcia, Gino and Jermiah are threats to us all, they have to be taken out, there must be a mistake, we are letting these lowlife people destroy our stuff, this is bad "

Lee said "Ian and Jamie, two honorable members of our council, we need to stop the fighting with one foe at a time, we have a large line waiting for us, we need to humble their leadership down, Mansa is the bigger threat, we need him gone first, Gino is a Pathetic Thug, but at your insistence, we will make Gino and Jermiah go away, and Garcia too, not Ryan Garcia but a Thug called Garcia, too many Garcias anyways " and we all laughed, Sergei stood up.

"You are all talking intelligently, I believe The Bosses are meant to be attacked in the end, take the youngsters down, we need them gone, they multiply easily, killing them ruthlessly will be a waste effort, we can bribe them into going away, after all family comes first even in The West "

Archer showed us a Tape and told us, Youngsters have been bribed away into working in their sweatshops, and many have been killed by their own already and Raf ended the council meeting, Camille, Marlon and Jessy with me went outside and now, Mansa and Gino attacked and started shooting with 4 goons, Jessy and Marlon got clipped, shot and killed instantly, and Camille shot and killed one, headshot in the middle of the eyes got one killed.

Ian and Lee, were targeted too, when a 18th St and a Kkangpae Guy shot the tires and the car went flying into a Warehouse and exploded, our warehouse, but no damage done, the car went down the lake, and this was a protected area, we ran inside, the residents were our people and people our payroll, and we smuggle people in from all over the world, usually free of cost, and Gino and Mansa escaped, Mansa was taken in by the police, Gino and a Thug killed the police and ran off, when two more cars came in, 1 cop got killed and Gino's thug died too, when the other two thugs came out.

Gino, Mansa and 3 more came here, now 4 goons are still alive, and they began running from the Cops, Wayne, Mary & Lincoln found out their partner was attacked by Mansa, and they charged with a head – on collision, keeping Mary and Wayne quiet, we brought them Nightclubs and Warehouses away from Southern California and sent their families there, 4th Partner, forgot his name is under our payroll too, and he send his family to Japan and Mongolia, and he got there too, leaving LAPD and SWAT Teams, and now, the thugs hid and the cops left the neighborhood.

Ian shot down both thugs, underlings of Mansa and Gino, Jermiah was away somewhere, Jamal & Henry were plotting too and now, Mansa and Gino killed some goons and residents when a Biker from Red Feathers MC (no Criminal Record) found his sons held hostage, his wife is a Featherwood Member (she is cool too), she chocked Mansa out and drowned him, killing Mansa Williams, the wealthiest, Mansa was stalking her and she is a committed women, Gino wanted to have been the man who killed the wife and the daughters.

And now, I found Gino, and I shoot him with a dart, and we took him and put him in a Cage, where he was, cleaned an entire room up, and threw the body in a graveyard and now, with that, we got two men killed, Jamal bombed the murder building and killed many from Kkangpae, Surenos, Aryan Brotherhood, Irish Mob and Russian Mafia, also many Aztec Warlords MC, Red Feathers MC & Brown Bears MC Members lived here, these Bikers are Street Fighters, Lawyers, Security Guards, Businessman and Doctors, but they are known for their fighting too, Aztec Warlords MC have crazy skulls as motto, they will kill anyone who attacks their own, Red Feathers & Brown Bears are more like Laid Back and Normal, Punkish Wolves MC have some crazies too, Bikers, Mercenaries, Peckerwoods, Armenians and Rednecks among many more groups are not Criminals but they will fight if provoked, and now, with 2 of the top 8 gone, Jamal is rivaled by Cesar, that was his name the whole time.

Cesar and Jamal came to our rooms and brought a note, and they brought their guns, and I called in, a flock of Mobsters came inside, and I realized, it was Henry and Jair Garcia, and we captured them, when their people were there, I tried Bribing, they have a Honor, and accepted their own gangs over ours, and walked away, with a threat to our face.

Blood Members walked in and demanded our girls whored themselves, resulting is us beating them up.

Blood Member pulled out a gun and shot someone's daughter but Sergei shot him in the hands, and in the head, killing him down, and the other Bloods drew their guns out, Sergei snapped his finger, the staff got the girls out, the girls and guys who can't fight were asked to leave, and The Bloods tried raping, killing and beating Sergei and Anatoly who was also here, both middle aged men, and Anatoly shot another man down, 3 Bloods remained, who were taken into our Warehouse and beaten there, realising there is a Cop in there, he told the other Bloods who beat him to death, Anatoly killed both men and buried them, Russian Council members beat them all up and buried them down, and send an anonymous tip, turns out the stalkers had no families, except Jermiah, who got his men with Henry and Jamal do shootings again, and now, they came to the docks and started shooting, and they found them locked, they have moles in there, we paid 4 Blood Members to be our moles, half the earnings go to Armed Groups, Drug Addicts rehab, Law Enforcement, Rival Gangs and Contract Killers to keep quiet, they kill each other all the time, we don't even do Major Crimes, off the radar, we may be placed back anytime now, and now, the four men we paid were on phone with Anatoly when Gunshots were heard and someone mentioned it to us that the four men drove themselves into a neutral zone only for a shooting to happen as Crips and Bloods are Enemies for Decades like Main and Mortal enemies.

LAPD Patrols came inside and now what happened was this we paid Blake, Tyrone, Chris & Benny, taking burgers, their girlfriends were close by Shannon, Biance, Hanny & Vanda, all blacks, when Rival Gangsters pulled up and began unloading, Vanda and Hanny got killed, Shannon is shot in the head by a Mexican who killed Biance, and now, in the car, Benny shoots the Mexican Psychopath down, when Crips come around and go guns blazing, on the front Benny was on the Passenger Seat, Blake drove the car, Chris was Left Back and Tyrone was Back Right, and Crips Homies began shooting, impact killed Chris on the spot too, Vanda was killed by their Crip Boy who killed Blake too, Benny and Tyrone survived, Tyrone went down.

Benny took his gun and took cover, when another Mexican shot and killed Vanda's killer for being in the area, and the Mexican Cholos of Jair Garcia shoot the Crip Car, when 1 of the 2 was shot and killed, and Benny shot the other guy dead, taking a look at Vanda, Shannon & Haney who died, Biance was still alive, and he shot and killed a Crip in the car, and there was an impact, he made it easy, shooting Biance down and begging forgiveness, she did forgive him, and now, he rushed back, another Crip car had come by, Camille was witnessing it, and I was there too, Tyrone shot someone with double guns, opening the gate, Tyrone fell out of the car and was crushed, Benny and Tyrone loaded the girls in the car too, and they sped up, Benny drove the car Biance owned and Tyrone driving his car.

And Shooting happened, Benny killed another Crip, shooting the Steering Wheel and bang happened, shooting at a Biker Cop or a Police Officer with Patrol Bikes and escaping Armed Groups, Angry Mobs, Police and Gangsters, and seeking asylum somewhere, and SWAT Teams came after them, a Wire Transaction allowed them to gain Military Tech, I brought it down for them, and gave them, in a small motel, we owned the motel room and manufactured food as well as drugs, we sell Smaller Drugs most of us don't do or sell hard drugs.

And Benny and Tyrone shoot down an entire squad of Police Officers, since the Koreans and Peckerwoods ran it, they were hostile to the police too, we are secretly making more than other cliques, and giving to EME Members as their Tax Collectors come inside, and we push them away too, many times we give them more in advance only, and now, with that done.

Rooftop Koreans sniped down a Police Officer, killing all the cops, Tyrone got himself killed taking five cops out, Benny called his boys and narrated down everything, Crips were attacked, he was dating the sister of the shot caller, who green lighted him for letting Biance his sister die, Bloods came in here, and started shooting, killing many of our staff, when Kkangpae Members broke out and killed all of them in return, Jair Garcia was spotted with his son, wife and sister, a Blood Member shot his and killed his wife and sister, Jair killed him before his son could be harmed, and an angry driver ran over his son, when a Kkangpae Member offered him a glass of water, he cried his eyes out and ate food, his bills were paid and he left, I met him, he tried shooting me, Camille knocked him out, Cesar came to our Area, he belongs to the worst gang, you guessed it MS-13 or La Mara Salvatrucha – 13, Donald Trump offered a crackdown on this gang too.

And now, Gino and Mansa are dead, Jair Garcia got Henry Williams into a shootout, and had him killed there, 1 Blood Member, a 14-year-old survived, and now Jair Garcia and his 3 henchmen began looking for that Blood Member, Tyrone's Cousin Shawn, who shot and killed a Homie, and took his gun, he ran out of bullets and began looking for an exit.

Anatoly Drago and Ian went to see Jair Garcia, an old friend and told him a few things, Jair was a close friend once, and rekindling of that friendship was happening and a peace offering was being made, Shawn killed the 2nd Henchman and Anatoly offered to have him removed, Anatoly paid Shawn, Shawn was a good kid, and he was a Criminal but he was never a bad person or anything, Jair Garcia hugged both men before collapsing, a heart attack and Surenos and Russians and Peckerwoods, aimed their guns on each other, Anatoly Drago told the Russians & Peckerwoods to go away.

6 Surenos, 8 Bravta and 10 Woods, but now, Shawn killed down the 3rd Henchman, and took his Machine Gun, and found a Rack of Loaded Glocks, Rocket Launchers and Handguns, and he started frantically looking around and escaped, Shawn killed 4 of 6 or 2/3rd of the henchmen and escaped, realising a Blood Member was alive who tackled both Garcia Goons, Shawn killed both of them in a form of execution and ran off, Garica was admitted to a hospital when Super – Surenos threatened Drago and Ian, who left the place, Henry tried attacking or ambushing the Russians, Anatoly Drago and Sergei with their goons single handedly killed Henry and his goons, taking another enemy away.

Season 2, Chapter 5 and 6, Cathedral –

Anatoly Drago, Ian Jameson & Sergei were there, Sergei got the goons Vladimir & Marky there too, and they left when Drago and Jameson left with their cars, Archer got some Irish to go there too, and now, we all left, there were 3 cars there, One had Irish Goons, other had Sergei and Russians and the 3rd car was Ian, Drago and Alexander, Anatoly's closest friend and his personal driver, Alexander had Fedor, a goon too there, Fedor is quite a common name, Russian Legend Fedor Emelioenko is a Politician, Businessman and a Retired Fighter of Judo, Combat Sambo & Mixed Martial Arts, he is the main inspiration behind Russian MMA Superstar Sergei Pavlovich who met Fedor and Khabib

Nurmagomedov to a level was inspired by Fedor, George Saint Pierre and Anthony Pettis aka Showtime, a Mexican Homeboy, he is half Mexican and half Puerto Rican, Bravta Members do Martial Arts, Peckerwoods and Irish do Boxing and Wrestling, we learnt Muay Thai with Koreans who practiced Taekwondo instead.

Crips tried shooting Anatoly and Alexander, when Sergei and his goons open fired, from their windows, killing 2 Crips down, and they drove to the left, and a crip car was following them, and The Irish drove past and started shooting them too, and they crashed down, and I was in the 3rd car too with The Irish.

And now, we chased down, Crips had 4 Cars, 1st Car had 3 homies, all of them are dead, and we got the other two coming, when we backtracked.

And Drove out of their sight, I shot the tires of one car and one car stopped, MS-13 Area, MS Members began shooting at the Bloods, MS and Bloods have an ongoing rivalry too, and we escaped, I hid down, I do not have tattoos of 18 but they will come after us too, Irish opened their roof and started shooting at the Crips Engine, it was a thing that stopped them and we got them to enter a Car Park, where an Ambush waited, Bloods and Crips shoot each other to death, and now Jamal Wilson not Williams and of course Jermiah survived and now they were there too, and now we had to care for Jair Garica's friends too, Cesar and Garcia had a fight now, Garcia has been greenlighted, Cesar and his goons came here too, Garcia is now a member of our organization, he was our friend but he never owed anyone a thing, and now, Jair Garcia may be working with them as a play, Lincoln, Wayne, Mary and their 4th Partner Seth were retired and moved out of the organization.

Jair Garcia killed a few Crips, and we escaped, nobody had weapons and those who did stashed them down already, cops couldn't find anything on us, and now, after months of being inactive, off the radar again, and a new cop Potter or James Porter was here, sadistic and ruthless, he planted fake proof and did crackdowns, he will be suspended as the dirt on him is out now, he is unlikable, Allen Jenkins is close to him.

James Porter and Allen Jenkins raided our warehouses and got nothing but Baking Power and took it as Cocaine, James was angry, vowing revenge.

Allen Jenkins aka Punkish Criminal is a Career Assassin, and he broke into our warehouses where many Goons and their children were, and he threw a Bomb, killing all of them and landed down, realising he broke into the wrong building he escaped and Porter was angry hot, shooting a goon down too, raiding the place and killing 9 men and arresting 1, he was let go due to lack of evidence, Porter and Jenkins were disgraced for their actions, killing members with clean records and the children, brother and wife of the members who got killed too.

Jenkins and Porter escaped down, and now, we need to regroup, and we killed Super Surenos Coalition, and now EME ordered an end to the War against Black Coalition since they killed down 3 Brothers in Prison and all eyes went on them and their allies Romanians, Greeks, Israeli and Samoans.

Ian, Anatoly, Sergei and Kkangpae Council Members met with Raf and John, and began discussing the effects of these gang members and what they can do, and now, Super Surenos aren't done yet either and we checked the list again.

1. Javier Rodriguez
2. Jose Silva Calsada
3. Javi Romero Rodriguez
4. Jair Garcia
5. Mansa Williams
6. Henry Williams
7. Gino John Willliams
8. Jermiah Williams

Jermiah died, Henry died, Gino John is somehow still alive, Jair Garcia is no more a threat as he was arrested and deported to Canada or extradited for 5 years, Javi and Jose are approaching, Javier will be dead, we found out he survived an assassination attempt whereas Mansa is remaking alliances and stacking them up one by one, killing Jamal and now, Mansa wants us all dead.

In a Nightclub, Mansa was getting women forced into having tattoos, where he claimed to have owned them, our sisters and wives, and now, we found out he was taking advantage of sold women and taking them inside for sex and household labor, his children and wife left him for another man, he got a 2nd wife, she was Jamaican and now, we broke into the household of that man when he brought new leaders, Jerome and Collins, to help him out, serving Prison for Life and More, and now coming out, making a fake resume to look cool, Camille played it again.

[Verse 1]
Another head hangs lowly[41]
Child is slowly taken[42]
And the violence caused such silence
Who are we mistaken?
[Pre-Chorus]
But you see, it's not me, it's not my family[43]
In your head, in your head, they are fightin'
With their tanks and their bombs and their bombs and their guns[44]
In your head, in your head, they are cryin'
[Chorus]
In your head, in your head[45]
Zombie, zombie, zombie-ie-ie[46]
What's in your head, in your head?[47]

---

41.   https://genius.com/1321114/The-cranberries-zombie/Another-head-hangs-lowly-child-is-slowly-taken

42.   https://genius.com/1321114/The-cranberries-zombie/Another-head-hangs-lowly-child-is-slowly-taken

43.   https://genius.com/8560359/The-cranberries-zombie/But-you-see-its-not-me-its-not-my-family

44.   https://genius.com/13579206/The-cranberries-zombie/With-their-tanks-and-their-bombs-and-their-bombs-and-their-guns

45.   https://genius.com/4074082/The-cranberries-zombie/In-your-head-in-your-head-zombie-zombie-zombie-ie-ie-whats-in-your-head-in-your-head-zombie-zombie-zombie-ie-ie-ie-oh

46.   https://genius.com/4074082/The-cranberries-zombie/In-your-head-in-your-head-zombie-zombie-zombie-ie-ie-whats-in-your-head-in-your-head-zombie-zombie-zombie-ie-ie-ie-oh

47.   https://genius.com/4074082/The-cranberries-zombie/In-your-head-in-your-head-zombie-zombie-zombie-ie-ie-whats-in-your-head-in-your-head-zombie-zombie-zombie-ie-ie-ie-oh

Zombie, zombie, zombie-ie-ie-ie, oh[48]
[Post-Chorus]
Du, du, du, du
Du, du, du, du
Du, du, du, du
Du, du, du, du
[Verse 2]
Another mother's breakin'[49]
Heart is takin' over[50]
When the violence causes silence
We must be mistaken
[Pre-Chorus]
It's the same old theme, since 1916[51]
In your head, in your head, they're still fightin'[52]
With their tanks and their bombs and their bombs and their guns
In your head, in your head, they are dyin'
[Chorus]
In your head, in your head[53]
Zombie, zombie, zombie-ie-ie[54]
What's in your head, in your head?[55]

---

48.   https://genius.com/4074082/The-cranberries-zombie/In-your-head-in-your-head-zombie-zombie-zombie-ie-ie-whats-in-your-head-in-your-head-zombie-zombie-zombie-ie-ie-ie-oh

49.   https://genius.com/4275235/The-cranberries-zombie/Another-mothers-breakin-heart-is-takin-over

50.   https://genius.com/4275235/The-cranberries-zombie/Another-mothers-breakin-heart-is-takin-over

51.   https://genius.com/1320574/The-cranberries-zombie/Its-the-same-old-theme-since-1916-in-your-head-in-your-head-theyre-still-fightin

52.   https://genius.com/1320574/The-cranberries-zombie/Its-the-same-old-theme-since-1916-in-your-head-in-your-head-theyre-still-fightin

Zombie, zombie, zombie-ie-ie-ie, oh-oh-oh-oh-oh-oh-oh, eh-eh-oh, ra-ra[56]
[Instrumental Outro]

And now, Gino with Mansa, Jerome and Collins began looking into something about drugs and not realising LAPD & SWAT Teams as well as OCSD (Orange County Sheriff Department) are all after them, and now, Jerome and Collins, who is the only non-black, as he is Albanian, are planning an ambush and rush to take over, Williams Goons were attacked down and killed as OCSD, LAPD & SWAT Teams joint strike their houses, killing 20 members and arresting down 25 members as four men and their driver Jack Rollins escaped down, Rollins is a former Marine, he is White and by White a mix of Irish, German and Scottish ethnicity took them away from there, and now, with that, the leaders successfully escaped and of the 20 killed many were clique leaders and many more of high power and ranking, their empire had crumbled, and The Cartel struck them down, killing many more, under scrutiny from EME Group (Mexican Mafia, LA EME).

---

53.   https://genius.com/4074082/The-cranberries-zombie/In-your-head-in-your-head-zombie-zombie-zombie-ie-ie-whats-in-your-head-in-your-head-zombie-zombie-zombie-ie-ie-ie-oh

54.   https://genius.com/4074082/The-cranberries-zombie/In-your-head-in-your-head-zombie-zombie-zombie-ie-ie-whats-in-your-head-in-your-head-zombie-zombie-zombie-ie-ie-ie-oh

55.   https://genius.com/4074082/The-cranberries-zombie/In-your-head-in-your-head-zombie-zombie-zombie-ie-ie-whats-in-your-head-in-your-head-zombie-zombie-zombie-ie-ie-ie-oh

56.   https://genius.com/4074082/The-cranberries-zombie/In-your-head-in-your-head-zombie-zombie-zombie-ie-ie-whats-in-your-head-in-your-head-zombie-zombie-zombie-ie-ie-ie-oh

Gino & Mansa with Jack parted ways with Jerome and Collins and now, Gino stepped outside and was shot in the head by a Cartel Gunner, and Jack hit him and his 2 companions with the cars, injuring two and finishing the job, as Jerome shot the Gunman, but got wounded by him, and now, Gino is also dead, Cartel was manipulated by Super Surenos not EME, EME with The Brand, Nuestra Familia & BGF run their Warzones in prisons but everyone seems to be at peace for some good reason, no bloodshed is happening.

Mansa, Jerome and Collins survived and with Jack Rollins escaped to Jack's house, my neighborhood, and now, they regrouped there, ordered distribution with easy, Drug Dealers and Smugglers were the Moles after all, and the rackets shut down, Jerome avoided bloodbath and more raids, by ending drug trading and focused solely on weapons and added blackmailing, extortion, kidnapping for ransom and grand theft auto (and by grand theft auto doesn't mean the game but stealing cars away) and now, Jerome and Collins driven by Jack Rollins came in here and confronted us, shooting nobody down but at a neutral ally, demanding down we give away 20% to 60% and Kkangpae Council refused and a War was on, Kkangpae being better equipped after all, Jerry and the other council members voted in, agreeing to enter a better quality business like owning Nightclubs, Cab Services, Logistics, Bakeries, Clothing and Store Running and we will exit the drug trade majorly but continue identity theft, protection, gambling and murder for hire as well.

In El Salvador, Honduras, Guatemala, Mexico, United States of America, Canada and Spain, 18th Streets enemy Mara Salvatrucha – 13 exists, they are deadly and lethal, inhumane too, FBI got MS Task Force, levels.

Mara – 13 and Asian Boyz may come back to us and bit us down, and we will battle them again, and now, we had peace, and we got Police, Special Forces and Sheriff Dept off us and quiet followed, and now, Jessy and Marlon were pushing down fake cards and hanging out when Jerome and his hitman attacked them all, Collins the only white man there, and Jerome send me a message, it was between me and him, The Knights were his family and some Gangsters under them, and he wants revenge, and before anything, Irish Mob had killed his goons, leaving two enforcers and Jerome behind, and Kkangpae, Aryans, Irish, Russians and 18th all came in there, Jerome called in Crips, Bloods and Vice Lords around there, and Marlon got it all called off, Jerome threatened him again, Mansa is getting more and more paranoid, Camille and I decided to flush him out, John and Raf agreed and the council members voted in.

Solntskaya Bravta Council –

1. Anatoly Drago (he should have been Ivan Drago) (Head)
2. Aleksander Pavlovich (Sergei Pavlovich Fan) (Second)
3. Vladimir Malakyan (Smuggling)
4. Yuri Oleinik (Trafficking)
5. Sergei Popov (Warehousing)

Surenos Council –

1. John Castro (Head)
2. Rafael Alvarez (Second)

3. John Calsada (Smuggling)
4. David Lopez (Trafficking)
5. Camille Lopez (Warehousing)

Irish Mob –

1. Vincent McMahon (Head)
2. Fiona McCauley (Second)
3. Aiofe Grotto (Smuggling)
4. Vance Macdonald (Trafficking)
5. Archer Johns (Warehousing)

Kkangpae Council –

1. Chan Jung Song (Weird Name) (Head)
2. Sung Junkook (Weird Name) (Second)
3. Chen Jin Jung (Weird Name) (Smuggling)
4. Kim Chen Quin (Weird Name) (Trafficking)
5. Lee Sung Jung (Weird Name) (Warehousing)

Aryan Brotherhood Council –

1. Jerry Manson (Head)
2. Phil McCall (Second)
3. Arthur Bennington (Smuggling)
4. Jamie Price (Trafficking)
5. Ian Jameson (Warehousing)

Camille and I found Mansa but Police Officers were there and we had to leave, explaining that all, Jessy killed a Williams Goon, a group of them and escaped, realising it was near by my area, Jerome demanded we hand over 4 thugs, and we refused, Jerome took his gun out and shot down an entire 18th Family and walked away.

Season 2, Chapters 7 and 8, Retaliation Time –

And now, we are ready, as 18th Streeters, Kkangpae, Aryan Brotherhood, Irish Mob and Solntskaya Bravta together are attacked and EME Soldiers too joined in, and now, we began looking for Jerome, who is now in hiding and we do not plan to let him go off on easy mode, and I remember the list of people we have to deal down with already, most of them are dead and the other half is alive and seeking revenge already.

Status of the Red List –

1. Javier Rodriguez
2. Jose Silva Calsada
3. Javi Romero Rodriguez
4. Jair Garcia (Extradited, Canada)
5. Mansa Williams
6. Henry Williams (+)
7. Gino John Willliams (+)
8. Jermiah Williams (+)
9. Jerome
10. Collins
11. Jack Rollins (By Associations only)

Jack Rollins is a good guy, Marlon got hit by a Truck and Jack and his family (Wife Emily who is as old as Jack 32, Daughter Tiffany who is 16 and Diane 9 with Jess 3, Sons Donald 13 and Jim also 13 with Mike 12) came to the aid, and took him to our house, and they did treat him well, and I realized, we took the bounty off of him, and let him live, and now, we updated the list only, he is no snitch, we respect that, because if he was on our side, he would do the same, he never committed crimes or felonies, being a driver, he also is a Millionaire now, he employed Gangsters and Criminals to work it out at his firm, giving drivers and earned well, he also runs adoption shelters as well as restaurants of his own, still drives for dangerous men around the city, given they helped him out, Henry was the one, now he is dead, his debt is fulfilled too, Mansa is nice to him but he is a deadly man, or maybe Jack is the one killing off his men, for Human Trafficking and Animal Violence, he has 1 dog named Sweetie, a Saint Bernard who is 4 years old female.

Jack has friends in Red Feathers MC, Punkish Wolves MC, Brown Bears MC and Aztec Warlords MC as well as Local MMA Gyms, Mercenary Groups and Arms Dealers too, he served in The Marine Corps, State Guard and Navy Seals, and he is a part timer in Mixed Martial Arts, Submission Grappling, Professional Wrestling, Street Fighting and Judo too, earning himself a black belt too, getting bord and now trying to become a Doctor too, his wife is an engineer on the other hand plus an architect too with a business and journalism degrees as well.

Irish Mob and Aryan Brotherhood business partner given members of the two groups also work under him and for his family owned restaurants too, and he is a heavy drinker too, he and his family have red hair, green eyes and neopagan beliefs too, following Odin and Norse Gods with the Celtic Gods and Currency of the house are Books and Pages, he is also very big on Pop Culture too, he sounds like Jack Reacher from Jack Reacher books, the story is about a retired Military Police (M.P.) Officer called Jack Reacher, who once was a Warzone Child, born and raised in Military Bases and Camps both in and out of the United States of America, he is an orphan as Josephine Reacher died from Old Age and was his mother, a French National, Joe Reacher died in book 1 titled

Jack Reacher – The Killing Floor where a powerful crime family killed Joe Reacher and Jack had them all killed, this was featured in Reacher Amazon Prime Series, Stan Reacher is Joe and Jack's father who died in Military Base only.

Jack had many girlfriends and even children it is claimed, Jack has no house, no social media, no presence, he has a duffel bag with his Passport, Military Medals, Chains, a Wallet and other contents, he keeps buying stuff, he goes into boutiques and buys clothes when his old ones are dirty, in Jack Reacher's second book, he did get a job and an apartment in Florida Keys, Jack is a drifter, who has no fixed address, author of Jack Reacher is Lee Child, a British – American based off in New York area, he looks handsome Camille said, he must be 55 or 56 by now, Jack Reacher has 20+ books now too, 2 of them had movies with Tom Cruise in them like Never Go Back was one of them, where he got out of a car, into the bus and the car was auto driving and the police couldn't find him despite having him surrounded down, he escaped with a black gentlemen on the bus, the black gentlemen probably was a Vietnam War Veteran or Jack's Military Buddy, who was contacted by Jack, he cleared the name of Jason Barr, who was in a Coma, Jason was released and was not given the death penalty after all, the killer was killed and brought to Jack Reacher's brand of Justice after all, imagine Jack Reacher, John Wick, The Punisher and Anton Chigurh fighting off some Warlord or Corrupt Politician, Punisher is a psychopath, his fans too suck, being online and telling us if Punisher was real, he would end crime, crime would not go down, guys like Frank Castles don't die but they don't win against AB, 18th, EME etc either, Punisher was a good tv show btw, Daredevil was so much better though, The Man Without Fear is Matthew Murdock aka Matt the Daredevil, as Charlie Cox did an amazing role in there and John Bernthal too was good, Mahershala Ali as Cottonmouth the Gangster wasn't bad either, his character wasn't appealing to us West Coast Gangsters either.

Camille and I got a Kid already, he turned 4 now, his name is Marcus, we plan on having more, she was with me years ago, and we had a daughter named Stephanie who is now 6, and Camille is pregnant with my child again, and now, enough Marvel and Pop Culture, we had a Barbeque Saturday as AB, Irish, Koreans, Russians, 18 and Eme came by, Jerome and Mansa, came by with their goons, Rooftop Koreans, I got two words for you, Rooftop Koreans and Sneaky Russians, and now, we shot their goons down, and the two men ran again, Jack Rollins drove them away, we are cool with Jack, no shooting him, he helped Russians, Aryans and Irish too.

Jack can speak English, Korean, Russian, Irish, Gaelic, Spanish, Hindi and Japanese with Mandarin (Chinese) and now, he calmed us all down and drove Mansa and Jerome away, Collins killed an 18 member and they all drove away with a drive-by shooting and the children of the killed members demanded revenge, and I promised them all blood, which was a bad move, we don't do what other cliques do no more, we keep people off the streets now, giving them Coca-Cola, Sprite, Monster and even Beer, avoiding Drug Police Charges and whatnot, many Cliques aren't happy, claiming we are sucking big white balls and big Korean balls but everyone is okay now, and Jair Garcia was released from prison, we believed it was because of the lack of evidence, Jair did things on behalf of others and realising that everyone turned on him, he returned the favor and came back asap.

The Council needed to deal with another issue, emergence of a Paramilitary Cartel lead by El Unico, Amado Rodriguez & Joaquin Fuentes, breaking off from Sinaloa Cartel and now the Council got a message, Jessy and Marlon and Camille with me got there, Jessy and Marlon their parents died to illness, their siblings went to Texas, Jalisco, Bangkok, London and Grozny in Russia down.

Solntskaya Bravta Council –

1. Anatoly Drago (he should have been Ivan Drago) (Head)
2. Aleksander Pavlovich (Sergei Pavlovich Fan) (Second)
3. Vladimir Malakyan (Smuggling)
4. Yuri Oleinik (Trafficking)
5. Sergei Popov (Warehousing)

Surenos Council –

1. John Castro (Head)
2. Rafael Alvarez (Second)
3. John Calsada (Smuggling)
4. David Lopez (Trafficking)
5. Camille Lopez (Warehousing)

Irish Mob –

1. Vincent McMahon (Head)
2. Fiona McCauley (Second)
3. Aiofe Grotto (Smuggling)
4. Vance Macdonald (Trafficking)
5. Archer Johns (Warehousing)

Kkangpae Council –

1. Chan Jung Song (Weird Name) (Head)
2. Sung Junkook (Weird Name) (Second)
3. Chen Jin Jung (Weird Name) (Smuggling)

4. Kim Chen Quin (Weird Name) (Trafficking)
5. Lee Sung Jung (Weird Name) (Warehousing)

Aryan Brotherhood Council –

1. Jerry Manson (Head)
2. Phil McCall (Second)
3. Arthur Bennington (Smuggling)
4. Jamie Price (Trafficking)
5. Ian Jameson (Warehousing)

The Heads and The Seconds headed in this time, but Jerry decided only 5 heads should discuss this and now, The Cartel is coming, and that they want to take over, and Jair Garcia may become a threat, and he now, leading Super Surenos into a Gang Warfare, as Javier and Javi attacked our compound, realising we killed the wrong people, and now, they kidnapped Marlon, but well The Red Feathers MC, Californian Rednecks, Red Mercenaries and Armed Mexicans ambushed and killed Javi's goons, and now, surrounded him, shifted and brought a plant, Super Surenos causing mayhem and killed many Bikers, Rednecks, Cowboys, Mercenaries and Neopagans, and now the whole small town turned against them, Javi and Jose were there, Jerry came out, Jose tried shooting him, Jack Rollins was there too, Jerry turned both men to his locked room, and made them surrender, Jerry and Ian, beat both of them up, okay that did not happen, it was Sergei and Anatoly who beat both of them up and made them surrender, Super Surenos Leaders have bowed down, and now, Jair Garcia came out, shooting down the two leaders for accepting defeat, Jair wanted full control and wanted them all gone, and killed them down, when Surenos started shooting, and Aryan Brotherhood members being in touch didn't partake in, instead they saved the civilians, and now, OCSD & SWAT Teams came by, Surenos killed them too,

Brown Bears MC Members drove by and were killed too, many bikers and mercenaries died, and now, Kkangpae Members took their swords out and began stabbing them down, and the Surenos got surrounded, Jack Rollins killed and turned on The Surenos, Jair Garcia escaped with his closest associates, I chased him down, Marlon, Jessy and Camille too, and Marlon and Jessy killed 2 of his 3 associates down, Jair Garcia, unnamed goon and an unnamed driver escaped, and Jair shoot and killed Marlon, wounding Jessy and Me.

The Cartel is called as Los Tigres, and they started shooting at our town, we brought all mining plants and paid off the debts, and the old owners were members of Russian Mafia, they accept everyone, Italian Mafia has Italian Men as Members or "Made-Men" and Non-Italians as Associates or "Friends" working for the Organization or a particular crime family, and now, gave back to the people while government cracked down on us in EL Salvador, Guatemala, Honduras and Mexico, 18th Members are getting killed daily, many have left the organization in fear now, Marlon was buried and tears down my face, Jair Garcia is a dead man, Jessy got targeted, as a Cartel Hitman, named Anci drove by, they are Native Mexicans mostly, killing Jessy by shooting him too, Camille and I survived, but other captains also got killed, and ran over the Bikes, Red Feathers MC Members attacked them because they are Human Trafficking their family members, Scamming Nursing Houses and Stealing from Homeless as well as Harsh and Brutal killing of Homeless Dogs, a member of Red Feathers MC mentioned owning a diner, and one day, they burned it down, and didn't apologize to him, killing his waiters, kidnapping and selling his daughter, cutting his dogs tongue down too.

They killed The Biker, his dogs and his entire family later, posting a video about it too, Harley Ares Fitzgerald, Damon Maxwell III & Dennis Miller are all against him, Miller and Yuri

Ivanov are Bikers but they are not Criminals, Ivanov joined Russian Mafia and Red Feathers MC, killing a few people too, Ivanov lost his friends to the Cartel.

The Council Members agreed and put out a hit on Jair Garcia and now, he was hot on our wheels, Marlon and Jessy were the last of their own families and their bloodlines aren't over, but now, we buried him down, and with there, we started plotting vengeance against Jair Garcia, killing his sister and nephew down, and making it look like a Car Accident, I cried a lot, never cried this hard since the deaths of Mom, Grandma, Grandpa and Dad and Garcia that bastard will pay for it, when Mansa Williams, Jerome Romero and Steven Collins aka White Boy in here and now all of them made a deal with Los Tigres, Jack Rollins is now training to become a Submission Grappler, Professional Wrestler, International Wrestler and a Mixed Martial Artist (Professional Wrestling & International Wrestling are two different things) and I like Ring of Honor, TNA/Impact Wrestling, All Elite Wrestling, World Wrestling Entertainment as well as New Japanese Professional Wrestling too.

Antonio Inoki founded Inoki Gnome Federation and New Japanese Professional Wrestling, he organized Professional Wrestling, Mixed Martial Arts & Submission Grappling under Inoki Gnome Federation where Legends Kazushi Sakuraba, Lyoto Machida, Josh Barnett and many more competed in.

Giant Singh now Great Khali is also awesome many MMA Stars like Hammer Mark Coleman, Beast Dan Severn, Predator Don Frye & Monster Kevin Randleman (+) did time in Japanese Professional Wrestling, Mark was the strongest of them all in my opinion.

Los Tigres attacked and killed Jack's sister and her family, Rollins will never forgive them actually, and he is no way interested in becoming Jack Reacher, John Wick, The Punisher, Ghost Rider,

Jax Teller or anything like that, he is going to go down like a Jack Reacher tbh, and now, we began working on Jair Garcia, and we found out where, he was hiding and we went after him, lost many friends and remember the old crew we had, Shot Caller and Leaders are all dead except they survived and went to join another clique, and now, returned and became inactive, Felipe and Maya are joined by Jessy and Marlon, young boys now 19 and 21 when they died down.

Ishika died in Texas, well MS 13 and her boyfriend too, MS 13 they robbed and killed both of them, Angel and Ishika were working for a Hardware Storeroom and now, leaving a daughter behind, Herman who was working with us the whole time, and was out due to his struggle with Heart Illness, we decided to relive him of his duties only, he works and sells at our restaurants and nightclubs only as well as running a conference center too, he cleans up nice, and his girlfriend turned fiancé Karla went to Texas and later Kansas but returned.

Season 2, Chapter 9, Los Tigres vs Border Brothers –

And now, we were out here, and a police officer came in here, and told us we may need to shut our hubs down, and we made him come in and showed him everything, mentioning he can come anytime, we have no drugs in our Cassitas anymore, and now, he went away, happy we turned a leaf around, Heroine and Cocaine Trafficking = Misery and we needed Income but it is better if we are all alive and we do False Identity Thefts, Car Jacking, Heist Robberies and many more, and I came up with a Heist of Diamonds, we entered illegal sales of Diamonds, Silver and Gold as well and Counterfeiting is not my cup of coffee either, and now a grand heist was ready too, and now, Xavier was out of prison, and remember the old crew.

1. Armando is the oldest member in here at 34, he runs the gang and smuggling and family businesses too, he does IT Work as well, just became a Widower, brother is in jail with La Eme aka Mexican Mafia (+)

2. Herman is half Indian and half Mexican, his parents died due to Illnesses and his brother is also a gang member but moved away to Texas and Kansas later, he is in love with the sister of Xavier named Carla, not a gang member (+)

3. Jason is another member, he is born to a Hmong Dad and a Samoan Mom, he is having Red Hair and Blue Eyes, a lot of us have them too, partially due to Spanish and English Heritage or just we have the same pigmentation too, dude has a Japanese Girl named Jenny it's a White Name not Japanese but that is her name

4. Xavier is a member who loves to kill actually and isnt like anyone else around in here, Gangs here do all kinds of stuff together, not just Crimes and Terrorism or Smuggling but also Businesses and all too, he is a Human Calculator actually, loves a Chinese named Marie Zhang Yung, Triad Members sister, we have ties with them too, would marry her soon enough

5. Angel is another member, quiet guy and driver, his sister is Fernanda and she is my girlfriend, and his girlfriend is Ishika, Herman's sister, he is a calm killer and seller too, increases price but saved many from over dosing out as well too, good hearted dude actually (+)

6. Jamie is another member, he is on the run, and he killed members of Bloods, Snakehead and Arabic Armed Groups too, he is a known killer and he is older too, his wife died due to Cancer but left two kids in his name, he had four but the other two died away too, killed by a Crip even though they were friendly to him (Incarcerated, he

killed his mother's killer and his family, got remarried and has kids)

7. Felipe is a Samoan – Mexican Man, who dates a nurse named Maya, he is not into Drugs or anything, but still fights for us and attends meetings and stuff, handles packaging and warehousing instead and does well too, good guy actually (+)

('+' = Dead)

Xavier and Marie are back, Jason & Jenny work for a Warehousing Unit under The Council, and got we have a crew ready now, as Me, Camille, Xavier, Marie, John and Rafael scoring it this time big, Council will not kill us or ask us, 6 of us are all we need, maybe get 2 more gangsters.

Dave Jenkins, an old friend and Castro Jonathan too joined in, we have about 25 members now, we are in low rankings with the other cliques but we earned high back, we don't need to be druggies and killers to make money, and now we got ready, here was the role of all the members too.

1. Jenkins is the operator, checking Cameras and whatnot as he will handle safes and passwords easily. Alias is Iowa.

2. Castro is the Negotiator, who will talk to the Bank Staff and make sure, they do not, call the police. Alias is Kansas.

3. John is our Grifter, he will grift inside the crowd and make panic distractions. Alias is New York.

4. Camille is the Thief, if Bank gives us the diamonds and money, she will take it and leave, she will be wearing wigs to disguise herself. Alias is California.

5. Jenny will be the Getaway Driver as she will stay in the Car and wait till coast is clear and we can drive back home. Alias is Alaska.

6. Marie is the Field Medic here in case anyone got injured, she will treat the wounds, becoming a nurse she is. Alias is Texas.
7. Rafael is The Scout and he will make sure Nobody Goes in or Out without his permission. Alias is Arizona.
8. I, David Bullet Lopez will be the leader and order giver, and will roam around the shop pickpocketing people down. My Alias is Tennessee.

Council wont ask for money either, they got their own things, they have so much money, Russians and Irish, they don't even do anything or ask money in return, lazy they became, and happy they are, Koreans and Aryans work somewhat hard, 18 Members are living life too, united we stand and divided we fell, we don't want divisions and work separately for a reason, I have been a Council Member after all, I forgot my own sometimes lol.

And now, we arrived at the bank scene, and we began looking at the cameras, and now, we needed someone to access the mainframes, and I asked if they needed a new camera officer, I bribed their Security Officers, we got a few of them to leave their positions, they got 2 Guards, this is a Shop, I keep calling it a Bank, they got 6 Guards, 4 Field Workers and 12 Diamond Workers as well as 4 Gold, Silver and Platinum smiths there.

And now, I went around and came across a security guard, and I came with better prospects, realising he is an Avenue who killed the brother of Marlon and tried killing me once, he was there, he said he would not do it again, being a heart patient (con artist) and now, with a crew of 5 there, we had competition, on the other hand a shooting happened as Tigres and Border Brothers + Avenues started shooting, and the 5 Guards went there, and we stopped them, Jenny and Marie dragged one of their and healed his wounds, and we got them to work with us, they have taken from many, it was 10 people actually, 4 of them retired, 6 of them now, but 1 is away on a vacation, leaving just 5 guys, final score and retirement.

Using Cartel shootout, The 5 Avenues killed everyone, and took some money, lunch break was their final break, 1 of them disabled cameras actually, and I realized it all, we purchased Tasers, Handguns with Silencers, Batons and Knives, keeping them all ready for a silent robbery, and we learned about the wires, Jewel Shop also sold clothes and whatnot, the shop was under Los Tigres, they had already killed many friends of Anatoly, Sergei and Jerry, pissing the council members off only.

Bravta and Kkangpae are already ready for a War, Albanians, Ukrainians, Yakuza, Peckerwoods, Paramilitary Mobs here, all of them are pissed at Los Tigres, and their leaders, the three jokers are Raul Martinez aka El Unico, Amado Rodriguez & Joaquin Fuentes.

Enemies List now includes –

1. Javier Rodriguez
2. Jose Silva Calsada
3. Javi Romero Rodriguez
4. Jair Garcia (Extradited, Canada, now dead)
5. Mansa Williams
6. Jerome
7. Collins

8. El Unico
9. Amado
10. Joaquin

Jair Garcia is now running, but today, he got hit by a Car, Irish Mob flushed him out, and he started shooting, when Aryan Brotherhood Members shot and killed him down too, and his son ran off, only to be hit by a Car and killed too, it was Canadian Marshals and American Police, his son flaunted a gun and shot down a Police Officer, and they had it coming, I will explain it fully.

Jair Garcia, Jair Garcia II, Unnamed Driver and 2 Unnamed Gunman let us call them Kyle, Rob and Daniels were there, and 6th Person Anthony, and they were driving around running from Canadian and American Law Enforcements, and they made a run in on an abandoned building, a team of 14 officers were send after them, Anthony killed 3 of them, and escaped, there was a chopper too, Jair Garcia II landed a Bazooka on them, killing 4 of them, and shot down a Cop when a Sniper sniped and killed him, and Anthony.

Kyle and Rob, shoot down two female officers and a 3rd Biker Police, Patrol Bike guy, and stole the bike, ramming it into another Canadian Officer, and a shooting happened, Kyle and Rob ran, taking his gun and shooting with it, killing 2 Canadian Cops down, 9 Cops dead, 5 more to go, turns out 2 were dirty cops in there, attacking and shooting their officer dead, and leaving the scene, it was the wounded Canadian Guy and 1 Mashal, who killed Rob, and wounded Kyle, when Daniels the driver shot and killed him too, Jair had 10 Goons in there, Canadian Officer regrouped, killed both dirty cops.

Took their Handguns in, and went back, he was high on drugs too, shooting Daniels, Kyle and Rob dead, and he went in there alone, and shoot down 3 goons from behind, and stabbed their necks down, and walked to the top floors, Jair had backup called in too, he had 10 goons with Daniels, Kyle, Rob, Jair II, Dirty Cops let us call them Dave and Jack and 3 Goons, he had 3 goons remaining let us call them Pablo, El Limon & El Chapo.

Chapo went down, looking and was shot in the back of his head, the Canadian Badass named Finn Macdonald aka Canadian Vigilante, The Red Assassin, another Rogue, went on in, sniping the ear off El Limon, Pablo and Limon went down, and got killed, Jair Garcia and Red Assassin went toe to toe, Garcia was killed and backups arrived, Super Surenos were cracked down on, Javi and Jose were killed, Javier died in a shootout too, and they all were imprisoned down under Human Trafficking, Piracy, Terrorism, Hate Crimes, Drug Trafficking, Smuggling and Arms Dealing with Gambling, about 89 Members were convicted and imprisoned, Super Surenos shot down, 47 members turned against the organization only.

Jerome, Mansa and Collins remain now, Jack Rollins quit his driving job, driving for Korean Gangsters as well as Arms Dealers, Smugglers, Fake ID Sellers and Con Artists now only, being on good terms still and now, Collins was found with Jerome and Mansa Williams, Mansa killed a female member, he had raped her and her child, and now, I furiously marched there with 18 Members, Kkangpae, Aryans, Irish Mob and Russians in there, and in their area, we had Aryans and Irish check the areas to detect and kill Gang Members, and now, we had 4 Gang Members killed there only, Mansa Williams and Jerome were found and we broke into their households, with Masks on, killed a few female gang members or gangsters, Jerome had a Puerto Rican and Thai Girl on him, I broke in, and shoot him in the face twice, killing him, and told the other two to scream, Camille and Xavier killed Mansa Williams and we left quickly and quietly, as the last of our ranks escaped, minor injuries, gunshot wounds and open bleedings, LAPD & SWAT Teams raided in and arrested 59 Gang Members, out of which 16 in record high numbers snitched, ratted, bailed out, tapped out or turned the other members over and escaped, so now 59 – 16 = 43, 42/43 Members are now in Prison for Rape, Pedophilia, Sexual Assault, Drug Trafficking, Assault, Kidnapping for Ransom, Attempted Murders, Murders, Gun Possession, Drug Possession, Gambling and Loan Sharking.

Collins was the only sole survivor, and he came back at us, Jack Rollins stopped him and he made peace, rejoining his street crew instead and Williams and Knights are both gone now, leaving the Cartel and now Border Brothers to handle up, EL Unico is an issue after all.

Asian Boyz joined them with MS 13 members too.

We went into Mexico, 1 day before the robbery, witnessing Lucha Libre, I plan to go there one day, and maybe become a Luchador for a while, just kidding, not that big of a fan though, and now, we got back into the heist, I saw a kid running with hotdogs from a stall, the stall owner ran after him, caught and slapped him, when I and Anatoly showed up, cut a big fat cheque and told him to give food to homeless and street kids, he agreed and now, we brought lands of food in Mexican Border Cities too.

Increasing Lands, most of us are Non Vegetarians, but we freed Animals from Meat Factories too, made Schools as well as Churches, funded Tournaments and Festivals and did Good in Mexico as well as Ireland and Russia even rural California and Korea too, we made a Legitimate Business and Police was off from us, we did not do Drug Crimes, we did not do Terrorism or anything to get their attention towards us anymore and send off many kids to college, people did not believe it, we stopped it all and we don't have Funerals anymore here, Crips and MS have Funerals every other day now too.

We enlisted into Private Military Contractorship, Local Security, Protection Rackets work out fine too, Street Fighting and Professional Level simultaneously too, and now, we had Restaurants, Law Firms, Warehousing, Taxi/Cab Businesses, Motels and Stadiums under our control only, different business owners and billionaires, we don't use AI, it can replace us Mexican Workers if that happened.

And Diamond Robbery was happening, this was somewhere near the Valleys, don't do things in City or Small Towns either, but in the end we switched to another Diamond Shop, Damo9n Max3well owned that and had Red Feathers MC & Brown Bears MC guarding it down, preventing Crime, Loot and even Attackers, as many attacked the staff and did Vandalism too, The Owner was a

Scumbag, Robert Johnson, he did do bad stuff, he was a different criminal, blue collar maybe, and now, once again the crew –

1. Jenkins aka Iowa.
2. Castro aka Kansas.
3. Xavier aka New York.
4. Camille aka California.
5. Jenny aka Alaska.
6. Marie aka Alias is Texas.
7. Jason aka Arizona.
8. David Bullet Lopez aka Tennessee.

We got 2 Big Getaway Vans, with Marie and Jenny driving them, Xavier and Marie driving, Jenny and Jason driving, and now, we made the plans and time to execute them all, and we found out the area, next to a Macdonald Burger Joint/Fast Food Joint and we began unloading, Lovebirds Xavier and Marie got Diamond Van and Jenny and Jason the other pair of lovebirds got Jewelry Vans.

Season 2, Chapter 10, Execution and New Enemies –

Los Tigres bombed another area now, Tigres control entire towns, expelling The Police and The Mayors away in Guatemala, Honduras, El Salvador, Ecuador, Puerto Rico, Dominican Republic, Dominica, Greenland and Cannada, taking over farms like nothing, Greenland and Canada cracked down on them and had many killed, imprisoned, expelled and detained down.

El Unico, Amado and Juaquin Fuentes recruited Mexican Marines, Kalibites (Guatemalan Military), Pirates, Police Officers, Paramilitaries, Contract Killers and Mercenaries as well as Average Frustrated Chumps (AFCs) too and now, they had small timers, part timers and legal business entities too, and now, we had them coming in waves too.

Los Zetas like professionalism many would state, Rising Knights lost a War to them in Mexico, a deal in some Mexican States made many Factions quit trafficking Narcotics and work on other small things like Protection, Smuggling, False ID Sales and Running Businesses only, Los Tigres members on Western Coast became Lifeguards, Firefighters, Teachers and Doctors too now as well as Basketball and Badminton Players too, and now, I mean some just haven't changed, and now we are here, El Unico is issuing threats too and new players come in as well.

Avoiding The Bikers, Armed Rednecks, Paramilitary Guys and Mercenaries here, and now, we got the vans ready, and now, we locked and loaded, I shoot down a Cop, and nobody noticed, he was tasered down, we realized his partner was battling MS 13, and I recognized the members, my targets brother, shooting him in the head, and his female companions too, and now, The Cop overpowered and left, rescuing his teammate, and I ran off, climbing the diamond store down, we got rich baby, I'd climb down, and now, before the cop could have done something, we realized something, MS13, ABZ, Crips & Los Avenues were there, waiting, and we went inside, we counted about 4 MS, 4 ABZ, 4 Avenues and 4 Crips, 4 power 2 = 4 x 4 = 4 square = 16 Assassins, and now, it was 8 of us vs 16 of them, outnumbered 2 ratio 1/ 16 : 8 = 2 : 1 and now, we went in, and now the positions, let us remember them all again.

Here we go again, we are 8 members in here, and we got this, the council of Solntskaya Bravta, Irish Mob, Kkangpae, Aryan Brotherhood & 18th/EME does not even bother with that or anything –

1. Xavier (mistook for Jenkins) is the operator, checking Cameras and whatnot as he will handle safes and passwords easily. Alias is Iowa.
2. Castro is the Negotiator, who will talk to the Bank Staff and make sure, they do not, call the police. Alias is Kansas.
3. John is our Grifter, he will grift inside the crowd and make panic distractions. Alias is New York.
4. Camille is the Thief, if Bank gives us the diamonds and money, she will take it and leave, she will be wearing wigs to disguise herself. Alias is California.
5. Jenny will be the Getaway Driver as she will stay in the Car and wait till coast is clear and we can drive back home. Alias is Alaska.
6. Marie is the Field Medic here in case anyone got injured, she will treat the wounds, becoming a nurse she is. Alias is Texas.
7. Rafael is The Scout and he will make sure Nobody Goes in or Out without his permission. Alias is Arizona.
8. I, David Bullet Lopez will be the leader and order giver, and will roam around the shop pickpocketing people down. My Alias is Tennessee.

I went inside with Camille, who pickpocketed down a lady, stole some cash from another lady, and walked out, Rafael began talking to the guards, distracting them enough and Camille walked out, and well her tools caused another distraction, car-jacking and crashing them all, she parked them elsewhere, and ran off, and now, Marie was close by, we had two trucks near Macdonald Joint, which was on some holiday after all, and now, we went out, Camille broke into the backdoor and with Rafael began taking from their truck, and I mean, they tasered down everyone and killed them, just kidding nobody was there, Diamond Shop had Diamonds, and we took them all, some of them were taken down, they were Mega Rich, they can cover the thefts easily like peanuts to them, and now, we began looking around, and now, before anything, one of the staff members thrown in a gun and came inside, and Rafael and Camille double shot him down, tasered him and threw him out, and we moved the trucks back, took the goods and loaded them, Marie and Jenny and the others were pleased, when Bloodbath happened, well remembered everything, we all had a Gun, we all know how to aim and fire too.

In Truck one, Ladies (Jenny, Marie & Camille) drove with Rafael in it, and away from there, Xavier had truck number 2, and he drove out alone, we brought nobody other than Guns, Tasers, Batons, Bats, Brass Knuckles and Knives, and now, 5/8 members gone, remained 3 of us, John w/ Jenkins came in, and now, we were out there, with a Bag, and we had paper bags in them, and asked them to put whatever diamonds they had, 5 customers in there, when Crips and Asian Boyz came inside, and we all ducked, and now, they yelled, and we knew what was happening, I called The Others, told them to drive to Northern Californian Cities and change Number Plating or something, and we got a Phone Call, Police are after them, and we needed something Jenny shot the steering wheel of a cop car, and the Cop Car hit a Truck and there remained 2 Cop

Cars, they were chasing one truck only, the other truck was manned down by a single individual only.

Kansas (John Castro) was sleeping in the 2nd Van, he woke & chose Violence, shooting the tires of a Police Car, sitting in the front with Xavier (Iowa), okay I am a little high, let me tell you the crew again, I am so tired man, here is the crew, forget Medic, Grifter and Operator, enough Choices Heist Monaco thing.

I am David Lopez aka Tennessee (I forget my own name), Xavier is Iowa, John Castro is Kansas, Marie is Texas, Jenny is Arizona, Camille is California, John (Jason, False ID, stole a friends that too) is New York & Rafael is Alaska now, okay so Tennessee, Alaska and New York stayed behind, Johnny Cooley I remember his name now, okay we are here.

Texas, California, Arizona and Alaska in Truck 1, with more Gold chased by 3 cop cars, one being shot down and both cops dying, 2nd car shot by truck 2 with loss gold, silver, diamonds and platinum in it with Kansas & Iowa on it, New York & Tennessee remained in the shop, doing shoplifting, when ABZ, MSX3, Avenues and Crips members rolled by shooting the valley and small towns, when some Fringe Rednecks and Armed Group guys started a round of shooting, New York and I started shooting, and now, Police and Sheriff got around, we were screwed, and now, I saved the cashier, shooting an ABZ Member, took the dead guy's gun and tossed it around, the staff were Ukrainian and Israeli Gangsters after all, Cashier took the gun, when MS member shot and killed him, I shot that guy in the head, 2 men down, New York killed 3 of them, Avenues and MS members, and we ran off, taking some gold and diamonds, and taking the car, we got trucks 1 and 2 fighting police cars, and Kansas, got out of his car, and shot the glasses of the police car with Texas and California, killing some cops and now, we got off with that, Truck 2 loaded their goods to Truck 1, Kansas, Iowa and California were coming to the save, and now, that was that, small towns song, Jason Aldean was right, sucker punch somebody on the sidewalk, car jacking old lady at a red light, pull the gun on the owner of the liquor store, you think it is tough, like to fool up, burn down the flag and stomp it, you think it is tough, try that in a small town, see how you far you make it down the road, right here we take care of our own, you cross that line and it wont take long for you to find, I recommend you don't, try that in a small town.

California hit ABZ Car, and we shot ABZ and MS Members down, towed the Crips too, and helped Rednecks and Cowboys, who killed the other Gangsters, only one shopkeeper was alive, an elderly, I took his hands and took him to the nearby house, and told him we wont hurt him, when an ABZ walks up, he was Harley Ares Fitzgerald the whole time, shooting the 3 men down, different gangs, when a 4th comes by, Magnus Von Stahl stabbed and killed him down instead.

I and New York sit in Truck 2 and escape, Sheriffs and Police were nearby, but we drove off, and the townies come by, everyone gave statements, they couldn't catch us, and we escaped, Council had another meeting, we were investing in Fortune 500s, Coffee Shops, Boutiques and Makeups, Surfing and Skating Contests, Libraries & Cab Businesses.

EL Unico, Amado and Fuentes with Collins now, a new ally were coming, Jack Rollins came in and mentioned it all down, and Collins and Crips entered the residential areas we had, and they started shooting at our shops and churches down, killing more people, LAPD Officers and Crips engaged into a shootout, when MS Members came inside and started stabbing children, disabled, elderly and laborers down, and now, Russians and Irish went down, Koreans sniped a MS member, we went to a War, full on Warfare or Warzone Mode happened.

Koreans and Aryans began stabbing and being stabbed by MS Members and Crips, Avenues started shooting, The Cartel Members were there, The Special Enforcers from Kkangpae and many residents joined the fighting, MS was getting out of hand, and now, we don't do business in Los Angeles, but in a small town with Mexicans, and now, I got there, with a few Bats and Batons, beating down Crips and MS Members down, and walking past killing many of them Gangsters and now, trouble always had a way of finding me, Camille and Russian Leaders on one side killing and shooting down Salvadorians and Mexicans, side by side, and now, we spotted Collins, Jack Rollins was there, killing MS Members and Avenues Members, Jason went to him and shot him in the head twice and walked by, and now, Collins was dead too, I remembered the man who killed Marlon and Jessy, Acalan was never his name Atzi was his name, and he ambushed me down, and Camille pulled the trigger on his shoulders and he was injured and we took him inside, and tied him down, he was a Federal Agent the whole time, it was a rumor, he was Native Mexican, and cannot speak Spanish or English properly either, and he escaped, he got a Cartel Runner in there, we hid, Anatoly killed the Cartel Runner and Cartel

Members, and Atzi attacked Anatoly, only to be beaten down, had both his hands and legs cracked down, and now, before anything LAPD, SWAT & OCSD Raided the place, finding weapons, guns and knives, many members took Cocaine and Heroin, Atzi and his crew got deported, we were all arrested down, lack of evidence made me and many more get out, Anatoly, Sergei, John, Rafael and Camille went in for a long time, Allen Jenkins and his friend made the raid, we flushed them down, we did not kill them but bribed them to go away, and now, well minor offences and shorter sentences happened, as Council Leaders did not have a Criminal History, Korean Leaders were pardoned, Aryan Brotherhood, Irish Mob and Russian Gangsters went to Prison with Camille, John and Rafael.

Cartel remained at large and we needed to flush them out too, and end the bloodshed, Koreans suggested we make a deal with them, a peace deal which failed, ICE began raiding our churches, we do Illegal Alien Immigration, and they did not find anything, we just made it work, we saw them a Mile Coming, Jason was a Police Officer after all, working on the inside for us, we still needed Cops off our backs and Jason wanted to end some Gangs personally, we don't allow this, many 18 Cliques will disagree with us on this move too.

Living in Los Angeles and buying Small Towns too, with Mexican Population, Native Population and White Population as Browns, Reds and Caucasians together worked harder, many Mixed Race people were here too.

And now, Jack Rollins quickly and quietly plus skillfully killed down enemies and helped us all out, Collins got killed too, who are the new leaders of Crips another family of clowns actually, and now who are they, their names are –

1. Devon Stone
2. Adam Stone
3. Charlo Stone
4. Judy Stone
5. Charlie Stone

Stones, Williams and Knights are all related to each other and pretty close, kill one family and another one comes up, I am going crazy, cannot remember names, dates, people, addresses and I am crazy, Camille and I had a son Bishop or Maverick, God help me, please and now, finally, Carnage Cleared and Cartel blew up a Church and declared War upon us, Jack Rollins joined hands with us and brought his crew of Mercenaries along too, and now we are ready for a Big War, Council Members met at a Building and it exploded, leaving us all injured, and now, I took a step up, retired them all and gave them land, I stood up and decided to end Stones & The Cartel once and for all, DEA Raided my Apartment, and could not find anything, a Killer was on Loose too, and now, we began seeing it all up, the heist happened, I was injured and had to go away for months too, and now here I am, working on my health.

1 Year Later, we are having a party, remember the new enemies we got, Cartel took over Super Surenos, retiring the old leaders away, sending them to Europe, Iceland, Mongolia and even India, far away.

Enemies –

1. Devon Stone
2. Adam Stone
3. Charlo Stone
4. Judy Stone
5. Charlie Stone
6. Raul Martinez aka El Unico
7. Amado Rodriguez
8. Joaquin Fuentes

Charlie Stone and Devon Stone fired at our party, killing many Russians, Irish and Koreans down, straining relations b/w Mexican Mafia or EME and Aryan Brotherhood + Peckerwoods alliance too.

Stones are marked now, Cartel too, Jack Rollins is on board too.
Season 3, Chapter 1, Cartel & Stones –
Enemies –

1. Devon Stone
2. Adam Stone
3. Charlo Stone
4. Judy Stone
5. Charlie Stone
6. Raul Martinez aka El Unico
7. Amado Rodriguez
8. Joaquin Fuentes

And now, we met up, with MS, ABZ and LAV leaders, with leaders of 38th Street, Florencia – 13 & Latin Kings Nation, and a sitting happened, where MS and LK Members attacked the father of a Russian Gangster, stabbing him, falling into a trap, Asian Boyz came to our aid, we saved them from their leaders who were Police Informants and Undercover Agents and now, new alliance happened down, ABZ and 18 made peace as TRG Members joined MS Members, Fresno Bulldogs saved by ABZ, Russians & 18 St turned Bulldogs into attacking and killing MS and Crip Members down, and now, Bulldogs began keeping quiet, Crips and MS dying, TRG Alliance caused peace between TRG & ABZ Members down, and now, The Cartel and The Stones began sending us kidnapped people and Stone Brothers and The Cartel stood outside, killing 2 Koreans down, Kkangpae tattoos, and I realized, Koreatown was on fire, LAPD & SWAT & OCSD were all over, and Fuentes pressed a button detonating a big building down, killing Koreans, Chinese and Russians, other Solntskaya Bravta clans came by, Council dissolved, we didn't do that, we were underground, now we don't sell drugs and stuff, nothing to meet up for, and now, The Council Members retired, Jerry, Ian, Sergei, Anatoly etc moved their family to Scottsdale, Houston, Coconut Creek, Iowa City, Alberta, Saint Petersburg, Dublin, Belfast, Mexico City and Other Cities, we just became a group of friends conducting actual businesses instead of drugs and war weapons.

With Anatoly, Sergei and The Others going to EL Paso, Texas, Kkangpae Members took their family to a quiet suburb in Modesto, Aryan Brotherhood Members went to Colorado, Irish Mob members went to Florida, and 18th Board will go to Arizona and start a new life there only, The Cartel killed many more, and now Greater Influences came by, Anatoly and The Others were never that good initially but retired richer then ever, Sergei and Anatoly have their own food branches in Siberia, Ural Ranges, Moscow and Many More.

Council is no more into Heroine and Cocaine industries and now, we began our line of work but enemies still prevail on us and this is the end hopefully, and Anatoly Business was attacked by a Jamaican Posse under Williams command probably, I mean Stones discount – discount Knights as discount Knights are Williams and they are Discount Williams, and now, our job was to locate and bring him to Justice, and a Red Feather MC Member Jack Rollins CCTV Footage showed us, it was a Jamaican named John Edwards aka Sniper Boy, and he killed someone's daughter and son too, an Armenian Friend, and now, Armenians and Russians together, we began a search for him, LAPD & SWAT Raided our Warehouses, we didn't have a thing, and a Lawsuit on my behalf was filed and SWAT Teams had their jurisdiction limited, I mentioned how the residents are actually attacked, Stone Members are in having SWAT members and we filed a video evidence showing SWAT Members hitting and beating residents especially the handicapped ones and the harmless ones, and The Judge ordered to remove SWAT & LAPD from my area, and now since we live in a Small Town in Central Valley, things are different too, and now, we began making Firearms and now found out a Jamaican Posse group has attacked the Local Churches, when Aryan Brotherhood and Irish Mob Members attacked them, many got killed but Local Ranchers, Cowboys, Veterans, Bikers and Mercenaries attacked, and now, the Workers and Church Attenders attacked, Neopagans attacked them too, we did good work in the towns, small towns and farmlands nearby, Fresno isnt actually far off, Bulldogs may or may not attack us all only, and now, we came across the enemies once again as members of the Stone Household, their parents and grandparents etc are all alive actually, their grandfather and grandmother never approved of their bloodshed and wanted them to have actual jobs or do petty crimes instead and I for one agree with them all over this one, and now MJF is an amazing

Professional Wrestler, and I heard he played Football, American Football in both High School and College, he is the next AJ Styles, Kenny Omega, Rick Flair and Hulk Hogan of Professional Wrestling for sure, he must win in Impact/TNA, Japan and Mexico + WWE.

And now, we found out, they were all hooded and masked, and I began shooting them, using a Sniper, I sniped one member in the head, killing him, and now when we realize they wore full armor, we shot the tires and the engine, it exploded down, and now, 2 of their 6 members were killed and now, they escaped when more of Stone Family Goons (GD, Bloods, Crips, BGF) and all came by, and began looting and burning and now3, Russian Mafia Hitman and Trackers began doing their job, Jack Rollins killed down 2 of their members, strangling them down, and dragging them away, he knocked them out, and took their weapons away, he is like a Jack Reacher lol, and now, he began saving people down, and doing some nasty stuff, and he killed one member down and hid in, he is good with cover, and now, The Cartel blew the buildings out, this was a full scale invasion after all and now, Cartel Members came there too, Jamaican Posse joined hands with The Cartel I cant even remember the name off and Stone Family of Monsters and Scammers, they scammed down people and children too, and they are monsters for that straight up, thinking they are some Jocks from High School, I mean they are Basketballers, American Footballers, Baseballers and Track Runners as well as Shooting Champions and Boxing Champions, we got Wrestling and Boxing here too, and let me tell you something, we used to sell drugs, but we are redeeming ourselves, Doja Cat loves Samuel Hyde aka Sam Hyde aka Sameer Singh Hydruv aka Sa Mu Hai aka Samuel Hydestein, a Social Media Influencer, Co-Host of Million Dollar Extreme presents World Peace and Various YouTube Prank Channels, Frank Hassle aka

Chad King, Charles and Nick Carroll and Eric Hayden too are there too.

And now, we got that done, enough of MDE World Peace, and now, Jamaicans and Mexicans are still shooting, Cartel Paramilitary wants to take over, Fresno Bulldogs had a civil war and many joined The Cartel instead, what the hell is their name again, I do not recall or remember now, Tigres Cartel is what they call themselves now, they killed Arabic and Indian Business Owners in Mexico and took over their goods too, and now they were here too, and do all the3 harm they can do to me and my friends too, and now, we all are fighting them and they have thousands of members in their gangs too now and they got an invasion lined, up I killed down ABZ Members, MS Members, Fresno Bulldogs Members, Cartel Members and many more, and we are losing people in this war, Children with the guns of their fathers and grandfathers or mothers and grandmothers came outside and began killing too, many were shot and killed down, entire families massacred, and we pushed them all back, and the entire town rallied do2wn behind us and we threw them, out cold and they killed dogs, cattle, birds, cats, rabbits and monkeys too, and now, leftover Acalan and Atzi were both found, wounded and we rounded them up, and hanged them, not until death and Jack Rollins subbed two of their friends too, who were Javier and Micah, a White Boy, and now, with the four at our mercy, Acalan and Atzi didn't snitch, realising their own friends and family members disown3ed them, they joined us instead, but we did keep a close eye on them all, their families died in famine and floods, they had nothing, many married dudes send their kids to Canada, New York, London, Moscow and Mumbai away and now, Mumbai and Jaipur are amazing cities in my opinion too.

And now, Stones and Cartel Members are to be targeted, and Kkangpae, Aryans, Irish, 18th St, Bravta and Armenians together send in a large war party and we began doing things, locating their members down and began hunting them, we broke into a motel house and we found out where the Cartel members were and began looking out for them all, and now, with that being said, I broke into the room of one Cartel Member and we killed him, his wife and his kids, and yes you heard that one right, we killed his wife and kids too, and they threatened us down too, and we murdered down everyone Acalan and Atzi with Javier and Micah and Jack Rollins were at their4 houses, and now, Acalan and Atzi were learning Spanish, English, Irish, Korean and Russian from Jack Rollins and Kkangpae members down the lane, Kdramas are good as hell tbh and now, we need to not forget about somethings too, and we found their labs and cooks, shooting them and the friendly members no, we walked past them, shooting a camera down, they were revolving cameras, and we broke inside, killing 3 members of the Cartel, they were ruthless and sadistic too, and we killed them all, I put a lotion of Sleeping Pill and LSD in those lunch packs they had, and we overheard two members too and we hid in there, and I tasked Camille, John and Rafael, Raf killed both of them with help of John and Camille and now, we are in their turf, Armenians threw fireworks and began launching grenades and rockets into a building where Cartel Members were working out in, and many died, and a shootout happened, there only, Armenians and Russians attacked Georgians, Ukrainians, Romanians and Mexicans in there and we did a large scale shootout, and we shoot down Stone Family Members too one.

One after Another and now, we are killing it down too hard, Highwaymen showed up, Bandits or Looters and began killing Cartel Gunners too, and one after another, Cartel Members lost control, we had hacked into the mainframes and we had disabled their electricity and I planted a bomb in the water supply detonating it down toon and now, police patrol cars showed up, a Cartel Sniper gunned them both down, Armenians killed the other two, and Sniper disappeared, he was our member only and now with that being said, we marched towards down the area, and rounded 6 members and took off, nobody was left behind and we moved on and Stones and Cartel Members didn't speak, and they knew they wouldn't get killed, we found out their families and threatened them, when they talked, they were told later we will never harm their families and we did keep them locked in a room for days, many members of various gangs and groups now, Kkangpae organized a grand heist from a Diamond Jewelry shop in a small town suburb nearby, we had to wear masks and get it all done, and I, Camille, John, Rafael and Xavier signed up for it, and now, we began looking when a new member named Michael Perry aka Bentley showed up from another clique and now, he replaced Xavier, he had a girlfriend named Leticia Johnson aka Lil Feather, they both plan to join a Biker Gang or a Biker Club and live a peaceful life, both are 28 and 32, and now, both are expert thieves, Lil Feather served for Irish, Aryans and Russians only, and now, Perry joined the team of 5, and began looking at the place for its credits, Kkangpae Members will take a large cut of the profits made from the loot, and we needed to rob a bank too first, maybe some grocery shops too.

And now, Michael Perry and I went out somewhere, and we began looking around, and we went into a shop room of a Stone Owned House, and Perry winked, and as the guy turned around, Perry used his phone and hacked his electricity and shot him in the head, and I kept the door guard and we took some money and got out, and yes, he was not friendly, he tried killing me that small town invasion too, and now, we took the money earned from yesterday, the day before, last week and today, and we split it down 2 ways, Perry and I walked happily, I sent the kids away, and we had a daughter too, Annabella and her twin Brother Jackson, sending them away too, time passes by pretty fast actually, and now, we smuggled into another area, a shopping mall, killed their security guard down, and pickpocketed him down too, and left him somewhere and now, we got out, and Perry is good too with his job, and we were never suspected down and out either too, and now, a MS13 Member hit us, and Perry and I hit the accelerator and we hit fast and they were shooting, when Perry hit them breaks and moved left, MS Car was hit by a truck and they exploded and LAPD was after us, and we escaped them too, and we entered a shop and got the number plates and color switched, and now, we ran into and hit the son of El Unico and a Cartel member, I shot the member down and we escaped down too, MS Member hit his son and ran off, killing the 5 year old and his 6 and 7 year old friends too, EL Unico never found out who did this and now, we had 3 MS Cars chasing us down, each car had about 4 members each and Stones came into the play too, John, Rafael and Camille came into the play too, and now we began running into the Car Park, and parked away, and we shoot down a member too, before anyone.

And now, we killed one member, Perry and I took his phone, gun and wallet too, throwing his IDs and taking the Cash, I packed 6 Pistols in me, and I mean 4 in most cases, and all of them had Silencers on them and now, we began running around, shooting and killing 2 more members and moving past them two too, and now, we stole food, guns and money from their cars and vans too, and drank the coffees, Starbucks Latte and Oreo Flavored Coffees and Shakes too, we just drink and think actually, and now, with that, towed4 the car and came back inside, John killed 2 members down, and Camille sniped one of their members down, 2 of them got alerted, and we packed into a Sedan and hid, when an Armenian came by Arman Ivanov, and shoot both of them down, he was joining 18th St Gang on behalf of Armenian Power and he was in the crew too, Rafael is retiring from Crime and Arms trafficking and even Contract killing too, and now, we escaped the city only and began looking around town and ran to Bay Area, San Francisco, Southern California, United States of America and we began hiding, killing more bounty hunters, mercenaries, contract killers and gang affiliates and escaped down to Border Towns, where Mexican Hitman were after us, killing one of them down too, and now, Kkangpae was at War with Yakuza, Albanians, Fresno Bulldogs and Triads, and now, they did win the war, but Kkangpae got under a Crackdown too, and they had to pullout of their own Organized Crime, Smuggling, Terrorism and Arms Dealings, and now, the council just dissolved in a way, no drugs or weapons, EME is disappointed too, and now, we send their Tax Collectors with our money, while getting our people out of those cells and somewhere more productive instead and being normal citizens.

And now, we got ready, Lil Feather and Bentley got ready, Lil Feather, Camille, Xavier and Ishika robbed a spot, afterwards Xavier and Ishika began working at our shops now, and now, Camille and I are getting sloppier too, Devon and Charlie Stone began shooting at us all, and now, Bentley I mean Bailey lol, he has a Bentley obsession, Bailey attacked Charlie Stone and killed his gunman, there were 3 and now there were 2 of them, we shot their tires and driver down too, and now, a physical altercation happened, as Devon and Charlie attacked John and Rafael down, and Bailey too, it was me and Camille vs Devon and Charlie, Devon gloated about killing and slaving the children, he didn't rape them but he wouldn't hesitate doing that, and now, since grandpa and grandma died, Devon's father died in a Car Accident, and Mother is still alive, and knowing the things he and his wife Jamala are getting into, she doesn't want to see Devon die, she has another son and daughter twin named as Frankie and Laura, and they are in Wrestling, planning Wrestling, Grappling and MMA, they were also in Petty Crimes and Drug Addiction once but now it is all over, and now, Frankie, Laura and Mother Stone walked away, The Cartel of El Unico, aka Tigres and another Cartel, Baja California Cartel had a shootout, Frankie killed a Baja Hitman, and told El Unico he was with him, mother and sister got killed, Frankie was gunned down too, and Stones have been pissed off since then and now, we beat down Devon and Charlei Stone, and tied them up, as Kkangpae and Irish Mob members came inside and took them on a Van elsewhere, unlocking the phones too.

Season 3, Chapters 2 & 3, Stones and Stone Stealing –

Devon and Charlei Stone somehow escaped but Wong and Tongs of Chinese Triads made peace, they don't even do anything (Drugs, Gambling, Murder) and now, we captured them again, El Unico send a grenade in the building killing Russian and Korean Mafia Members down, and many Irish Mob Businesses were bombed down, LAPD and SWAT Teams attacked and began a crackdown on The Cartel Tigres and Stone Family, Jamaican Posse members too, and forgot his name but we got him maybe, Acalan and Atzi, began guiding us down, and we killed more and more Mexicans and one by one, and now, we were winning the war, and now, we may not get too ahead of it ourselves, as we still have another thing to do later on, Avenues and 38th St lead by El Albert and Javi joined Tigres Cartel and Stones Operations and now, we had issues John and Rafael had it with those two already, and now John started having heart attacks, and Rafael is diagnosed with Cancer and Heart Illnesses too, Russians, Koreans, Irish and Aryans are doing fine, and now, we needed to do something before anything, Devon and Charlei were saved as El Unico raided the households, and killed the members from our organizations, Russians and Irish moved to other small towns, Aryans started their own Household Business only, Kkangpae began running Restaurants, Hotels and Casinos only, council disbanded in a way and now we had new enemies, Albert and Javi joint attacked our compound killing a few Ogs too, and now we had a war, killing some of their younger members, and I have been losing it, cannot remember my own name or my kids names either, and now, I am going insane, Camille married a White Peckerwood named Bjorn Van Helvig who is a Red Feather MC Member, Professional Wrestler & Mixed Martial Artist, Mercenary, State Guard and Street Fighter as well as a Businessman, and I met Gabriella 'Gabby' Reyes again and she called me David 'Bullet' Lopez now and we began dating, and now, with that, we had a new members list too –

Leticia 'Lil Feather' Johnson
Michael 'Bailey' Perry
Jack Rollins 'Red Wolf'
Jesse 'Taylor' Calsada
Jose 'Sniffer' Daniels
Angel 'Blue' Lopez
Jey 'Joker' Raul Martinez
Tom 'Tommy-San' Soto

And now, with we organized our own crew of thieves, and Council has changed now, EME joined instead and we left the council only, and EME works directly, but they left the council on good terms and Armenian Power joined on EME's behalf and now, El Albert and Javier are actually brothers of El Unico, Joaquin Fuentes and Amado Rodriguez too, they think they are El Chapo and Pablo Escobar.

Tommy-San, Joker, Blue, Sniffer and Taylor decided to go with me The Bullet on a Grand Theft Mission, we were planning to loot a Diamond Merchant store in downtown Los Angeles and needed the muscle, and I came up with a plan, Gabby is a Doctor and a Drug Smuggler too, and she also did Illegal Alien Smuggling without payment too.

And now, we met with The Yakuza Members and made a deal, since the deals with Kkangpae are over, Yakuza and 18th St made a deal, we met some Yakuza Members too and here are five of them.

1. Tamaya Hideki, Ryu
2. Jochi Kanemaru, Dragon
3. Seiya Ishimori, Tanaka
4. Kenji San, Tenryu
5. Takeshi Mousasi, Mist
6. Daimyo, Tetsuya Okada
7. Underboss, Kenta Okada

And now, we fended off some Avenues Goons for them, as an Avenue Member attempted to Rape and Kidnap a Yakuza Daughter, we found out and killed him and his 4 friends one after another, the girl died in a Car Accident and now, Arman Ivanov aka Neville, Michael Perry aka Bailey and Lil Feather aka whatever name was

Enemies –

1. Devon Stone
2. Adam Stone
3. Charlo Stone
4. Judy Stone
5. Charlie Stone
6. Raul Martinez aka El Unico
7. Amado Rodriguez
8. Joaquin Fuentes
9. Javier Fuentes
10. El Albert Fuentes

Crew Members –

Leticia 'Lil Feather' Johnson
Michael 'Bailey' Perry
Jack Rollins 'Red Wolf'
Jesse 'Taylor' Calsada
Jose 'Sniffer' Daniels
Angel 'Blue' Lopez
Jey 'Joker' Raul Martinez
Tom 'Tommy-San' Soto
Arman Ivanov 'Neville'
David Lopez 'Bullet'
Gabriella 'Gabby' Reyes
Leticia 'Lil Feather/Letty' Johnson

Perry, Letty and Gabby now work backstage, John and Rafael retired down too, and now run a business, a restaurant and now, I am the only in-charge in here as Xavier and Ishika joined Rafael only and now, Council is still respected but here we are all free, and now we needed to do out Contract Killing, Gambling, Weapons Trafficking and Robberies perfectly without getting the public eyes too, and now, we prepared a crew, Kkangpae and Yakuza made peace because I told them so and now with that2, and now with peace making deals going on around, we focused on the issues and attacked a tattoo parlor ran by Fuentes Family, and now their 2nd and 3rd cousins are either Mercenaries, Professional Wrestlers/ Luchadors & Mixed Martial Artists, Security Guards, Thieves, Smugglers or Professors as well as Small Time Business Owners, anyways this was an Avenues Tattoo Parlor, and John and Rafael as well as Xavier and Ishika mentioned being attacked by them all, and I got a call the other day, Camille mentioned a shootout happened, and Xavier and Ishika got killed and their self was stabbed down and John and Rafael escaped and contacted LA-EME and the Aryan Brotherhood and EME Members being frequents and a EME Member's friend got killed in the shootout caused the Cartel to back off, the shooters got killed by John and Rafael only, there were 3 of them, and I heard to the news of Shooting and Mass Murdering happening all around the world, remembering the Mass Shooting between Armenia and Azerbaijan happened where Nagorno-Karabakh Corridor was the main area they fought over for years on and off, Armenians lost to Azerbaijan many say and the others say, both made peace and Karabakh is still in Azerbaijan and Azerbaijanis don't have a Gang here, one thing I noticed, never seen Azeris in LA, they go to NYC and Miami only.

And now, I assembled the crew once more, and now, we decided to do a massive home invasion, now we make sure there are no dogs in the house, I love dogs because they make good security too, and trust me, I have brought a new Husky Pair called Anna and Allen, and they bit like hell, Pet Monkeys, Rabbits, Birds and Cats don't attack you, okay cats can too and monkey bite sucks too, and now, we found out of a local car dealership sold down a car to a businessman living in Beverly Hills, he had two german shepherds living with him and we wont go there, like they can bite, I don't want anyone to be bitten on their ass at all, and what If he is some John Wick and now, well we attacked his house, his dogs and sons named Garrett and Mack as well as his sons Jack and Adam were playing around when we attacked the two dogs, and the children, and broke into the house, unknowingly members of Red Feathers MC were seen sitting in there, Mother was a Featherwood MC and formerly Pink Doves MC Member and now, we had to leave but a Biker came by and punched our members, when we took a gun out and cocked it at the kids, and we made a deal, he let us go, but a one of the dogs bit me in the ass, and one of the young boys called him off and told me to go away, and I went away, Anna and Allen don't bite, Garrett and Jack's owner came to my house, brother of Arman Ivanov, meet Sigurd Thunberg (he is not related to Greta Thunberg, but has Northern European as well as some Native American and North Indian Heritage) and he was a Pagan, Odin tattoos were visible too, White – Americans are basically European – Americans, Central Asian – Americans, North African – Americans and Jewish – Americans and even West – Asians, Easterners and some Latinos are white, and even in Native Americans, Pacific Islanders and Hmong Groups, we can see Red Hair, Blue Eyes, Green Eyes and Yellow/Blonde Hair and now, forget that, Arman and Sigurd got into a fight, Arman got his ass kicked and I and Taylor apologized to his sons and his dogs, and now, he demanded the leader, which was me only, and well we ended the fight and made peace, turns out he is the one who has a partnership with my businesses too and now, we all made peace with him and Jack Rollins aka Red Wolf also knows him, they are cousins only, and now, I felt bad about myself, Gabby and I had a son, forgot about him, Angel was his name and Nikos was our second son, both were born during our fresh school passing out, my college funds went to rescue my parents cancer and both survived and died from a car accident only, and I was cool, living my life the way I want only, and now, well I decided to break off into another household and we found out about a bunch of people, Native American and White American Household Areas where Mexican Americans have been badly mistreated down and we broke off into the house of a Businessman, now there are Rich, Working Class, Middle Class, Poor Folks and Below Poverty Line, we attack classes 1 and 2, sometimes 3 and 4 as well too, and now, we ran into Devon and Charlei Stones who started shooting at our directions only and now they had their brothers as well as Fuentes and Unico too, remember the list –

Enemies –

1. Devon Stone
2. Adam Stone
3. Charlo Stone

4. Judy Stone
5. Charlie Stone
6. Raul Martinez aka El Unico
7. Amado Rodriguez
8. Joaquin Fuentes
9. Javier Fuentes
10. El Albert Fuentes

The Yakuza –

1. Tamaya Hideki, Ryu
2. Jochi Kanemaru, Dragon
3. Seiya Ishimori, Tanaka
4. Kenji San, Tenryu
5. Takeshi Mousasi, Mist
6. Danta (daimyo, boss), Tetsuya Okada
7. Kenichi (underboss), Kenta Okada

The Crew –
Leticia 'Lil Feather' Johnson
Michael 'Bailey' Perry
Jack Rollins 'Red Wolf'
Jesse 'Taylor' Calsada
Jose 'Sniffer' Daniels
Angel 'Blue' Lopez
Jey 'Joker' Raul Martinez
Tom 'Tommy-San' Soto

And Ryu, Kenta and all warned us off them and they started shooting at our Vans and we drove off, and now Tommy – San hit their cars down and we drove away on the highway, hitting a prison bus, and the inmates ran free and attacked Cartel Members, many Skinheads in there, a favor for EME & Aryan Brotherhood Members as well as Irish Mob and now, they attacked the cops and armed themselves and began shooting Stone Goons and Cartel Thugs, and now, Devon and Charlei Stone began attacking us, going into Gabby's workplace and trying to attack her, but Dennis Miller, Yuri Ivanov, Harley Ares Fitzgerald, Magnus Von Stahl and many more were there, when Allen Jenkins aka Punkish Criminal got there and took them all out, Damon Maxwell III was also there, his grandpa and father were suspected of being masked heroes called Red Punk and Punkish Angel, even though his father identified himself as The Typhoon, but Maxwell's book called him Punkish Angel, given the fan following of the Punks and how Maxwell III killed his only enemies when they tried attacking his son Damon IV, who probably would be a Superhero too, okay they attacked him and his girlfriend Crystal Scarlett down, Maxwell III is 38 and retired Professional Wrestler, Mixed Martial Artist, Mercenary, Bounty Hunter and a Dog Shelter Owner and Media books have mixed the ages and time periods up, and now, Maxwell has daughters and sons many of them in Iowa and Canada and even Finland, Norway, Japan and India and now Stones, Fuentes and Unico attacked our streets again, killing our people, and Perry cried as his daughter, sister, mother and grandmother got gunned down and El Unico yelled laughing, killing the father of Tommy – San, and he never had a good relationship with him either.

Tomko Sr, Tommy's grandfather was a Yakuza Boss turned Doctor, Professor and Greco-Roman Wrestler, and now, he has arrived in The United States, his clan once sold drugs now help the community and organizes charity, Japanese Government ordered a crackdown on The Yakuza too, now his clan emigrated the United States of America and hearing Tomko Junior and Honda (named after Samurai Legend, Honda Tadakasu, who by Oba Nobunaga once referred to as the Samurai among Samurais for his ferocious war skills, Honda fought in 55 active battlefields and was never hit once, he was so good fighting on the front lines, Samurai were a class of Warriors of Feudal Japan, serving Daimyo, collecting Taxes and Fighting Wars, Miyamoto Musashi is the most celebrated with one eyed dragon Dante Masamune, Musashi was undefeated in 1over60 duels in Japan and fought in the battle of Sakigahara at the age of 17 under Lord Toyotomi and Honda Tadakasu) and now both killed by The Cartel, Tomko Sr at 70 contacted Local Yakuza Clans and got a fair deal trade, El Unico and the Mexicans have attacked down Yakuza, Kkangpae, Triads and Asian Boyz, and now all of Eastern Asians and Hmong People with Pacific Islanders formed a collision against El Unico and now, we kidnapped Devon and Charlei again, killing 20 of their guards down, and stealing away a warehouse, and now, with that, we made the news again, and Grandpa didn't want to spar down Devon or Charlei Stone, they had raped and sold an old friends daughter and now Tomko Sr took 6 years to track and rescue her down, and now, he wanted revenge only, and now, we allowed him to execute down Devon and Charlei Stones.

Season 3, Chapter 4, Stone Stealing –

Adam and Charlo Stone are now furious, and a bloodbath happened as Jamaican Leon killed their parents and elders as well as their children, and was able to run off and with his gang too, and now.

Enemies –

1. Devon Stone
2. Adam Stone
3. Charlo Stone
4. Judy Stone
5. Charlie Stone
6. Raul Martinez aka El Unico

7. Amado Rodriguez
8. Joaquin Fuentes
9. Javier Fuentes
10. El Albert Fuentes

Crew Members –
Leticia 'Lil Feather' Johnson
Michael 'Bailey' Perry
Jack Rollins 'Red Wolf'
Jesse 'Taylor' Calsada
Jose 'Sniffer' Daniels
Angel 'Blue' Lopez
Jey 'Joker' Raul Martinez
Tom 'Tommy-San' Soto
Arman Ivanov 'Neville'
David Lopez 'Bullet'
Gabriella 'Gabby' Reyes
Leticia 'Lil Feather/Letty' Johnson

The Yakuza –

1. Tamaya Hideki, Ryu
2. Jochi Kanemaru, Dragon
3. Seiya Ishimori, Tanaka
4. Kenji San, Tenryu
5. Takeshi Mousasi, Mist
6. Danta (daimyo, boss), Tetsuya Okada
7. Kenichi (underboss), Kenta Okada

Danta & Kenichi and Ryu came in running and formed a new council as the seven and him ran over Samoans, Mexicans and

Easterners (Japanese, Mongolians, Chinese and Koreans) and now, Tomko got Tommy instead to run for him and retired to Nevada, and now, we had his blessing to execute down Devon and Charlie Stone down, and we will, the girl committed suicide, leaving behind a mixed race son (Japanese and Russian) she was married to a Russian named Anatoly (the council member's driver and hitman) and now, the son reunited with Bravta and his Father and now, went off, and now Adam, Charlo & Judy Stones now want their brother back, sending assassins, that killed more and more, we tracked them and banged them down too, Bjorn aka Sigurd and the Bikers as well as Mack and Garrett who liked Anna and Allen too, helped us as well as Jack and Adam played with Nikos and Angel, Judy Stone and Fuentes were our next big targets down the lane, and we tried shooting Judy down, the dude would not die and now, Stones and Fuentes attacked The Yakuza, and we came rushing, Tomko Sr and his assassins killed the elite down, Acalan and Atzi joined Tomko Sr, who turned out to be Dante only, Tomko Sr passed away a long ago, Dante is a Con Artist as well and now Devon and Charlei were kept in a Storage Room and made to do Manual Labor and kept under a different location, Unico and his goons got there, and we had them all gunned down only, captured two of them down too, they shot and killed the dogs, sick assholes got what they deserved and now, I called the Crew for a Meetup, Eliminate Judy Stone or her goons, Judy is a Girl, I mistake her for a man sometimes and now with that, we saved a Kkangpae Gangster's friend from being kidnapped by Stones and Kkangpae was happy with the progress, got Triads to make peace with Yakuza and Kkangpae, Kkangpae are Korean Mafia or Gangsters and they are awesome actually, and now, we attacked El Unico and weakened his cars down, and tipped the police off, Blue shoot the goons down and was identified down, but Kkangpae killed the Cartel Goons and cleaned the bodies down by burying them all again, El Unico was arrested where EME Members, Fresno Bulldogs, Nuestra Familia, Latin Kings and Texas Syndicate Members are waiting for him, he was kept in Solitary Confinement and now, he was behind bars, and forced to stop working, and now, we turned on the enemies remaining, and now Judy Stone got arrested for Prostitution as she kidnapped and sold 30 year old unmarried girls and they were FBI and ATF Agents, and ATF killed many Cousins and arrested Judy down, Charlo and Adam Stone are the ones remaining, and now Devon and Charlei Stone attacked us again, and we told him that and now, Devon and Charlei were sold down, turns out they were decoys, Devon and Charlei escaped to Nevada, and were found down, it was me and Gabby vs Devon and Charlei, and we killed both of them, Devon was shot twice in the chest and Gabby shot Charlie or Charlei Stone down, and they were standing and a Car of Skinheads killed them when AB Leaders came by and stopped them from attacking me, and now, Council Abides man, and now, with that Sigurd Ivanov and Biance Ivanov, two dangerous individuals, they do not sell drugs but are Street and Professional Fighters, Mercenaries, Ex – Military and Security Officers too, and now are feared, Biker Clubs are feared, not all Biker Clubs are Criminals but some are Drug Gangs with Patches only, and now, LAPD Officers were on the move, Jenkins and Lincoln were fired and now are Vigilantes and Lincoln is an actor now and a mixed martial artist too, Chris Daukas was a Policeman turned MMA Fighter and Johnny Hendricks former UFC Welterweight Champion is now a Texas Policeman and fought off drug cartel, skin heads, organized crime, smuggler dens, theft groups, school shooters and many more there, and now, we got the crew here, and had a beer session in there, and now, with Devon and Charlie Stone dead and now, it was all over, they were nuesver dead, they were kept hostage under our command and we plan to kill them, but the two ran off.

And now, Stones and Cartel had a falling out, when a Cartel Member killed the mother of a Stone Family/Crip Goons and now, EL Unico Goons killed Devon and Charlie, Judy was in Custody, Adam and Charlo were captured but Samoans killed some Mexicans, and put trackers on the Cars, and LAPD showed up with a SWAT Team in there, and arrested everyone on the spot and Samoans escaped, and now Dante aka Tomko Sr in disguise and now, he stole art and whatnot, his assassins worked for Senators, Business Magnates, Military & Special Units, Police Force, Judges and Security Contractors too and now, they took out Cartel Members too, and weakened them all, El Unico, reunited with The Fuentes Family Members and Avenues gone wild, attacking MS13 and killing Stones cousins aka The Saints down, and the guys think of themselves as Alphonse Capones or Al Capones, National Crime Syndicate/Murder Inc., the Country Boys and the Council I mean Frank Lucas and Leroy Nickey Barnes were dangerous too, American Gangster movie is one of my favorite for a reason, and that is something too, and I mean we don't have Anton Chigurh types running around in here either, No Country for Old Men was a horrifying movie, imagine finding out your son is Anton Chigurh, don't want Nikos and Angel in Crime, Arms Dealing or Labor, wish they become something like Business Owners or something, and now, Gabby and I planned a heist in downtown Los Angeles too, and I hope Canada rekindles their friendship with India, Justin Treadou was wrong there, and we have no ill will and now, we needed to work in somewhere and I called the crew again, The Yakuza and The Crew 18 are meeting somewhere to discuss a grant theft and now, we got it.

We are breaking into the house of a successful businessman, and stealing his money, my guns are locked and loaded, and now, we were driving to another neighborhood and began looking around and see the guy leave, we wore masks and raided the house, by going inside and seeing the house down, we realized he had a family too, two sons and a daughter, Blue took over and shot both of his sons dead and retreated down, the Businessman came running and I shoot him in the neck and chest, backside of the house and we found his wife and killed her too, and using the keys unlocked the house, dragging the bodies, Blue made sure everyone was in the backyard, and now, with 4 people dead, we broke inside, and we ventured inside, and now the crew had -

1. Bullet
2. Blue
3. Tommy – San
4. Neville

And now, Tommy got out of his car, and killed the wife, how did he do so? When father and sons split up, and went to the backside from two different directions, he called Blue to hide, he shot and killed both brothers down easily, Tommy walked up to the wife and put a gun on her hand, taking her backyard and shot her dead too, and now unlocking the doors down, we broke inside, their daughter died by falling off the stairs, and speaking of dogs, Pitbull Princess and Golden Labrador Elise were locked in the Garage, and we opened the door, and got them into the Van and had Tommy drove them to my house, I said Anna and Allen will have more friends now, and we looted the house, and walked away, we called in another Cab and Gabby drove it down and we walked off as Adam Stone attacked us on the way in, and Adam was in revenge mode for what had happened, he killed a few cops too, Devon and Charlie were killed by Gabby, a Skinhead snitched out, mentioning it unknowingly and a highway café footage mentioned it too, Gabby taser down Adam Stone and we drove past him when Avenues attacked us, and we walked past it, Ryu and Yakuza had snipers planted killing 2 of their 6 members down, while that happened, the other four got trapped inside a room and now, killed one after another by chocking out, and now Danta and Ryu took out 6 Avenues as Fuentes and Unico were outside, they shot and killed Yakuza and Kkangpae Members down, and raped some of the wives and sisters too, and now, we killed Unico's sister in revenge only, and now, Raul Martinez was disowned by his family already, grandmother died, mother died, father died, brothers don't want him around, uncles don't want him around, mother died and his children walked away, joining 18th St and from there Avenues, some chose to go to College instead, and now, we meet with Joaquin Fuentes and he sniped down a new recruit and his mother, killing both of them, as well as the father, leaving behind a brother and a sister, who demanded revenge, and we agreed and the crew was handed guns and snipers and now we made a plan, to make the cartel surrender and put an end to all of them, we called out other 18th Street Crews and now, demanded their help in an all-out war where other Shot Callers mentioned being killed by Stones, El Unico and Avenues and we bonded together, taking many members from other groups, we stormed the house of Avenues Assassins, and one by shot and killed some of them, in a shootout that happened, 18St and Avenues, we outnumbered the Avenues, and now we kept moving forward, killing anyone in the Avenues wounded, was shot in the head, and yeah dogs do bark, I ordered the gangsters to not shoot at the Dogs and Rabbits, and keep moving forward, one member Jesse was too scared and Javier pointed a gun at a Pitbull when I told him to not do it, Pitbull leaped out and attacked, when Avenues began shooting and we had a bloodbath happening, Javier was with the LAPD and SWAT, I shot him in the head, and now SWAT & LAPD came by, and all Surenos began shooting at them only, and now, we targeted down the Cops and broke their phones and car tires were torn down, and now, many cops did kill, I shot and killed the main officer and his second, and we took out the driver, when members of Stone Family and Yakuza too began shooting the cops down, and now, the streets were filled with blood, and that was when a Chopper was sent in, and some Avenues shot to the Chopper and it fell down, and I woke up from a nightmare, and I went towards an all 18 meeting and told them, we need to take out The Avenues Assassins down first, and then attack down Stones Crips and Bloods alliance too, and someone mentioned El Unico and Fuentes Family, Joaquin Fuentes was there a few hours ago, coming with a Cartel on the Highway, and began shooting down on 18th Members and we shot at them back, realising they had weapons, I attacked the nearest one and Blue and Taylor stole his pistol and handgun and shot his friends and him down, we picked the guns up and began shooting back, Joaquin was shot in the legs and shoulders and he ran off, and now, we turned the tides and attacked the local police too now, and killed all of them too, and escaped the law again, this was a Kkangpae Zone and they had it under control, the cops don't accept down Bribes or anything either, and now, we took in members of various crews in, took in some rental vans and trucks, at midnight struck the houses, and now we targeted about 6 houses, we went inside, a German Shepherd, a Pitbull, a Siberian Husky and a group of Golden Labradors barked, we adopted the stray dogs, they went to the members of Armenians, Aryans, Irish and Russians, who fond over dogs, and now, we walked in, and shot down a member of Avenues, his tat said MSx3 instead and now, we shot down and killed 5 more of his friends, with silencers and sound modulators on them, it was a lot easier, Joaquin Fuentes was attacked and kidnapped down, we knocked him out cold, and took him in the van, shooting 1 of his 2 sons down, and killing him, we had his son and him in the boot of a Van and now, we kept moving forward, killing a Cartel Hitman down too, and we moved in, broke into a house and performed a SWAT Team 6 Strike down, killing everyone down and walking away, shooting 2 more on our exit, nobody was left behind, a Golden Labrador Stray came running and I ordered Tommy to let him into the truck and we walked by, and now, Russians began buying the whole area down the next day, and headlines happened, during the night many gangsters were found dead and LAPD was believed to have done a strike on them and now, we celebrated Joaquin Fuentes and his son escaped by, his son got hit by a Jeep and killed and a crying Joaquin curse me down and out cold, and I saw it all, and shed a tear too, I have 2 sons and a daughter named Josephine too.

And we went down, and I killed him down too, and now, not really, he escaped and ran off again, and now, Adam Stone broke into Gabby's apartment, and killed her friends down, Gabby took a pan out and smacked a goon down and stabbed him in the shoulder with a butter knife, and strangled him down, and used his knife to scare him down, but using a chord to strangle him down, and from there she used a gun and overpowered the other goon locking him out into a bathroom and Adam and Charlo got there, Lil Feather and Bailey attacked Charlo and Adam, and now, Gabby got them both on their knees, and now Tommy San and Blue got inside, taking the two and their goons to my apartments and we were attacked again, they had a tracker on them, Stones broke into the household and rescued everyone, Adam shot and killed a dude with a headshot and now, we tracked their areas down, and began looking when El Unico and Fuentes Family hit us too, and now, they destroyed entire windows and doors, and puddles of blood became everything, we shifted from Los Angeles to Central Valley and now they brought that shit there too, and now, we needed to wipe them out, Joaquin, El Albert and Javier were there, El Unico too was there and now, Joaquin was target no 1.

And now, we began attacking others and now, Joaquin's daughters and wife also got killed, I did it, and we found him sleeping, took him to a bathtub, and asked him his last wish as well, he cut people down with a sword too many times.

Season 3, Chapter 5, Joaquin and Javier deaths –

And prior to that day, Joaquin and Javier had taken over our lands, and said Children are fair games, Camille and the other exes are all out of here and now, we needed to figure a way out and I called the Yakuza and the Crew down once again.

Crew Members –
Leticia 'Lil Feather' Johnson
Michael 'Bailey' Perry
Jack Rollins 'Red Wolf'
Jesse 'Taylor' Calsada
Jose 'Sniffer' Daniels
Angel 'Blue' Lopez
Jey 'Joker' Raul Martinez
Tom 'Tommy-San' Soto
Arman Ivanov 'Neville'
David Lopez 'Bullet'
Gabriella 'Gabby' Reyes
Leticia 'Lil Feather/Letty' Johnson

The Yakuza –

1. Tamaya Hideki, Ryu
2. Jochi Kanemaru, Dragon
3. Seiya Ishimori, Tanaka
4. Kenji San, Tenryu
5. Takeshi Mousasi, Mist
6. Danta (daimyo, boss), Tetsuya Okada
7. Kenichi (underboss), Kenta Okada

Taylor, Sniffer, Tommy-San, Bullet, Neville and Joker planned in, Red Wolf is now a member of Red Feathers MC and turned out and killed many from a Human Trafficking and Animal Kidnapping Gang, and was released from Prison after he was deemed not guilty of killing anyone innocent, with his biker club, wife and some lawyers filed defamation lawsuits when Professional Wrestling, Mixed Martial Arts and Submission Grappling Fighters he fought too joined in and now, he earned Millions and Bikers and Fighters all formed their own businesses with that, Rollins last case actually, fighting in Japanese MMA as well as Russian MMA and Canadian Professional Wrestling circuits too, Iron Claw is going to be a good movie with MJF and Zac Efron in there are Von Erich Brothers, speaking of MJF aka Maxwell Jacob Friedman is an amazing Professional Wrestling and his persona of being a Goodfella, Tool and a Jerk is just amazing, his tag team with Adam Cole called better than you Bey-Bey is amazing, Cole and MJF have AEW World Heavyweight Championship under MJF and Tag Team of Ring of Honor together.

And now, we attacked the goons, as Joaquin took the kids on a Vacation in an Inn, a Motel, we found out his room and the door keeper was a member of Avenues only, and we killed him too and now, we broke into the household, and strangled his wife down, and killed her with that, and strangled both of his daughters and son with wires and pillows too and found him alone, and tasered him down, and dressed as EMTs Gabby, Lil Feather and Bailey took them all somewhere, Adam and Charlo Stone were also there, and Ryu and Dante were the Drivers too, and now, we took Joaquin somewhere and killed him there only, and walked away, and now, with that being said, we found out about Joaquin, opening his phone up and disabling all of his passwords down and calling in Javier Fuentes and now, we set up am Ambush for him, Gabby mentioned beating Judy Stone up once, she was stitching an inmate at the prison where Judy attacked him, and stabbed a nurse, Gabby dragged her down and chocked her out cold and landed hard punches and elbows on Judy, and a Warden came inside and taser down Judy Stone and she saved the patient's life, who didn't speak a thing, not knowing who had stabbed her down, what for or why she was stabbed down, and Javier Fuentes was coming by there too, and now, we began having a little jetpack joyride, and now, Yakuza brought the Motel and threw out Adam and Charlo Stones down, Dante was the new owner and now, many Cartel Hitman, Psychopaths/Serial Killers, Sexual Predators, Animal Abusers and Kidnappers, Human Traffickers etc were killed down by the Yakuza and many handed over to the police and now, we began unloading down, Javier had a Bodyguard, Henchman and Sniper with him, and now I mean driver not sniper lol, and his wife was also there, and Dante fooled her into drinking a cup of coffee, he had Sleeping Pills on them, and that killed her only and now, Yakuza buried her and Joaquin and his entire family there and now, Javier and his Henchman got inside with the Bodyguard, the Bodyguard was knocked unconscious, he was a Russian and a Bravta Member but loyal to Javier Fuentes and now, Sniffer and Joker killed down a Drug Lab Gangsters and called in LAPD, OCSD & SWAT Teams down, and now, Surenos Lab Bust happened, and now, with many more dramas happening in here, El Albert Fuentes is the only one alive now, and his family got killed, David Lopez aka Bullet was the one, I am also running a Business as a Sous – Chef lol, and I killed all of them weeks ago and buried them down too, and now, I have a lot of Innocent Blood on my hands too, and Cops don't even know, truth was 38 St did that, and I guided them to the right directions, wearing a hoodie to cover my arms and all up and a mask pretending to be a worker there and they killed everyone and walked away and when Cops came by, I told them I saw nothing and pretended to be blinded by a light and they left me down, after a cup of soup, coffee and a soda can, Albert is heartbroken too and now, Adam and Charlo Stone ran off and away as Javier pulled him, his bodyguard and henchman were restrained and Javier got shot and killed in the chest open wound and stomach, and I shot him in the head too, $2/3^{rd}$ of Fuentes Brothers are dead already, they may have a 4th brother and a sister, who well aren't here, and second, would most likely not attack, their brother and sister died because of Illnesses, David Fuentes had a Heart Attack and Blood Pressure, Sister Amelia died from Cardiac Arrest only and now, the mother and the father.

The Parents are alive, but recently, the mother died in her sleep and the father died too, he had Cancer and Old Age too caught up to him, losing a lot of people, grandmother's death by hands of MSx3 Goons wasn't enough, well MSx3 Henchmen got gunned down by the Avenues, who were their friends, and one of them was the cousin of Tommy – San named Hideki – San, who ended an entire crime racket of Avenues, no more Human Trafficking and Avenues under him are an organization of Assassins as well as Smugglers, Security Protection and Arms Dealing but they run a legit business too now, and they do not do anything as of now, and Javier and Joaquin got buried down too, and the Bodyguard and the Henchman got a new paycheck, I paid them to go away, leave the gang and go start a new life somewhere only and now, with that being said, El Albert Fuentes and El Unico aka Raul Martinez were the ones, Acalan and Atzi got more and more to desert El Unico and Raul has been weakened down too, and now, I ordered a grand heist, in a Shopping Mall? Never but maybe a Bank? Never and we chose down a Diamond Shop where Polished Diamonds of Israel and Mongolia are coming from Nebraska and Connecticut and now, we are robbing it all, and now, a crew was called in as Bailey, Lil Feather and Gabby got their jobs coming in, Elijah Wayne aka Black Wood came by and joined the crew, and he did something too, and now Black Wood is extremely talented, he never robs a house with dogs, never robbed elderly or handicapped, never robbed Veterans and he has morals and principals, being a member of Dirty White Boys but staying away from White Supremacy, claiming America is a White Country but Red Tribes, Black and Brown Americans, Yellow Americans aka Asians too deserve respect especially Indians, Mongolians and Hmong, Samoans, Tongans, Mauri as well as Mexicans, Brazilians and Dominicans out of all of them for their dedication and hard work, he praised the Irish, Scots, Nordic and Cuban Communities too once, and now, Black Wood was here and he is like AJ – Styles (Allen Jones, as AJ's real name is Allen Neal Jones, AJ probably means Allen Jones, his first name and last name or surname, third name too works) and now, with that being said, Black Wood, went to the Diamond Store, it was a Luxurious one, with Dark Walls, Red Carpets and Hollywood Bigshots coming in there, and now, we identified the stale room, and we came up with a plan too, Black Wood or BW came with that one now.

1. I, Bullet will go inside and take the guys in the shop to the back room

2. Sniffer will take over the doors, the glass doors, and will

keep the limited guest hostages

3. Blue will take out anyone who comes in, will kill Security Guards down too if there are any

4. Taylor will keep the Trucks and Vans ready, as there are Multiple Vans and Trucks, here 4 to be exact, and we will have them stationed in the back of the shop, making it easier to rob and loot people

5. Black Wood will snipe down any cop who comes by or anyone with a gun who comes running to save the shop

6. Neville, Tommy San, Joker and Taylor will drive the trucks one by one whereas Bailey, Gabby, Lil Feather and Dante will run the Vans down, we will also try not to attract attention, Stray Animals and Homeless are already in a shelter here, we never rob LA, we rob nearby valleys and this was in Los Angeles, but then again, we decided to remove down, since BW and I were making plans, we rent down 4 Vans instead, and now, we brought in big vans and black in color and now, as plan being made, Neville, Tommy San, Joker and Taylor had the Trucks, Bailey, Gabby and Little Feather are now busy with some work and Dante too had business, now Blue, Taylor, Black

Wood and Sniffer stayed aback with Vans and a 10th member showed up, Acalan as Atzi works for Gabby only now, and we began working, Acalan sniped the two guards down, and he sniped one guard, and I shot the other in the stomach, Acalan sniped him dead, and he moved down, and now, Blue took out a Hollywood Bigshot and strangled him down, and now, we stole him and shot down 3 more celebrities, 4 dead bigshots and their cars were robbed down too, and now, Adam Stone, Charlo Stone, Albert Fuentes and El Unico with their goons, broke in and started shooting, bringing away the attention

of FBI, DEA, ICE, ATF & HIS (Federal Bureau of
Investigation; Drug Enforcement Administration;
Immigrations & Customs Enforcement; Bureau of
Alcohol Tobacco and Firearms; and Homeland Security
Agency) and now, Cartel brought 3 more Cartels and a
City Wide war with Romanians, Ukrainians, Albanians
and Latin Kings had happened, many Fresno Bulldogs
members too broke in and attacked The Police, LAPD &
SWAT & OCSD (Los Angeles Police Department; Special
Weapons and Tactics; and Orange County Sheriff
Department) too came by, and now, a full blown war
happened when Arms of Freedom, White Cross and Red
Assassins who are newly emerged armed groups and
Skinheads too showed up, and now, an open five way
shooting happened and now, people all over were arming
themselves up and fighting each other, Racial Riots
between Pacific Islanders, Russians, Nigerians, Japanese
and Brazilians also happened and now, we opened the
door and attacked down everyone, I killed Adam Stone
and walked by his dead body, Skinheads came and didn't
attack me, but attacked down the Cartel Goons, I killed a
cop, and got identified, and Taylor sniped the cop down,
and we all went inside, and El Unico and I began shooting
each other, Judy Stone was released but stuck in a traffic
and now, we both began shooting at each other, missing
the bullets, I shot Raul in the leg and knees, and his goons
and Albert dragged him, killing 2 skinheads down and we
ran after them, and now, we killed many Cops and Law
Enforcement Officers and now, I ordered the Skins to
leave town, and we all ran off, Yakuza, Irish, Dirty White
Boys and Council had a meeting now, and we sit down
there, John and Rafael, were killed, Xavier and Ishika,

they too got killed, by Judy Stone and Adam Stone, and we killed Adam Stone down, Judy Stone and Charlo Stone are next, and we found out, it was a Bulldog, who killed their children down and they falsely killed John, Rafael, Xavier and Ishika down and now, we are out here for revenge down, Devon, Charlie and Adam Stone are all dead and Stones Family and Fuentes Family bonded up together, Albert found out, we killed Joaquin and Javier Fuentes and their families too were killed because of us, Atzi and Acalan and Dante saved many shops from being looted down and burnt alive, saved a bunch of cops too, and now send them their ways.

And now, with that, we began operating there, and smuggled drugs and sold them, I got some drug addicts into a truck and into rehab, Gabby worked at a rehab, took Drugs, Marijuana, Beer, Alcohol everything down and now, Riot Police and State Guard was deployed Politicians and Political Groups were organizing it all down, elections cancelled and presidents rule has happened and now, with that we got calmed down, and we took away dead peoples wallets, diamonds, gold bars and cash and ran off, and now, with a police force coming there, and they open fired and killed a member of 18 and we open fired, head sniping happened and now, 3 members remained and I saw them kill 7 more and it was 3 vs 3 when backups came in and we attacked them all down, sniping them in the head, and now, we were all under scrutiny and now, a war happened, I killed the main cop, and shot his comm too, and Bailey shot his second and third in the head, and took the comms away and now, Bailey risked being shot down, Lil Feather sniped a cop and saved him, and now, El Unico and now, Albert Fuentes was also there, trying to show up and shoot someone down, and now, Central Valley and Farmlands we now own became another Warzone and now, we were ready, I played down BFMV song Lead of Faith, BFMV is Bullet For My Valentine and their song Lead of Faith, Waking the Demon, Tears don't Fall etc and newest one Halo with Pendulum was amazing one too, and now, we were shooting them all down, Cartel Members began killing down and shooting more and more members down, and Blue shot their drivers, and Taylor took a car and drove away somewhere and the drivers chased down.

Blue and Bailey called in Armenians, Russians, Irish, Aryans, Koreans, Yakuza and 18th Crews and now, The Cartel Members were outnumbered, Acalan and Atzi killed down their own best friends and broke down sobbing and crying too, Gabby and Lil Feather treated down the wounds and saved a lot of people too.

Crew Members –
Leticia 'Lil Feather' Johnson
Michael 'Bailey' Perry
Jack Rollins 'Red Wolf'
Jesse 'Taylor' Calsada
Jose 'Sniffer' Daniels
Angel 'Blue' Lopez
Jey 'Joker' Raul Martinez
Tom 'Tommy-San' Soto
Arman Ivanov 'Neville'
David Lopez 'Bullet'

Gabriella 'Gabby' Reyes

Leticia 'Lil Feather/Letty' Johnson

Acalan

Atzi

And now, War was happening, Red Wolf came and sniped down some big gunners and saved the day.

Season 3, Chapter 6 and 7, the Stone's demise –

And now, Adam Stone was the next target we had, Judy Stone, Albert Fuentes and EL Unico were next assholes, Leon the Jamaican came to our aid and gave us some information, and told us where Adam Stone is and we forgave him down and now Jamaican Posse and Latin Kings are at War, Romanians, Ukrainians and Albanians are fighting off Israelis, Bulgarians and Native Mob too and now, a crackdown on Ukrainians, Natives, Bulgarians and Jamaicans happened and the war came to an end when Jamaican Posse took down many LK Members and won the War and now, we all worked down on Adam Stone's Target and he planned to visit down and now, we went down and realized, Acalan and Atzi lost their families, but got their sons and daughters like, Acalan had a son surviving and Atzi had 2 daughters who are now living in Foster Care where Rednecks and Cowboys, some Bikers, Armed Group Guys, Peckerwoods etc too work there and now, Adam Stone has a friend, and he is Puerto Rican, he married a girl, she is Indian, someone else's Arrange Marriage Wife, and her name is Sumitra Singh Rajawat, she works with Gabby, she mentioned how her sisters were all never allowed to talk to boys and the oldest two got married to Rajput Boys only, and they were all in their caste and all were in Canada too, they were Half White and Half Indians, and their father and mother threw them all out, even attacking their children born too, their boyfriends and now Love Marriage Husbands were Redhaired and of Scottish Origin, and given her aunt married a Mongolian, another redhead and blue eyed

Siberian, the family is strict, her other sisters died in Car Crashes, they all had Arrange Marriages, live a fine life, and now, Sumitra got a job there and he is upset with it, demanding she comes to India, she married a Peckerwood named Brian Mason here, and her father had him and his entire family killed, they were all Bikers, Red Feathers MC and now, The Bikers filed a lawsuit against her family over it, and she escaped New York and came here, Brian Mason was her best friend and not lover or boyfriend and now, with that being said, we were attacked by Judy Stone and her goons, who kept firing, Acalan and Atzi got shot and killed there only, Atzi shielded me, Atzi daughter also got killed, Acalan lost his son too, Atzi daughter stood there crying when a bullet hit her down too, and now, we went down, Taylor shoot down a Gunman, and Blue left a bomb in the car, and ran off, Gabby shot and killed Judy there only and went upstairs, Acalan and Atzi laid there dead in a pool of blood, and now, Judy Stone goons ran off, and were shot dead, and now, Tommy San and Dante tracked down and began their style of raiding down together and we met the others again and not this deep a conversation usually happens either and now, we went down, and began working around, and we went to eat at the local McDonalds too, and now the yakuza members –

1. Tamaya Hideki, Ryu
2. Jochi Kanemaru, Dragon
3. Seiya Ishimori, Tanaka
4. Kenji San, Tenryu
5. Takeshi Mousasi, Mist
6. Danta (daimyo, boss), Tetsuya Okada
7. Kenichi (underboss), Kenta Okada

Kenichi, Danta, Mist and Tenryu have never talked much, Dragon and Tanaka too, Ryu is a frequent visitor too and Dante is also a member too now, and we began talking about Adam Stone's death and Judy Stone's death and now Charlo is all alone and Albert Fuentes is to be eliminated down too, and we agreed unanimously and Yakuza mentioned MSx3 and Avenues issues with

Border Brothers joining them but they later left and now, 38th St is coming for us too and we mentioned we will keep them alright too and now, with that being said, we began working on around it and now, we brought more and more weapons, we have a plant for that only, Russian Mafia members gave it to us and now, we will began making them and go there, buying Sound Modulators aka Silencers too and began working around there and now, we hit a few Stone Thugs from their Barber Shops too first, Teenage Recruitment doesn't happen here with us, BW shot them down like a Professional or Pro Chad, and now, we went down and began looking around at what to do and came across and we needed to do something too, spotting El Unico and El Albert together too, and we decided to let them off for now, and we focused again on what the matter at hand was and now, we decided to watch some MMA Fights with Yakuza Members and we watched the following –

1.   UFC 1 to 12
2.   Fedor Emelioenko vs Mark Coleman
3.   Fedor Emelioenko vs Mark Coleman rematch
4.   Fedor Emelioenko vs Kevin Randleman
5.   Fedor Emelioenko vs Little Nog
6.   Fedor Emelioenko vs Little Nog rematch
7.   Fedor Emelioenko vs Tim Sylvia
8.   Fedor Emelioenko vs Pitbull Andrei Arlovski
9.   Fedor Emelioenko vs Chael Sonnen
10.   Fedor Emelioenko vs Frank Mir
11.   Fedor Emelioenko vs Rampage Jackson
12.   George St Pierre vs Carlos Condit
13.   George St Pierre vs Nick Diaz

14. George St Pierre vs BJ Penn
15. George St Pierre vs Johnny Hendricks
16. George St Pierre vs Matt Hughes
17. George St Pierre vs Matt Serra
18. George St Pierre vs Michael Bisping
19. Mighty Mouse vs Ray Borg
20. Mighty Mouse vs Tim Elliot
21. Mighty Mouse vs Henry Cejudo
22. Mighty Mouse vs Joseph Benevides
23. Mighty Mouse vs Ian McCall
24. Mighty Mouse vs Adriano Moraes
25. Dreamcatcher Gegard Mousasi vs Austin Vanderford
26. Dreamcatcher Gegard Mousasi vs Salty John Salter
27. Dreamcatcher Gegard Mousasi vs Phenom Douglas Lima
28. Dreamcatcher Gegard Mousasi vs Jacare Ronaldo Souza
29. Dreamcatcher Gegard Mousasi vs Prime Time Uriah Hall
30. Dreamcatcher Gegard Mousasi vs Chris Weidman
31. Dreamcatcher Gegard Mousasi vs Phenom Vitor Belfort
32. Dreamcatcher Gegard Mousasi vs Dan Hendo Henderson

Henderson book Hendo – the American Athlete is going to be Legen Wait for it Dery for sure, it is a how I met your mother reference in here, and now, Yakuza and I enjoyed down UFC 1 to 6, and now we took a break, UFC should have similar tournaments instead, championships weren't Cringe back then and imagine Kevin Holland defeating down Jack Hermanson, Darren Till, Du Plessis and Adesanya on the same night and becoming a tourney world champion, Kevin Holland aka Big Mouth/Tranquilizer is an amazing fighter in my opinion and now Dragon Lyoto Machida and Antonio Inoki are worshipped here, both are Karatekas but

Machida went to the ufc and Inoki created New Japanese Professional Wrestling where AJ Styles, Great Khali, Mark Coleman, Luke Gallows etc have fought, New Japan Professional Wrestling is also good, and I miss seeing Kenny Omega and AJ Styles in there, and Edge aka Adam Copeland may fight Okada there, Seiya Sanada and Tetsuya Naito are also good, LIJ Stable or Los Ignorable De Japan, Just 5 Guys, Bullet Club & BC Japan, Guerillas of Destiny and House of Torture are all in Stables/Groups/Teams and now, that aside, Ryu agreed to help us all out and find out where Charlo Stone is and we began looking around for him and end him too, for once and for all, Knights, their cousins Williams and now, 3rd cousin Stones, who is next now, Edwards 4th Cousins and 5th Cousins Carters aren't attacking us, because they are all dead, EME killed them all already, and now, we began walking around and entered Compton Area, and there are many gangs shooting around and running pay per views, and now Charlo Stone was burying down Judy Stone and vowing revenge, and he killed down some of his own people.

And Samoans and Armenians killed down his top gangsters, and hence I became looking into him, and Judy Stone, joins Adam Stone, Charlie Stone and Devon Stone as well as Joaquin Fuentes and Javier Fuentes being dead, and now El Unico and El Albert aren't going to be there at the funeral with it being all blacks only and now, we kidnapped and killed 2 of his closest gangster friends, and they are from Black Disciples and Gangster Disciples, and now, camera caught us being there and we had to get out of there, and 4/5 of Stones are dead now, and we have forgotten Amado Fuentes, fun fact El Chapo rival and cousin was Amado Carillo Fuentes, leader of Fuentes Organization and Juarez Cartel, which works with Barrio Azteca on the Texas – Mexico Border, Barrio Azteca is involved in –

1. Trafficking (Drug & Human)
2. Arson
3. Murder
4. Assault
5. Auto Theft
6. Burglary
7. Extortion
8. Intimidation
9. Kidnapping
10. Robbery

And their enemies or rivals are –

1. Border Brothers
2. Sinaloa Cartel
3. Los Mexicles

Allies –

1. Juarez Cartel
2. La Linea

And now, we attacked the Stone Family down, killing their relatives and the children down, and we began attacking them all down, shooting up the funeral house and found out where Charlo Stone was, he sniped down a few of my Samoans, Armenians and Tongans, and we held some more of his family members hostage and attacked him down, and we climbed up, he took the backdoor exit, killing Church Fathers, Pastors and Preachers, we had Gabby stich them up with Lil Feather and Bailey and they saved a few more passer by people and we began chasing after him, and he and his final four members Shawn, Latrelle, Jamal, Tyrone and Sweet a new member began shooting down, I killed Sweet with two gunshot wounds, and now, Tyrone was his older brother, and we killed him too, and Jamal, Latrelle and Charlo escaped when an angry uncle came, Bailey fooled him down and got him back inside, and now, we wore masks and all, and we had all our members escape down, and the funeral had about 20 – 30 people in there and 11 Gangsters or Gang Members are already dead in there, Ukrainians ambushed us all in there, and now, a wild west shootout had happened down the lane, and we lost all of our members, and we dragged them to the cars and drove off, and now, with nobody from our side in there, Bailey, Lil Feather and Gabby made it out too, given she saved a Gang Member too and now, Stones were done.

And now, with them being gone, Amado began shooting at us, killing more and more of ours, with Ukrainian Firing Squads, and Slava are dangerous people, Amado has been absent for a while and now, we found El Albert and shot him in the kneecap and escaped from there, and Gabby killed a Fuentes Goon and we escaped and now, in a Car Chase that followed out of Los Angeles outside LAPD jurisdiction and now with that being said and now, we attacked everyone down, and got into a shootout with a bunch of Deer Hunters and Cartel gunned them all down, camping families too, and allowed us to gun down 2 members, a Hunter (who resembled Jim A10 Miller) killed 3 gunman, and he was a Mercenary and retired MMA Star Bjorn Stahl from Iceland and Canada, he killed all Cartel Hitman, he doesn't eat Meat anymore either, he doesn't hunt bucks or bears, he hunts Gators and eats their meat instead and The Hunters hunted down The Cartel Members, they were Mercenaries working for FBI and ATF and we ran from there, away from there and we began working away, and now, swerving into a farm house and shooting down Stone Goons, and Charlo hid down, and Amado and El Albert also came by, with El Unico too, and now a shootout happened and fire happened, the farmer killed a cartel gunner down, and when other farmers and townsfolk came in running and attacked down Cartel Hitman with knives and whatnot, shooting the tires down and Dogs of the town mauled the younger hitman and hitwomen down, and out cold, many townsfolk died, both men and women alike, and many dogs too got killed into that too, and now, we found out Charlo got a gun and killed and he was out of bullets and he got hit with the fall of legs, a leg sweep happened and he got tripped down and stabbed in the legs down, and he escaped, and remember Tyrone and Latrelle, teaming up with El Unico, Albert and Amado, escaped down, we shot down Tyrone and Latrelle and killed both of them down, and now, began shooting our way down, and attacked Sheriffs and Townsfolk too, and now, Amado was the one Allen and Anne mauled, killing 1 of 2 henchman too, Analise was saved because of them and now, I will remember it, I killed the daughter and sons of Amado and his wife and sister in laws too, and now this is a bloody game and we kept running on after him and his goons, El Unico is now powerless, Acalan and Atzi got everyone away from him and both men are now gone, they worked for me and chose me over him, and they knew Unico never cared for them or did any charity, Cartels do charity too and helped people out so many times and Raul was unlikeable actually and now with that being said, and now, Daedalus was their Greek Torturer, Acalan mentioned him as his biggest rival and second in the organization, half Greek and half Mexican and he was the Underboss, the Second and the Heir Apparent too, and now, he brought in some tricks and tools too, and we just threw a toaster on his nose and punched him on the forehead and tripped him down, he fell from the top to a table below him, and he was out cold, and now, Unico, Amado, El Albert and Charlo were escaping, Daedalus, Tyrone and Latrelle realising they were backstabbed and we did not shoot either of them and recruited them all into the group and Daedalus mentioned how Unico used to beat his dogs up too out of anger, and now, we gave him a chance to strike back and Half of the Cartel sided with Daedalus and the other Half started shooting Daedalus Soldiers removed the helmets and rolled their sleeves up and a shootout happened, the farmer and townsfolk are all dead too and now, we moved out, killing down a Loyalist, and kept our move, taking a chopper, Bailey took the GPS and a SUV and with Daedalus, Tyrone and Latrelle (who are actually Half African and Half Puerto Ricans named Miles and Domingo) started riding with me and we hit down the SUV Sedan of Unico and killed his henchman, who shot and killed Tyrone for real this time and Latrelle stomped him down, Amado and Albert escaped with Unico, driver got killed too, and Charlo Stone did not beg at all for help and accepted the death and attacked, Bailey and Blackwood killed him down and we ended up finishing Stone Family and now, Fuentes Family was next, Tyrone was saved and both men left Los Angeles with their friends and shifted to another state and got another job, and we got the job done, and EME Members called in and congratulated us, and now a riot had happened as Mexican Inmates and Native Inmates have attacked the Black Inmates down, and now a Race Riot happened, and now Asians and White Inmates chose Brown Inmates and Red Inmates too, Indians and Samoans too joined Mexican Mafia down as Middle Eastern and Puerto Rican inmates chose down Black Inmates and an all out brawl happened with bodies laying down everywhere, Stones are all dead, next is El Albert, and we found him too.

Season 3, Chapter 8 and 9, EL Albert –

70% of our enemies are dead, 7/10 or we will make it 8 or 4/5th and now, we needed to make sure it is official as El Albert is still breathing down and we laid low, and now, Yakuza Members Ryu, Dante, Danta and Tommy San had a party in their house when Tiny Rascals and Born to Kill attacked us down and we had another war happening, Daedalus went in there and killed some of them, he put the fear of god in people and was a scared personality in many ways.

And now, The Yakuza opened up a hotel and members of various ethnic gangs got better jobs, we love selling drugs and weapons, but we don't want to die or kill each other anymore, no wonder we do petty things, MSx3 Members too work in here, and yes we will kill but it is time we don't, and now, we began working in here, I spent more time with the children and the dogs now, and we all lived a happy life, and with that being said, welcomed another pair, twins named Willow and Surge (Call me a Celebrity Worshipper, the girls are named after Jeff Hardy and Matt Hardy Personas, Willow the Wisp and Just Surge) and now, Gabby and I lived, Bailey and Lil Feather joined new biker clubs and now, we do steal to this day, and now we also do festivals and all and we began working on a new way of living and life and remembered that we did kill Williams, Knights, Stones, Fuentes and many more and now, El Albert, Amado and Unico grew more powerful, killing many of EME and now, we wanted them gone too.

And now, we had a greenlight thing going on, EME and Yakuza made peace and now, Yakuza value loyalty and MSx3 keeps bothering us all, and now, Jack Rollins aka Red Wolf is back in town too, and he killed 3 MSx3 Members down and buried them somewhere, leaving them at a MSx3 Neighborhood only and walked away, killing a 4th and a 5th member, a male and a female too, escaping down, his dog started running, he wore a hoodie and began roaming around, and a MS Member asked him the value of a car and he said, it was his owner's car and he is looking for his dog, he said he works for Damon Maxwell III and well found the dog mating with a female dog and an issue happened, Jack took the dog and got into the car which was stolen, Jack and his dog were spying on MSx3 and tracker was there, and Jack got his friends to locate the car, the dog named Jimmy helped find it and Jack recruited the car thieves into his group to fight Human Trafficking, when the Gang Members/Gangsters or Mara laughed, and Jack had his friends shoot them all dead, and down cold, and Jack took the car back again, and now, Jack Rollins killed people he had a split personality disorder too atop of that, and now, we began looking around, Jack assembled the Crew, we will enter the house of a Scammer, Murderer, Rapist and a Corrupt Businessman, Eric McIntosh and we will beat him down, he now has an army of his own too, we wore down masks and got ready to rock n roll down too, and now, we went to watch Lucha Libre or Mexican Professional Wrestling, and now, we should do that too, and now El Albert and Amado with 6 guards are there too and now, with them and now, I began my way up and down, and began to like know the guards and we went outside, and somehow a bomb went kaboom, and like once the Wrestling Show ended, the attached venue had a concert, a Musical Concert where the bomb went boom, the Wrestling Venue was closed, trapping even LAPD, the SWAT Team and OCSD as well as State Guard among Biker Clubs, Rednecks, Cowboys, Peckerwoods, Mercenaries and Armed Group Members, and I went out, and came across a member of El Albert's Gang, shot and killed him down, and killed 2 more of his companions down too, and now, we began swooping around and doing it all rightfully and now, I began seeing if anyone else was watching, I shot the guy at the head, after pretending to trip at him, and killing him, before anything, and now, we went there and now, I swooped around and began searching for other goons, CCTV

Footages exist for a reason, wore a luchador mask for a reason only, one by one I got away and now, with that, I took down an angry psychopath too, and tripped him down as well, and now, with that, I swooped back in, he bombed the concert and I killed him for that and now, I walked back in circling down, and I saw Blue and Taylor come out and Tommy San with Ryu and Danta and we shot down and killed the cops and the cartel in a 3 way, 18 man shootout and now, with that, we killed all the guards of El Albert, Amado and EL Unico.

And now, Cartel Members and Other Cartels did a shootout when some of the Marines and State Guard attacked them and in a shootout, I mean another shootout that happened, Amado's Tigres Cartel members got killed one after another, and now, we walked back inside, El Albert, EL Unico and Amado had one active guard who tried shooting but got tackled down by a Marine Solider, who Amado jumped and in a Kimura got his hand broken, and we had them surrounded and LAPD Members arrested them all down, and took them into Custody and now, the Maniac bombed the entire building but Damon Maxwell III, Allen Jenkins, Harley Ares Fitzgerald and Dennis Miller somehow got the police in and bomb deactivated when the maniac tried shooting, we had him killed and now, the Maniac was El Unico and Al Albert, Amado escaped down from the grips and Albert and Unico recognizing the dude left off, that man was Jack Rollins, who saved their lives many years ago, Red Wolf mentioned it all too, and now, we walked off, and organized another grand score, a team of 6 was all we need down here actually, I meant when I was on Tinder, Bumble and Hinge, girls who dropped their Instagram down, never replied to messages, I mean don't drop your Gram ID if you don't want Strangers, Dating Apps are where Strangers go and meet each other, like why is it an issue, and 6th Street Interviewers are so goddamn cringe man, Desirable Truth and Israel Padilla going to get their asses kicked someday, I am so sure, Andrew Tate worshippers, do you even think John Zherka asks a girl her body count (Body Count means the amo9unt of people you have killed and these fucking assholes use it for the number of sexual partners, I am not sure who follows them) and now, we walked down, and I assembled a crew –

1. Bullet
2. Tommy-San
3. Blue
4. Taylor
5. Blackwood
6. Vacant yet

Yakuza Council –

1. Tamaya Hideki, Ryu
2. Jochi Kanemaru, Dragon
3. Seiya Ishimori, Tanaka
4. Kenji San, Tenryu
5. Takeshi Mousasi, Mist
6. Danta (daimyo, boss), Tetsuya Okada
7. Kenichi (underboss), Kenta Okada

Mentioned Fresno Bulldogs and Latin Kings took over their mansions and are hosting down Dealings, Beatings and Killings there as DBK – Crew happened in there, Rapes of many Yakuza Girls happened too when Cartel Members arrived, paying Latin Kings & Fresno Bulldogs Leaders, many members got recruited down and into Yakuza Compound, and we got the score in and called a 6th Member, Red Wolf answered the calls down and came by, but he later got a call and had to go to his family, no ill will and asked him hold down and we will have someone else in there instead and yes the crew –

Crew Members –
Leticia 'Lil Feather' Johnson
Michael 'Bailey' Perry
Jack Rollins 'Red Wolf'
Jesse 'Taylor' Calsada
Jose 'Sniffer' Daniels
Angel 'Blue' Lopez
Jey 'Joker' Raul Martinez
Tom 'Tommy-San' Soto
Arman Ivanov 'Neville'
David Lopez 'Bullet'
Gabriella 'Gabby' Reyes
Leticia 'Lil Feather/Letty' Johnson
Acalan (+)
Atzi (+)

Sniffer joined in, and now, we needed 2 more actually, Gabby and Neville signed up, we had a new recruit joining in tonight, her name was Breonna Lopez aka Typhoon and she worked at the Café and all, going to college and car jacking too, her family passed away, illness and all, and now, she came from Dallas, Texas and planned big for herself, but wanted to keep LA safe for her family, she is my sister and speaking of the other Lopez Angel also my cousin, and now, the kids were doing fine, the dogs are a great company too, why do I keep forgetting their names, and I am such an absent father, and anyways, I began working on it all and now, after being with the children and the dogs, I walked out and began working, College Funds are all ready now, and we began working, and now with that, we began looking around, killing more and more goons, no but avoiding them, and the police, and other gunners from local armed groups, and making our way out of here, and the Crew and the Yakuza and the Council began looking for Amado, Albert and Raul Martinez down the lane too, and began looking around, and now, the trio and a driver were there, Sniffer, Blue, Taylor and I with Neville hopped in and began chasing them down, and they were driving at a low speed and we drove around, following them too, getting the others to go back to their homes and now, we are all at the brink of getting them, Bailey and Lil Feather too joined Gabby and the rest of the Crew down too, and now with that being said, we arrived to their destinations.

Taylor was watching Tom Holland and we had a whole Tom Holland playlist going on for some reasons, I never really liked him, and there was his playlist –

1. Spider-Man Homecoming
2. Spider-Man Far from Home
3. Spider-Man No Way Home
4. The Devil all the Time
5. Uncharted

6. Heart of the See
7. Cherry
8. Civil War

And now, I mean, Girls love Tom Holland and that is for sure a fact, and a true thing to be honest, and I am also a fan of Harry Potter Series and this is my ranking –

1. Chamber of Secrets
2. Deathly Hallows 1
3. Prisoner of Azkaban
4. Deathly Hallows 2
5. Goblet of Fire
6. Philosopher's Stone
7. Half – Blood Prince
8. Order of Phoenix

The Directing and almost everything was done wonderful, like Draco Malfoy and Harry Potter were the two main characters in an unique way actually and that was true too, like Ron Weasley was my favorite character in my opinion, like Domhnall Gleeson and Robert Pattison aka the Batman were my favorite actors like Robert acting career was amazing and beautiful from Twilight and Harry Potter, Cosmopolis (a personal favorite), Devil all the Time w/ Tom Holland, Lighthouse w/ William Dafoe, Water for Elephants, Remember Me (a personal favorite), Good Time, High Life, Damsel, The King w/Timothee Chamlet (a personal favorite), Tenet w/John David Washington (a personal favorite) and The Batman (best Robert Pattison is the Batman) cannot wait for Part 2 actually.

Albert, Amado and El Unico are all in there or were all in there and began discussing, and when a man came out, we just shot him down, sound modulators were in the gun, Taylor had and Tommy San dragged his dead body down and we got it out, and opened the hose, watering the blood down, and it swerved inside, and we counted the gunman in there and gunwoman too, and now, we saw one of them coming, we closed the hose, got the car to go away, and I shot the women down too, and took her gun as well, and we walked by, when Anatoly and Sergei came by with The Russians, Aryans, Irish, Koreans, Armenians and Mexicans too, they had some Mexican Mercenaries and Armed Groups in their friends list or a mutual friends list, Gabby called them all, John and Rafael were personal friends too, after all, and house was cleansed down, and the dogs were not killed, all Gangsters have Pet Dogs who also serve as guard dogs, British and Irish Actors are amazing at their jobs like British Actors have that in hand – Michael Caine, Taron Egerton, Tom Hardy, Domhnall Gleeson, Colin Firth, Tom Holland, Andrew Garfield, Rupert Grint and Daniel Redcliffe.

And now, with the War over, El Albert, Amado, El Unico and a 4th Gunman were interrupted when two more gunwomen came out and were shot by Anatoly and Sergei, and a Russian Goon attacked and killed the last bodyguard, they all had, and now, realising shooting wouldn't help them out, and now, Unico had kept Anatoly's son hostage, the son alone killed down all the goons, training in Boxing, MMA, Judo, Combat Sambo and Freestyle Wrestling (wanting to be a Professional

Wrestler and Mixed Martial Artist as well as a Gangster and a Model) and now, Anatoly realising Unico and Amado had him, pleaded, Sergei pointed a gun at the last son Amado had, Amado pushed Anatoly's son, and Anatoly shot and killed the son of Amado and Amado realising Anatoly found out about how 2 of Anatoly's children were killed by Amado, Anatoly became a Widower, he has 6 daughters and 2 sons with the youngest being 4 and oldest being 24, and now, Amado lost his only child, Anatoly and Amado's children were friends, Amado's 2 sons died in a Car Accident, 1 got killed by Anatoly and 1 got killed by me, the other 2 died because of a Turf War.

El Unico, quickly and quietly left the room, Amado and Albert got shot multiple times in the chest, and EL Unico ran away, and we followed him, killing his wife, daughters and sisters.

Season 3, Chapter 10, Sparing El Unico –

And now, El Unico had his last guards killed too, as Armenians and Russians and Mexicans outnumbered and killed them with the Yakuza showing up too, and now, we had him surrounded down too, and I tipped the Police of his Allies, and a Crackdown happened on his gang, all of his allies were killed down too, Avenues, MSx3, Tiny Rascalz Gangsters, The Other Cartels among more, and now, Unico was running away, and now, he was pleading us to stop, he was a Soldier and a Mercenary, he became a Security Guard, and after being a Cartel Leader, he decided to stop for MMA and Professional Wrestling as well as having Cartel goons work as

Mercenaries and all, Raul Martinez pleaded for life, and told us he would retire asap, and wish to be spared, when his grandmother, who Raul's grandmother revealed, Raul's own son killed his grandfather and parents, Anatoly did nothing wrong with killing him, she turned out to be his sister, and Raul realising how much his own son brainwashed him down, revealing all of that, and now with that, Martinez and Tigres stopped Drug and Arms Pushing, and many of them turned to farming and bare knuckles and now, most of his goons were Luchadors who got fired and now, Martinez was spared, Amado and Albert were buried down too and we got a call, Gabby mentioned it all, my sons were born as Michael and Maverick Lopez and daughters were Christina and Elizabeth and now dogs Allen and Anne too, Gabby had send them to her father, since he needed them and walked out, Christina and Elizabeth mentioned down that Yakuza Members Dante, Kenichi and Ryu mentioned it that MSx13 Members & Almighty Latin Kings wanted to fight us all, and now, we are ready for Bloodbath too, and now with that, we are all ready, The Yakuza members Ryu had a member in LK who was their friend, he joined a chapter of Brown Bears MC and Cherokke Arms, a Native American Armed Group too, and now, he was named King James or Javier Rodriguez and now, with exiting, no friends in LK were spotted, but turns out LK and 18 made peace, MSx13 Members joining down Tiny Rascals, Vice Lords, Asure13 and Black Dragons are going to war with Yakuza and 18th and we had a new member, Sons of Samoa and Tongan Crips joining us in there too, and now, who are the Black Dragons and why do they want beef with us, answer is simple because they can, they wish to survive and thrive and our routes too, we do not sell anything now, and with that being said, El Unico and his goons to which there weren't any, walked away, Tigres Cartel in Arizona, Tijuana, Guatemala City, Tongan Isles, American Samoa, Domingo and St Johns stopped working soon as native government crackdowns followed down, and once back home, Police raids happened, Michael and Maverick were attacked too down, when they were revealed to bs MSx13 Members, the daughters and the dogs were kept locked by Maverick, but one of my daughters got out and MS members gunned them down, Christie survived, Gabby had Mackenzie, another daughter born, MS Members killed us down because of a disagreement and I woke up from my dream, I got the kids out of Los Angeles, to a cheaper city in El Paso, with my aunt, and now, with them gone, Allen and Anne also gone, we began focusing on the gangsters that opposed us down.

El Unico started Wrestling as the Winged Eagle, and began competing in and became a rival of Magnus Von Stahl too, and now with that, we watched Iron Claw, I mean the trailer again, MJF and Zac Efron and now, Bang-Bang Gang (Jay White, Austin Gunn, Juice Robinson & Colten Gunn) and the feud with Maxwell Jacob Friedman aka the MJF is something amazing, hopefully Adam Cole shows up too and maybe we may have The Golden Elite vs Bullet Club Gold too given Adam Cole was in both The Elite & The Bullet Club, and Jay White aka Switchblade being the one to betray down Kenny Omega aka The Cleaner, it only makes sense too, Bullet Club got so big, it had countless sub-groups, quintet, trios and tag teams of their own, title changed within clubs when Good Brothers, Guerillas of Destiny or Young Bucks fought each other often a lot, and I hope Kenny Omega, Adam Copeland aka Edge, Chris Jericho and Christian Cage form a group called The Canadian Elite anytime soon they are all Elite Professional Wrestlers and Canadian atop of that, Kenny Omega and Chris Jericho dominating Music Industry as Jericho is the lead singer of Fozzy, Kenny Omega having a YouTube called Being the Elite (B.T.E.) and Adam Copeland getting Movie Roles of his own and Christian Cage running his own Businesses.

I wish Cage disbands with Luchasourus & Nick Wayne.

Imagine Adam and Cage being joined by Chris and Kenny, who btw were formal rivals or enemies in New Japan Professional Wrestling, as Chris Jericho debuted in New Japan attacking down Kenny Omega and a Ringside Worker too, and Tetsuya Naito was Chris' second rival, as he lost both grudges actually, Naito teamed with Sting & Darby Allin and defeated the team of Sammy Guevera, Chris Jericho and Minoru Suzuki.

Another fun fact is both Minoru Suzuki and Kenny Omega both fought in Mixed Martial Arts (MMA Rules) and Kenny is 4-3-0 and he debuted against UFC Superfight Champion Dan 'the Beast' Severn and lost, but Minoru Suzuki, Kazushi Sakuraba & Shinia Aoki fought in both MMA & Wrestling with Sakuraba and Aoki fighting in both plus Submission Grappling, Suzuki is 30-20-0 in MMA and King of Pancreas Openweight

Champion too, brother defeated Ken Shamrock and lost to his brother Frank Shamrock twice too, losing that championship to him, MMA Superstars Ken Shamrock, Dan Severn, Don Frye, Kevin Randleman, Mark Coleman etc fought in Professional Wrestling rules too, and Mark Coleman & Kevin Randleman defeated the team of Jan the Giant & Giant Singh (Great Khali) where Mark Coleman pulled the pin on Great Khali, Kevin's and Mark's Wikipedia read so, I wish Great Khali continued his persona of being the violent Indian Dude, and kept the World Heavyweight Championship, I mean Khali is 7 feet 2 inches tall, and organized down shows in india, WWE India happened under Great Khali and there were videos of Khali and WWE Stars having dinner or lunch together in Khali's village only.

Khali is awesome, my favorite, now he was a Security Guard, Police Officer, Laborer, Professional Wrestler, Actor and now has joined a political party in India called Bhartiye Janta Party or BJP, in English it means Indian People's Party which is currently the ruling party in India, the Minsiters came to Texas once too, I am currently reading his Wikipedia, Prime Minister Modi likes Texas, Howdy Modi was that event, not much into Politics, but he seems like a cool guy, and anyways, I am a Gangster, not sure if they would ever dine with me lol and anyways now, 3 more dudes joined in, who was the new girl we added, and the crew now –

Crew Members –
Leticia 'Lil Feather' Johnson
Michael 'Bailey' Perry
Jack Rollins 'Red Wolf'

Jesse 'Taylor' Calsada
Jose 'Sniffer' Daniels
Angel 'Blue' Lopez
Jey 'Joker' Raul Martinez
Tom 'Tommy-San' Soto
Arman Ivanov 'Neville'
David Lopez 'Bullet'
Gabriella 'Gabby' Reyes
Leticia 'Lil Feather/Letty' Johnson
Breonna Lopez 'Typhoon'
Christopher Guzman 'Skipper'
Demetrius Goldstien 'Dementus'
James Maxwell 'Ashton'

Demetrius is Jewish, James is White and partially Native American and Christopher is also White (White = Europeans, Jewish, Northern African, Caucuses, Turkic and Upper Indians to a level, White People have 90% Blonde Hair and Blue Eyes etc but many Hmong, Pacific Islanders like Solomon Islanders too usually and especially and even Persians may have that characteristic too) and now, with that being said, Indian Groups of Rajputs too started buying our weapons, we thought they were Armenians or Azerbaijanis, and now, other than that, they seem cool dudes, super-friendly and all, Great Khali is also of a Rajput Family and a Punjabi Family like a inter-caste one, and now we found out they are members of no such gang but a paramilitary robbers and they called the Black Tigers, they rob Banks too, and they have White Names somehow, and they called each other Tiger 1 and Tiger 2, other than that, we worked with them, and now MSx13, Tiny Rascals, Vice Lords, Asure13 and Black Dragons were the collision has changed down.

Black Dragons –

a. Chan Chong

b. Zhang Li Chong
c. Zee Ling Chong
d. Xiang Chong

Asure13 –

a. Scally Calsada
b. Acalan Pineda
c. Javier Lopez
d. Atzi Soto

Tiny Rascalz –

a. Tajiri Ken
b. Rye Kenichi
c. Kyomi San
d. Sho Tonga

Vice Lords –

a. Raymond Jones
b. Franklin Jones
c. Xavier Jones
d. Brandon Jones

MSx13 –

a. Kabil Rodriguez
b. Naycon Guzman
c. Patley Lopez
d. Ovidio Calsada

Anatoly mentioned he is a member of the Rodnovers (Russians are Eastern Orthodox Christians & Slavic Pagans) MSx13 Members are of Aztec Origin and their names are not like Jose,

Yair, Brendon, Javier etc and now, we were out here working on them when we got a call and we stepped outside, Black Dragons were there and we proposed down a friendly treaty, we demanded what they wanted and we told them, we will allow them to run their Operations of Gambling, Protection and Thefts here as well as they can own and lease rent here too and they agreed with the following –

1. Black Dragons & 18th Street Crew will have a pact which allows Black Dragons to come to 18st Neighborhood and conduct Gambling Operations, Assassinations, Grand Theft of Automobiles (GTA is Grand Theft Auto lol), Trafficking and Hideouts from Enemies

2. 18th Street Members will honor their words to Black Dragons who in turn will not attack members of 18th Street Gang and will always help them out financially, mentally, physically and business wise as well

3. 18th will come on the fore front if Black Dragons face an attack from a predominantly Hispanic Organization or Assailant whether be Surenos, Nortenos, Bulldogs, Cartel or Latin Kings

4. Members of Black Dragons and 18th Street Gang will treat each other as Brothers and always invite each other to deals and gatherings too and offer protection services

5. Conduct Thefts, Robberies, Burglaries and Businesses together and will keep a form of secrecy from others outside the business conducted between the two groups

6. The Alliance pacts are meant to be honored and fulfilled by both parties and no 3rd party is meant to be involved in the agreement pact unless both sides unanimously consent to it

7. 18th St and Black Dragons Members can switch sides and join the other gang if they wish to and battle enemies together as well and during funerals of Black Dragons, 18th must send in 2 representatives as a gesture of respect

8. No Civilians, Pet Animals whether be Dogs or any other animal, No Elderly or Children are going to be involved and if conflict happens, it will be solved peacefully

And We agreed to the terms and conditions, our clique only has a few limited members and we signed the deal or sealed the deal down, and they hugged us down and we met the leaders, since the Knights, Williams and Stones murder, they have been impressed and found it strange how Drug Operations as well as Violent Attacks have been stopped and how we began working quickly and quietly and now, we taught them our ways out and we began working together, and now, we make deals and work as a group.

Black Dragons –

a. Chan Chong
b. Zhang Li Chong
c. Zee Ling Chong
d. Xiang Chong

Chong Brothers and Yakuza became friends too and Kkangpae and Triads too have made peace now, and Chong Brothers and We shared territories in a way, their neighborhood is next to my neighborhood, we did not leave down Los Angeles or LA either, and now, Chong Brothers member Chao Ding, Lei Dong, Jian Heto and Song Chong began working as my personal bodyguards and joined the crew, I learnt Hindi, Russian, Chinese, Armenian, Korean, Irish and Ukrainian by now as well as Spanish, English and Aztec Tongues, and now, with them we decided to loot down a Major Shop at the Mountains, I mean where the Wealthiest are, like how many classes there – Business (Shop Keepers and Drivers), Middle/Working (Lawyers, Writers and Teachers), Prosperous (Bankers, Doctors and Filmmakers) and Elitists (Politicians, Celebrities and Socialites), many say 3 classes – rich, poor and those in the middle, I disagree there, and now, Black Dragons made peace with us because I didn't tell anyone, but I actually am friends with Chong Brothers through my school life and now, I made a deal and got a crew assembled down too for that, we are looting cars from car dealerships of Honda, Toyota and Mercedes and giving them at a lower prices to some interesting characters too, Business Rivalries are far more deadlier and sinister, we may keep them for ourselves too.

Season 4, Chapter 1, the Discussions –

Chong Brothers came to our house and we got the list of Crew Members ready too now.

I said, handing them the list, and said "this is my crew, and we worked with Armenians, Koreans, Yakuza, Russians, Aryan Brotherhood and Irish Mob among more " –

Crew Members –
Leticia 'Lil Feather' Johnson
Michael 'Bailey' Perry
Jack Rollins 'Red Wolf'
Jesse 'Taylor' Calsada
Jose 'Sniffer' Daniels
Angel 'Blue' Lopez
Jey 'Joker' Raul Martinez
Tom 'Tommy-San' Soto

Arman Ivanov 'Neville'
David Lopez 'Bullet'
Gabriella 'Gabby' Reyes
Leticia 'Lil Feather/Letty' Johnson
Breonna Lopez 'Typhoon'
Christopher Guzman 'Skipper'
Demetrius Goldstien 'Dementus'
James Maxwell 'Ashton'

And I continued "and for the robbery, we will need 5 different groups, 5 different locations, and now we will steal cars from Honda, Toyota and Mercedes, we will require 8 people for the job, and on the other hand, we will steal from a moving train from Central Valley and steal down Polished Diamonds, Platinum and Jewelry, we will commit a Bank Robbery in San Francisco as well as Fresno, and the 5th Group will be there for backups and for loading all the goods " and now, the Chong Brothers listened and finally Chan said "David, plan is risky, but with the risk comes the reward and that is all we want, but no deaths must happen, we agree " and there are four brothers – Chan, Zhang, Zee and Xiang.

Zhang – "how do we divide down the responsibilities and began working? "

I – "You Guys can have 4 and I can have 4 people stopping the loader trucks and disarming them down, or maybe we can hijack and kill the guard, but again no innocent blood, maybe we can steal directly from their plants and oceans 11, you must have seen the movie, you and I were there together "

Zee – "if the car truck isnt there or plant closed, our group can return or steal something else valuable too "

I agreed and nodded – "Zee very well actually and Xiang, you have been quiet"

Xiang – "well, David, you and I are very well friends, we will do this and we will have more heists, it is the other gangs that are making nonsense, you got your collision to side with us, but MS and their allies are issuing things "

I mentioned we will have something figured out and that enemies come and go and now, we found out, the train isnt stopping there and car dealership is shut down for 11 days, and now, we made another plan, robbing off town casinos, shops, malls and houses instead.

And now, we chose the location of a truck and came across members of MSx13 and their partners too, Vice Lords are related to Stones, Williams & Knights Family and now they are here too, they will be followed down by Kingston and Johns, and now, they are all Black Gangsters in BGF Gang and now, here is the list again.

Asure13 –

   Scally Calsada
   Acalan Pineda
   Javier Lopez
   Atzi Soto

Tiny Rascalz –

   Tajiri Ken
   Rye Kenichi
   Kyomi San
   Sho Tonga

Vice Lords –

   Raymond Jones
   Franklin Jones
   Xavier Jones

Brandon Jones

MSx13 –

Kabil Rodriguez

Naycon Guzman

Patley Lopez

Ovidio Calsada

And now, we began watching Dhar Mann, or Dharmendra Mann, he makes cringey videos and now, Vice Lords think they are Jon Jones, like seriously, fanboying too badly, John Jones is a big fighter, and these guys, Jon maybe a drug addict and a part-time criminal element, Jones would never approve of a Gang killing people for betting against him, they aren't related to John Jones or anyone like that, and now, as Jones Brothers and Kabil's Crew came by, Guns Blazing and we called in Rooftop Koreans with Kkangpae began shooting them all down, and we ran off too, Kabil Rodriguez & Raymond Jones said they will have my head, and I am like fuck you, and we were going to War with them all, as Ovidio, Patley, Naycon and Kabil came from MS-13 Gang, and now, with them it was war, in the beginning about Middle 1990s, Mara Salvatrucha Stoners aka MSS was formed when Salvadoran Peasants trained to be Guerilla Fighters came to Los Angeles and formed a gang now Mara is a Gang, Salvatrucha is a term used to honor Salvadoran Peasants trained to be Guerilla Fighters, Stoners meant uses of Weed and LSD, they dropped Stoners and added 13 to denote the letter M, which meant they pay tribute to The Mexican Mafia aka La EME.

18 and MS got into Shootings and Gunfights, and that was bad for drug business, when members of Mexican Mafia aka LA EME called in members of both groups and called in for a meeting in a Basketball Courthouse and sat down some rules, where they demanded we pay them taxes and divided down Westlake Neighborhood aka MacArthur Park down, we got a zone and they got the other zone, and murders rate dropped by, and we both branched out, and now, when members got killed, arrested and deported down, members in Honduras, El Salvador, Guatemala and Nicaragua began to recruit more people, and since the local police was ill-equipped, many gangsters began joining the Military and the Police, and now, MS 13 and 18th ST gangs fight reached down here, Criminal Activities included Trafficking (Human, Drugs and Weapons), Extortions and Murders, Terrorism Activities included Mass Murders, Bombings and Piracy too, in Central America two gangs caused mayhem, Government Crackdowns cannot do anything, Honduran President Juan Orlando Hernandez who did a Crackdown on both gangs was caught Smuggling & Trafficking Narcotics and imprisoned in The United States only, Brazilian President Jair Bolsonaro may also be there with him, and now, MS' brutality is why Los Zetas use them as a recruitment pool, the ones who can follow orders are selected in their wars against Mexican Pirates, Communist Insurgents, Native Aztec Armed Groups, the Famous Sinaloa Cartel and Jalisco New Generation Cartel.

And now, we had it as the enemies Vice Lords, MSx13, Tiny Rascalz and Azure13 leaders, and we started some boxing too, like the five main bodies of boxing are –

A. World Boxing Association (WBA)
B. World Boxing Council (WBC)
C. International Boxing Federation (IBF)
D. World Boxing Organization (WBO)
E. The Ring (should have put WBO after WBA and WBC, it would have looked cool)

Let me do that again, the five main bodies of boxing are –

A. World Boxing Association (WBA)
B. World Boxing Council (WBC)
C. World Boxing Organization (WBO)
D. International Boxing Federation (IBF)
E. The Ring

There are 5 World Champions in each division and they all have a Mandatory Champion every 3 to 4 months, imagine if Boxing allowed Kicks, Wrestling, Holds and Weapons, it would be so funny or imagine if MMA, Professional Wrestling or Kickboxing had similar governing groups, NWA and WAMMA or National Wrestling Alliance and World Alliance of Mixed Martial Arts exist for a reason, WAMMA Heavyweight Championship's first, only, last and one champion was The Last Emperor and Russian Bear Fedor Emelioenko and their division was as follows –

1. Heavyweight Champion – Fedor Emelioenko aka Last

Emperor or Russian Bear

2. Lightheavyweight Champion – Lyoto Machida aka the Dragon
3. Middleweight Champion – Anderson Silva aka the Spider
4. Welterweight Champion – George St Pierre aka Rush
5. Lightweights Champion – Jay Dee Penn aka BJ Penn (didn't know what BJ stands for here)

And now, Asure13, MS13, TRG and Vice Lords all came in there and took their guns out, Snipers (Koreans, Mexicans and Chinese) gunned them all down and now, we had them grounded and now, we had Armenians and Russians break in, and now, we held the leaders down as hostages, and now, they had been taken hostages now, but EME Members came to out door and had Azure and MS leaders taken from Prison, our hostage held, and BGF Members came in with Vice Lords taken out, TRG Members held Blackwood at Gunpoint and we agreed to let them all walk away, and TRG Member killed a Mexican Vendor and now, we are at War now, Warzone is on.

Black Dragons exiting the scene and we made a pact and they refused and we called in other 18th St and a full on War was going to happen, and so MS and 18th were stopped by EME Enforcers and now, they had set up new rules, we exited everything solely being thieves and whatnot.

1. No Innocents and Family should be hurt
2. No Mutilation, Kidnappings, Torture etc
3. No Dogs or Other Pets involved

4. No Police should be called in
5. No Infighting if we enter Prison Walls
6. No Disrespecting EME Members and Customers
7. No Rape or Sexual Assaults
8. No Disrespecting Dead Enemies/Rivals

And now, we agreed and backed off, and now, we had all the leaders there, and now, they didn't have families, they all died, and now, we send the dogs and the kids away to grandparents, her parents house and now, with that it was just us and we had send in enough cash to keep them in colleges too, and now, this is it, no more gang warfare after this big one, maybe we can all retire down after this major score only and now, with that, Black Dragons and Yakuza run Motels and we brought some too, and I called the crew in and we planned to monitor them all for 6 weeks and start eliminating them all one by one, before any move can be made, only MS will agree to those terms and now the others won't.

And now, 4 LAPD Members came in, and we recorded their names, they are fellow thieves only and their names are –

1. James Potter, White
2. Zhang Chow, Yellow-Asian
3. Matthew Carter, White
4. Dakota Hall, Red American

And LAPD Cops mentioned a list of other cops, with their Badges, Phone Numbers, Names, Police Numbers and Addresses, about them and 12 more, 16 Cops are accepting bribes, we bribed them in advance only, and they all cops wanted MS-13 Members dead as well as Vice Lords and for every MS and Vice Lords Member we killed we would get 12,000$ and the Mayor and The Sheriff were paying us to get rid of them, we had 12 more Cop Cars pulled over, I told these cops to get transfer to Smaller Cities, and we will handle them, too many cops here, and the cops were from other cities only, Anatoly and Sergei from the council got them to go away, and now, it was our job to take out Vice Lords, MS-13, Tiny Rascalz Gangsters among more including Mass Shooters, Gang Members, Human Traffickers and Many More.

And now, in exchange for an Immunity for 18th St Members, we signed the bills down, and now, with the Cop Cars gone, we made a score, there was a Black Market Arms Dealer meeting some Bloods over a Gun Deal, Greek Dealer, once he had left, we will kill the Bloods and take those weapons to a Greek Café and meet the desk guy, from there, we will get a large sum of money dumped in our trunks, Baily and Blackwood cleared their trunks from camping gears, and we were ready for the big scores, about 2 Million Dollars and from all the old MMA + Boxing Gambling, Thievery, Logistics, Mercenary Work and Café Jobs, we have made a Bank and with more of this cash, our families wont ever have to work again, Jack Doherty is so terrible with those Street Interviews, he is the guy to break into another man's house, attack him, get beaten up and lose the fight and call the Police on him and act like a Victim, like all his fights have happened whenever he provoked a man, got slapped and called the police and security guards after that, and he is so pretentious about that too.

And Patrick-Bet David calling Khabib the GOAT of UFC ignoring the milestones by John Jones, Georges St Pierre, Anderson Silva, Demetrius Johnson, Frankie Edgar, Mark Coleman, Dan Severn, Don Frye, Ken Shamrock, Dan Henderson, Henry Cejudo, Dominick Cruz and don't know how many more, Gegard Mousasi and Rory MacDonald + John Fitch are all Goats if there is a Goat, Goat List and Conversation is so ridiculous and Patrick is the same guy who didn't talk to his mother for five years and fucking blocked her, that is your hero, I don't see how he is so likeable or anything he does, I doubt he watches UFC, UFC 294 was a literal shitshow, not impressed, Tim Elliot is 36 and is doing wonderful, but everyone else sucked, Islam finished a short fighter, haha fight someone like Colby Covington and Justin Gaethje man, not dwarf stars like Alexander Volkanovsky.

Season 4, Chapters 2 and 3, The Big Scores –

And now, MS and Bloods were all there, and now Greek Arms Dealer called Apollo was attacked and we shot down the MS Members, like5 of them, Bloods were all killed except Looney, the target was called so, he worked and killed many of ours, and we sniped him down, and we noticed 3 more MS Members, and 2 more inside, and now, we sniped the tires of the car, and now, we bolted down, I came into the Car Park from another side, and met those two MS Membmers shooting them dead, and Blackwood my 2nd took their guns too, and handed me one, Gabby and I marched in there, Gabby killed a Blood Gang Member and we walked by and began searching down, and retrieved the cases, Apollo and Us raced to a Greek Café and now, we got till there, and we got the money and weapons sent in, Apollo takes Protection from us, he has a few members in the gang, and now, we hired a new dog, this one is a Caucasian Shepherd named Lauren and Joseph and now, we began to make the scene, like Mexican Boxing and Professional Wrestling is so much better in my opinion and now atop that, let us get down to business lane, and we got the milk and now we have the cow, I am with you man, and with that, we met the leaders again, Vice Lords with MS-13 and Ti8ny Rascalz Gangsters, Gangland made badass documentaries on all of us actually, Gangland made 3 on MS-13 alone only –

Season 1, Episode 2, You rat you Die

Season 1, Episode 11, Root of all Evil

Season 7, Episode 6, Capitol Killers

Where they talked about MS – 13 in American Soil, You rat You die, where they mentioned how MS-13 Gang works in Virginia, Texas and California and how deadly and they can be mentioning Brenda Paz, a Honduran-American or Honduran born American Girl who ran away from home and began working for and dating many older MS-13 Members, at 13 she dated a 20 something year old Dennis something and another shot caller who killed an innocent man named Javier Calsada in Houston, Donald Trump and the Republican Party of America had a crackdown, and the FBI have a special task force dedicated to Mara Salvatrucha – 13 only, shows you how dangerous they really are.

Root of All Evil show an episode where they attacked, paralyzed and killed an Iranian Immigrant called Wally and talk about the connection between that and a 2nd incident where members of Ms-13 open fired at a bus carrying laborers where Man, Woman, Children, Crippled and the Elderly alike where, and how it was all connected as LAPD and Honduran Police Officers were also present there, the history of MS-13 began as how they were shunned from 18th Street Gang (which comprised of many cliques and sets and many being Mexicans only as Salvadorans formed their own gang using Spanish Word Mara which meant Gang and Salvatrucha which was to honor Salvadoran Peasants trained to be Guerilla Fighters and Stoners as many 1st Generational Members only smoked Marijuana and LSD and later added 13 to denote homage to the Mexican Mafia aka LA EME (Spanish for the M) and many 1st Gen Members were interviewed down too) and now, most of them being deported Salvadoran Members only, the opposition leaders are Salvadoran born Civilians and many have Argentine Blood too.

3rd one was about Washington DC Chapters of Mara Salvatrucha – 13 and how the broad daylight murders were happening under their watch and the movie we die young was about Washington DC Chapters of MS-13 Members only and how Lucas and Miguel with the help of an Army Veteran and a Young Friend escaped the gang, emotionally heartbreaking movie.

Sin Nombre was another movie about MS-13 Gang Members in Mexican State of Oaxaca which killed and raped a Member's girlfriend who in revenge killed his girlfriend's rapist and killer and saved a young Honduran Girl from their clutches and sacrificed himself, dying in the process only.

Tiny Rascalz Gangsters and Vice Lords too had an episode where a Northern Californian Resident called Vanna In mentioned and detailed his time as a member of Tiny Rascalz Gangsters, his initiation and crimes, his time in prison, and how he reformed himself and a member called Jim, who had to run away, the police officers in the documentaries were shown a Chinese and a Mexican one who met a guy called Little Badass, funny scene but Little Badass died in a shooting at age 12, Vice Lords one was boring and corny.

We had an episode, I thing Season 2 Episode 7, called or titled as Murder by Numbers where we talked about the history of 18th Street Gang, we were always Multi Ethnic and Multi Racial and pre MS-13 timing, how we had an issue with a Gang called Clanton – 14 (now 14 usually is associated with Nortenos and Nuestra Familia but Clanton – 14 is a lot older then both Mexican Mafia and Nuestra Familia) and how many Koreans, Africans, Mexicans and Arabs were all into this gang, everyone wasn't in for Drugs and all but we were in this together too, and how Juan Romero aka Termite created one of the most successful branches of 18th Street Gang called Columbia Lil Psychos and how miscommunication got him expelled, attacked and how he survived an assassination attempt from the people he thought were his brothers, how he and his driver escaped them and got 42 members in for prison time, he solely collected taxes and sold little bit drugs too.

Gangland is an amazing television series or show, my favorite were about American Gangster, MS-13 Episodes, 18th Street Gang, Fresno Bulldogs, Aryan Brotherhood, Aryan Circle, Public Enemies Number 1 Death Squad, Bloods and Crips and Latin Kings among many more, like Rappers like Tupac Shakur, Snoop Dogg and many more had Gang Ties, Tupac got killed over them only, and Latin Kings one was very interesting, as we didn't make eye contact with TRG, MS and Vice Lords Members and slowly drove out and now, we were getting shots fired, and we drove off fast, and they killed some Aryan Brotherhood Members who began open firing and killing down MS-13 Members and Vice Lords, nearly wounding one of their leaders, what was his name Raymond and we had Azure13 Leaders on our trail, we shot the tires down and loosen them down, and now an Open Warfare between Aryan Brotherhood and Affiliates and MS – 13 Coalition was called abruptly when Council Members took money exchange for the damages and now, we confronted Azure13 Leaders and they made a deal, all 4 of them + Black Dragons will work against Raymond and his Brothers and will have them killed by our hands, and we together ended a Set of MS13 Members, by shooting their engines and they caught fire, on a highway and escaped down, Avenues and Florencia – 13 joined us against MS-13 and now, we were having a good hand against MS-13.

Latin Kings episode Kings of New York talks about a guy called King Blood aka Luis Felipe, who escaped Cuba during an expedition and came to Miami, Florida and went to Chicago, Illinois and from there went to South Bronx, New York and started Bloodline aka New York Chapter of Almighty Latin Kings & Queens Nations, and began working, they killed even their own, cutting limbs and burning people alive, even the innocent, King Blood was send to ADX Florence, Supermax Prison in Colorado where famous Cult Leaders, Terrorists, Spies and Criminal Figures like Theodore/Ted Kaczenski aka The Unabomber formerly, Joaquin Archivaldo Guzman-Loera aka El Chapo, James Marcello of Chicago Outfit, Oklahoma City Bomber Terry Nichols, 1993 World Trade Center Bomber Ramzi Yusif, Army of God member Eric Rudoph, Richard Reid British Al-Qaeda Member, Irek Hamidullin of Russian Republic/Region Tatarstan who served both the Russian Army and Taliban is the newest inmate, Jose Padilla a Puerto-Rican born Al Qaeda Member, Dhzarkov Tsarmev Boston Marathon Bomber who was sent to Terra Huete for Execution was a Kyrgyz-Chechen (Kyrgyzstani as well as Chechan-Russian) who bombed Boston Marathon and threw away an Engineering Career for Life without Parole plus we have inmates like that and so many more.

El Chapo or Joaquin Archivaldo Guzman-Loera, he was the founder and leader of Sinaloa Cartel, and in Sinaloa

Mexico his cartel handed our Free Internet, Electricity, Water Supply and created Schools, the villagers saw Guzman as a Hero, and his family and associates too, many Mexican Cartels during Covid-19 were seen handing out Food and Clothes and maintaining a Curfew to help Mexican Villagers out, and now, another inmate a Cult Leader, Rapper, Child Molester & Rapist Dwight York who ran a cult of Black Supremacy is also locked in there, I never support anything like Child Rape and Molestation, Animal Cruelty, Elderly Abuse, Domestic Violence and a lot of other things, Yakuza and Black Dragons met us and we all decided to break into a compound of Almighty Latin Kings and Queens Nation in California and they were guarding down Diamond Shops, they stole our Diamonds and Gold as well as Cars and we are getting them back now, we shot and killed Latin Kings Members, they weren't partying, but doing watch, keeping watch or patrolling and we killed them all down.

And they were working for a Cult Leader named Daniel Markins, he thinks he is Dwight York, he is no Child Predator or a Predator in general but a very terrible dude, wannabe terrible joker like those Sigma Males man, like their reels make no sense, Daniel Markins is neither African or Latino, he is some Indian – Arabic dude who got kicked out of his own community, Dhananjay is his name, he sells us Cocaine yeah he is a cool kid, he and Apollo are beefing down actually, Asure13 and Black Dragons with us kidnapped away 5 members of Vice Lords and we asked them the location promising down Freedom in another city, and the Vice Lords mentioned the leaders of Vice Lords and MS 13 are hanging out at a Brothel where they kidnap people at, and we decided to end them, ever since I have children, I told myself nobody is for sale, and end human trafficking and Anshul Jubli is going to be like the Great Khali, a Major Star Player, Man Great Khali was different, I am sure if he was 6'6 or 6'7 instead of 7'2 He'd probably be a lot different, him bullying Batista was funny though, I am fluent in Hindi now too btw, another language in my collection, Dhananjay is my teacher.

And now, we saw the leaders of MS-13, Vice Lords and Tiny Rascalz Gangsters aka TRG which is Home Invasion expert actually.

Tiny Rascalz –

a. Tajiri Ken
b. Rye Kenichi
c. Kyomi San
d. Sho Tonga

Vice Lords –

a. Raymond Jones
b. Franklin Jones
c. Xavier Jones
d. Brandon Jones

MSx13 –

a. Kabil Rodriguez
b. Naycon Guzman
c. Patley Lopez

d.   Ovidio Calsada

And now, Ovidio and Naycon with Raymond and Sho T9onga went inside, and now, I was seeing an opening now and we were seeing the other leaders, as Azure13 and Black Dragons on our side now, Blackwood and Gabby killed 3 members and made them vanish, 1 Vice Lord

and 2 MS Members and disappeared and when a 4th went there in a dark alley, and as he entered, Gabby shot him in the chest and stomach as Blackwood covered his mouth, and now, they did not even realize it all, and now the crew was here with Yakuza Members behind us too.

Crew Members –
Leticia 'Lil Feather' Johnson
Michael 'Bailey' Perry
Jack Rollins 'Red Wolf'
Jesse 'Taylor' Calsada
Jose 'Sniffer' Daniels
Angel 'Blue' Lopez
Jey 'Joker' Raul Martinez
Tom 'Tommy-San' Soto
Arman Ivanov 'Neville'
David Lopez 'Bullet'
Gabriella 'Gabby' Reyes
Leticia 'Lil Feather/Letty' Johnson
Breonna Lopez 'Typhoon'
Christopher Guzman 'Skipper'
Demetrius Goldstien 'Dementus'
James Maxwell 'Ashton'

Ashton and Dementus looked around, and began taking out a few members too, and one by one, we got there, and now, the Vice Lords being the loyalist they claim to be, when members of Latin Kings came by and started shooting down members of Vice Lords, where Ashton and Dementus were taking members out, Dementus killed the unconscious Vice Lords and started shooting, Vice Lords saw a member with a soda bottle get killed and his son crash the car, only to be killed by a Latin Kings member down, the car crashed, more Latin Kings came by and shooting increased, this was a Gated Community with Closed Gates, at the outskirts in a farmhouse, I mean a gated farmhouse and now, Ashton and Dementus saved LK Members down and the one who killed the soda VL and his son killed 1 MS and 1 Vice Lord member before being shot in the head and killed down, the other members got out and a shooting happened, we began ambushing the Vice Lords, MS-13 and TRG Members with our cars hitting them and surrounding the farmhouse down, and now, with Yakuza under Tommy-San killing TRG and MS Members down, we made our way down, and into the farmhouse, where we spotted sex workers, who began pleading and we shot a Vice Lords member down, and got them to go with Blackwood and Gabby, I don't want to do this anymore, I had daughters too, and now we marched in, let us finish this, Child Traffickers must die.

Season 4, Chapter 4 and 5, The Ending of few –

Crew Members –
Leticia 'Lil Feather' Johnson
Michael 'Bailey' Perry
Jack Rollins 'Red Wolf'
Jesse 'Taylor' Calsada

Jose 'Sniffer' Daniels
Angel 'Blue' Lopez
Jey 'Joker' Raul Martinez
Tom 'Tommy-San' Soto
Arman Ivanov 'Neville'
David Lopez 'Bullet'
Gabriella 'Gabby' Reyes
Leticia 'Lil Feather/Letty' Johnson
Breonna Lopez 'Typhoon'
Christopher Guzman 'Skipper'
Demetrius Goldstien 'Dementus'
James Maxwell 'Ashton'

Jack Rollins aka Red Wolf got us to do this, secluded areas are where no police can come in and we got it done rightfully, Red Wolf took Children and Elderly Sex Workers, and now, Typhoon and Neville with Sniffer, Blue, Joker began leading the surrounded members to surrender and kill them as Skipper, Lil Feather and Baily rounded up the Money, Drugs, Weapons, Contraband and other things into Trunks and Boots of cars down, we were looking for the leaders who had guns too, Yakuza Members rescued their daughters, sisters and friends now.

Tiny Rascalz –

a. Tajiri Ken (+)
b. Rye Kenichi (+)
c. Kyomi San
d. Sho Tonga (+)

Vice Lords –

a. Raymond Jones (+)
b. Franklin Jones
c. Xavier Jones
d. Brandon Jones

MSx13 –

a. Kabil Rodriguez
b. Naycon Guzman
c. Patley Lopez
d. Ovidio Calsada

Many TRG Members snitched on their leaders being with us, because they didn't like Animal Abuse, Child and Sex Trafficking, Mass Murders and Terrorism, which was being planned down too, and now with most of TRG behind me and now, we began looking, last the leaders were spotted in the main rooms, and we began looking, speaking of Naycon and Ovidio, they escaped with a 3rd member and one TRG, hiding in the farmlands only, Raymond and Sho Tonga got captured and I order Red Wolf to kill them and he did end both of them, Tonga and Raymond were not even raping children, we don't use Bad or Good, they make no sense, we have Good and Bad, but it is changed in many ways, we use Unlikeable now, and with that, Sho Tonga and Raymond are now dead, and MS Leaders escaped by jumping the windows into a getaway car with that, speeding down, and we had firing and a few TRGs ducked and we broke down a door, and I killed a Vice Lord, raping a minor and another one came out, two in the bathroom, killed both of them, and Tommy-San killed the 3rd one, we dragged down members of The Tigres, remaining ones, and MS

Members and killed them, TRG Leaders were all found and captured and no mercy to Pedophiles and Child Seekers, as Tajiri and Rey got killed by Gabby and Dementus only.

Ashton, Gabby, Bailey, Lil Feather and Yakuza began treating down the wounded members, Tongans and Armenians rounded up Cartel Members and began executing them down, and LAPD Bribers came by, James or whatever his name was, their names are –

1. James Potter, White
2. Zhang Chow, Yellow-Asian
3. Matthew Carter, White
4. Dakota Hall, Red American

Dakota and Matthew paid us for the good jobs and got our names off the crackdown list, half the gangs are off already, Tongans and Armenians and Yakuza aren't even active now, TRG and 18 don't have anything to hide now and with that, their police officers came and fired more and more bullet shots in there, and upgraded list now is –

Tiny Rascalz –

a. Tajiri Ken (+)
b. Rye Kenichi (+)
c. Kyomi San
d. Sho Tonga (+)

Vice Lords –

a. Raymond Jones (+)

b. Franklin Jones
c. Xavier Jones
d. Brandon Jones

MSx13 –

a. Kabil Rodriguez
b. Naycon Guzman
c. Patley Lopez
d. Ovidio Calsada (+)

And now, Gabby and Ashton began running after Ovidio because he wasn't dead and we ran after him, when a LAPD Patrol car began coming, he broke into a farmhouse, this farmer didn't kill his cattle for meat, he is no meat farmer, he poisoned the waters of the horses, the dogs, the cattle and the birds, and now, he was shot down and killed by a rancher in there, and his 4 friends got surrounded and killed too, and LAPD and 18 Members had to go away, Government isnt supposed to find out about this and we kept it all under the rung, looting their houses down and taking the money down as well as valuables and whatnot, and James and Zhang took us to a meeting room, where we discussed childhood with Gabby being there with them, and I told them, the remaining leaders will be taken out one by one with Latin Kings joining MS13 in their crusade against MS-13 and now with Arabic Members as well as South Americans in there and now, we were ready, we found their Arabic Members and with a few tricks we got them in there, and we knew they weren't Arabs, they were Cubans and Argentine and we shot them all dead, we didn't, we had them snitched down, killing a commanding officer down, and buried him down and we realized it all down, we needed leverage and began killing various customers of Vice Lords, dumping them near their house, strangling and drowning, and now, there were no remarks of whatsoever and now, with that we began working our way down.

Tiny Rascalz –
Tajiri Ken (+)
Rye Kenichi (+)
Kyomi San
Sho Tonga (+)
Vice Lords –
Raymond Jones (+)
Franklin Jones
Xavier Jones
Brandon Jones
MSx13 –
Kabil Rodriguez
Naycon Guzman
Patley Lopez
Ovidio Calsada

Or the Alive Enemies are –
Franklin Jones
Xavier Jones
Brendon Janes
Kabil Rodriguez
Patley Lopez
Kyomi San

Forgot to mention Ovidio died in our hands on the bust day and Jack Rollins curb stomped down and killed Naycon Guzman who survived and made sure he was dead, and now, and with that, we were getting closer to killing them all now

Franklin Jones

Xavier Jones
Brendon Janes
Kabil Rodriguez
Patley Lopez
Kyomi San

And now, I remember meeting Black Dragons and Azure13 Members down, who mentioned spotting down Jones Brothers and now, we began working when Apollo and Dhananjay began fixing races and now, I went into a non-fixed race and won some of them too, giving back their cars, and killed some car racers, they kidnapped and sold our friends, and this way payback and the cops came back and brought fat paychecks, we had the money and now, we didn't realize it either, Ashton, Dementus, Blackwood and Bailey joined a Wrestling Show, or a Professional Wrestling show nearby and an American Football Team, Gabby with Lil Feather and Bailey got busy, and so the remaining crew members with me planned to do Wrestling and MMA and even Grappling after killing down Jones Brothers and making sure nobody is dead.

And now, Iced Coffee Hour is so retarded, that guy literally said Childless Marriages are so better and so many podcasters opening around and I just laugh at them like –

I cannot take Jokes on Andrew Tate podcast (Whatever Mansophere, I am sure whosoever this Andrew Tate guy is would laugh with the girls, they basically call some girls and slut shame them for their life choices)

Unfiltered Podcast (The Host asked the girls to rate them on a scale of 1-10, on physical beauty standards and calls one girl a stupid bitch and throws her out, I am sure he treats his own mother, sister, wife and daughter that way, I bet anyone likes that guy, he is a joker)

Fresh & Fit, imagine someone like Samantha Frank or Sam Frank, the nicest girl you can meet up, berates you in pure anger, Myron Gaines is a dumbass, Prince is actually likeable but his NBA Superstar Story was so rigged dude is describing a Human Trafficking/Slave Owners party

Desirable Truth, attacking Women outside Nightclubs and paying them to say they like a particular type, girls being exhausted, drunk, stoned or angry have no choice but to get clowned at

Israel Padilla, Austin Texas' 6th Street Interviewers, yelling like a Psychopath and being told off whenever someone (especially a girl) doesn't want him, but he made some good progress and im happy with that

Michaelson is also doing good, ask about jobs not marriageable man, they aren't marrying you or seeing you a 2nd time and anyone can figure it out.

No Jumper Podcast by Pornstar, Host and Creep Adam Grandmaison aka Adam22 as well as Plug Talks, Adam is accused of many assaults both Sexual and Physical, I would not say anything on the matter.

Tate Podcast, I don't care about redemption, he ran a Web Camera service, and lured innocent 18 and

19-year-olds into it, forced them to do Web Cam, and scammed people without remorse, Cowboy Donald Cerrone is right to be angry at him, I mean Candace Owens yes her too.

Candace Owens called Mia Khalifa and condemned her for being a Pornstar and praised Andrew Tate who ran a Web Cam Business and scammed people, who admitted scamming people, Owens is wanting attention obviously, she hates seeing people go to Bars, Nightclubs and buy Beer, hates people having a better life then her, hates movies which may not have political ties.

Patrick Bet-David is the worst of them, he blocked his own mother for five years, and never spoke to her, never visited her, never bothered talking to her and claims God made her talk to him, what a lunatic, are any of his stories real, I do not think so like he called Khabib the GOAT of UFC (Been a UFC Fan, don't know what a GOAT is, until someone mentioned Greatest of all Time, which has be Anderson Silva, John Jones, George St Pierre, Mark Coleman, Randy Couture, 100s more before Khabib, and Ukrainian Yaraslov Amosov in American Top Team is 27-0 close to breaking his record only, wait till he goes to UFC, beats Welterweights and Lightweights there too, I love Khabib but his fans literally don't do anything other than praise him 24/7, like get some jobs, I am a Khabib Fan, don't really watch UFC now, Bellator MMA and BKFC now)

Pearl Davis hopefully gets her dream lover who is –

Promiscuous and Abusive, Pearl being the only women who wants women to have zero rights, I mean she wants an abusive and cheating husband

No respect and her husband shutting her show down like Wife School is terrible, she cannot even cut that Chicken down

Attention Seeking from others and isolates her

Pearl cheated on her ex I heard but don't believe so.

Season 4, Chapter 7, Tigres last cell –

I remembered down Pearl Davis, her points are stupid as fuck, she lives in the freest country and supports Sexism, Promiscuity, Anti Women Laws and whatnot, like hopefully Pearls' husband is going to be A. Abuse, B. Beats her, C. Cheats on her, D. Does end her channel and make her do Wifey Things and E. doesn't let her meet her parents and siblings, how ridiculous can people be, pearl would probably support Bride Kidnapping of Kyrgyzstan and Kazakhstan.

Sneako is another idiot in this list, he tells Men that they have to watch this girlfriends and wives sleep with another man and go through out, Gabby or Lil Feather are from Promiscuous and second Sneako watched a movie glorifying Child Sexualization, Cuties was meant to be against sexualizing children and did the opposite and Sneako is a guy who wants attention only.

Jonathan Hogwood wants a Japanese Sex Doll to be his wife, like is this guy unwell or what, he seems to have issues, talks about how a man has a right to beat his wife and cheat on her, hates American Women for what? Going to College, Having a Career and not being Housewives, is this guy retarded, I am so sorry about my language, but I won't stop there.

Matan Ewan is another hothead, slut shaming an Only Fans girl and calling her an Online Whore, dude people post Only Fans content and content is not always Nudes, some bad day, he is going to be found with broken legs and arms, he should stick to school, not this trolling, man got arrested for Game of the Year stunt, it was funny btw but stained his name.

N3on is another underaged fool, what is he doing, how did his parents allow him to go to Romania and live with another man, he faked his own death and got famous for it and clearly loves shouting and yelling, Adam22 is probably going to beat him one day and Adin Ross won't protect him for sure.

Adin Ross is another Drug Addicted Clout Seeker, I am sure he called Mike old and yelled at him to shut up, I am shocked how Mike didn't hit him hard, two slaps alone can make him cry, he seeks attention from fans and Andrew Tate for some reason, let that guy live his life, what is his thing anyways.

Iced Coffee Hour, group of braindead people, giving clueless opinions on things and don't know who watches them anyways because I don't care about them, I found out many members listen to them for some reason.

Brett Cooper, she only has fans because she is beautiful and her opinions don't even make sense, Gen-Z and Gen this, what is this? And why is she chasing clout and attention, she makes good points only for views and is unlivable at its best, she wants to be God-Woman and shame people for being Pagans or anything that is not Christian (Christians I mean White Christians claim to be Liberal, attack Neopagan Houses and Atheists in Utah)

Dillion Danis is another one in this list, he wishes to be Mixed Martial Artist, Boxer, Businessman and Actor The Notorious Conor McGregor, and man all the things he has done, like fighting 2 MMA Fights and being inactive for 4 whole years, calling out UFC Fighters and YouTubers, pulling out of MMA as well as Boxing Showdowns like KSI Pullout, slut shaming Logan's wife who didn't even say a word against him, I am sure if Danis never posted demeaning photos of her, she wouldn't even know him, Nina Agdal (Logan Paul wife) Instagram posts are filled with people calling her a slut and a whore and claiming she is ran through (derogatory term for someone who had many romantic partners used commonly in Manosphere and Redpill Programs)

Jon Zherka and Nick Fuentes, two grifters who just want internet fame and have no life outside of it, Zherka was never a Bouncer I suppose, Fuentes runs a show and promotes Neo-Nazism while he is Mexican and goes to Adam22's show and mentioned how he isnt a Racist like dude pick a side.

Ben Shapiro, weird name and surname, seems nice and speaks too fast, I cannot understand a word he says, and he looks like he is made of woods and bricks, and poses like a Movie Star, I am sure he is a real-life Batman or something.

And now, speaking of that, it was made by some of us members to troll people online, I do think they are jokers and now, speaking of that, we had an attack planned down, some Redpill dude tried molesting Gabby and Gabby kicked him out, he with a metallic pipe beat her and damaged her hands, nose, fingers, ribs and many more parts, and we are finding those bros, and they are White MS-13 Members not surprised after all, I remember a Vice Documentary, shameful to see MS Members kill Women for no reason and we get blame too, they are responsible for crackdown, okay Gangs control Honduras is both our fault and I wish to make peace between 18 and MS-13 now, and end this War.

I mean seen enough deaths, Gang Survival means Making Peace, ending this all, and now, we began spreading Olive Branches around to Avenues and Mara-13 and some accepted too, and now, time to end the bloodshed, don't want more people dying now and well with that being said and now, we began working on there, opening up shops and starting a new chapter in our lives, kids growing up somewhere better and dogs too.

And we made a playlist of Television Shows to pass time as well –

1. Altered Carbon's both seasons and anime called Altered

Carbon Resleeved

2. Kengan Ashura and Omega plus Tekken and One Punch Man

3. Snowfall all 5 seasons in one sitting, as many as we can

4. Godfather Trilogy plus Goodfellas, Capone, Lansky, Gotti and Untouchables plus Irishman

5. Boyhood and many related movies and The Act, like Dhar Mann rip offs so much better

6. The Punisher, Daredevil, Defenders, Iron Fist, Jessica Jones and Luke Cage

7. Doctor House Seasons one after another with both Percy Jacksons and Artemis Fowl movie

We finished the 1st five already and now, Lego Batman and Lego Movies too, like Lord Business, haha what a funny name it is man, and Back to the Future Trilogy is also amazing, Martin Scorsese makes good movies in my opinion and Rocky is also good, I don't sympathize with Ivan Drago because –

1. He killed Apollo Creed purposefully in the Boxing Match

2. Didn't apologize at all to Apollo's Wife and Son, leaving them without Restitution Money to please Soviet Generals

3. Being Happy and having zero emotions on it and mocking Rocky Balboa for that too and losing in Moscow

And aftermath made no sense either –

1. His Wife defended Ivan killing Apollo but divorced him over losing a Boxing Match and leaving her son, I met many Russians and they hated that part

2. Ivan trained his son to be a Boxer and nothing wrong with

that, but I mean Ivan could have made him do MMA, Judo, Wrestling or Combat Sambo as well

3. Ivan losing all respect because Balboa defeated him is literally not adding up, like Russians are far more closer then Mexicans and Americans in Brotherhood and Belonging, his wife leaving him was just as senseless

4. Ivan allowing his son to train with Apollo's son too is just like burying the movies only

Sigma Males calling people fatherless should watch Apollo and Creed Movies, Creed is fatherless because Ivan Drago killed his father, how can you sympathize with a Villain, Apollo never insulted him or anything, like Sigma Males would support Rapists, Terrorists and Serial Killers because someone wronged them, like my son was killed by The Joker because Society wronged him, who the hell is he to kill my friends or my sons, like these guys make no sense, I was listening to Sigma Males music, while we spend hours discussing nonsense and broke into the houses, and surrounded the Sigma Males and Redpill Speakers, Gabby came in and pointed at the man who hit her, and I shot him in the head, chest and stomach, and we locked the door now.

Extraction Franchise is going to be awesome and now, Blackwood and Dementus took the phones away and broke the camera, and now, we had them all rounded up, killed one of them already too atop of that, like Gabby didn't even do anything to him, and now, we rounded them up, Sniffer and Angel killed the others in the building one after another, and they all started yelling, I shot and killed one of them, and told I do not like talking, and now, one after another, we found members of Vice Lords with Women who were Drugged and we killed them all, Gabby and Lil Feather used their kits and revived some, while the others overdosed, Bailey's sisters being 2 of them, and Blackwood's sister too, purposefully even Gabby's staff members who were reported missing and now, Gabby came up with a story of a broke-in and tracked the attackers down, and given her clean record she won't be suspected, we killed everyone and walked out, the main attacker died losing blood and in pain, and we took one of them, Jones Brothers to our house, and I don't like Pornography at all, and the way and we killed them all, and we asked him, turns out he was their 5th brother and we just killed him down too, Jamal Jones is also dead, and 6th brother Tyrone William Jones too, they tried killing down everyone too and with that, Jones Parents got killed by Black Dragons only and their uncles and aunts too.

With there, we began a journey downtown, and began eating around, when the Vendor, another 18 member got shot down and killed down by Jones Brothers.

And we began looking around and a shootout happened there, and the enemies who are alive are –

Franklin Jones
Xavier Jones
Brendon Janes
Kabil Rodriguez
Patley Lopez
Kyomi San

And now, we had Angel, Sniffer, Blue, Red Wolf in there and Red Wolf rescued people down to safety and began working on our way up, and yeah I was watching Being the Elite or BTE YouTube Channel ran by Kenny Omega aka the Cleaner, Matt and Nick Jackson, Adam Page aka Hangman, American Nightmare aka Cody Rhodes, Adam Cole and many more, like imagine Kota Ibushi and Demetrius Johnson aka Mighty Mouse officially joining in, Mighty Mouse wants Sammy Guevera down, maybe Johnson would be a Heel type character, I mean imagine Adam Copeland aka Edge, Chris Jericho aka Ocho, Kenny Omega aka the Cleaner and Christian Cage aka the Father Figure forming a group called the Canadian Elite and Edge and Cage winning Tag Team Gold, Jericho winning International and Omega becoming World Champion and going back to New Japan, crazy ending, and props to Sting aka Steven Borden for retiring at 65 years old.

16x World Champion (WCW, WWE and Jim Crocket Promotions maybe) Rick Flair aka the nature boy coming to All Elite Wrestling and being with Sting and Darby Allen, Nick Wayne is a dickhead, 18 year old, having a high paying job, he doesn't need a father figure, and if he wanted a father figure, Sting is there he is way better a father figure in my opinion.

Buddy Wayne passed away years ago, he will be proud, maybe Wayne disowning his mother is scripted, it is bad and damages family values, Christian Cage should realize Luchasourus & Nick Wayne would turn on him the same way he turned on Jungle Boy Jack Perry, Adam Copeland aka Edge was there for him, I would never make those comments anyways Sting is a Chad and he should have retired 14 years ago but anyways, he can have his world title shot against MJF.

AEW Twisted Family –

1. Nick Wayne – Kid
2. Darby Allen – Cousin
3. Christian Cage – Stepfather
4. Luchasourus – Criminal Stepuncle
5. Adam Copeland – Nice Uncle
6. Beth Pheonix – Nice Auntie
7. Sting – Grandfather who wants to end the drama and reunite the family
8. Jack Perry – Estranged Brother
9. Kenny Omega – 2nd Uncle, Distant Relative
10. Chris Jericho – 3rd Uncle, Distant Relative
11. Tonny Khan – Family Lawyer
12. MJF – Model Brother

Sting is like Batman and there is no denying about that, Sting will retire at 65 or maybe TNA/WWE Return and do something, he has won WCW, TNA and Jim Crocket Promotions World Heavyweights Championship as well as many Mid-Carders and Tag Team Championship, many even think he is the father of Darby Allen, this isnt true, Sting is a fan and is impressed and began training Allen to be an even wrestler and that is something positive about him there too.

CM Punk return to MMA and TNA Debut sounds fun too, like TNA is growing bigger soon enough, they need young stars like Darby Allen, Nick Wayne, Jack Perry and MJF, and they need the AJ Styles commitment from them all, Styles has a 20 year association with TNA being their Television/King of the Mountain/Global/Legends Champion, X-Division Champion, Tag Team Champion with various partners and World Heavyweights Champion too.

And we killed Tigres Members and got help from The Yakuza who executed them all one by one with Native Mob and we partied there only, I woke up next to a *pretty Native American girl.*

Season 4, Episodes 8 – 10, Killing Time –

And now, Whittier is a dream city, less then 300 people, either White, Red American, Hispanic or Asian, like one building to store them all, sounds peaceful, Los Angeles is love but crime is getting heavy, like we don't kill people like the MS and Latin Kings and now, we began looking around to drop them all, Edge and Beth Phoenix are a cute couple according to Gabby, Edge did wrong to Matt Hardy by sleeping with Lita aka Amy Dumas, like Matt Hardy lost both his girlfriend and best friend, Edge was divorced for that, he had 2 ex-wives one being the sister of Val Venis and 2nd not on good terms for sure, and Edge was wrong, being his fan, I must admit, Kevin Croom aka Crash did a similar thing to Tim Elliot, winner of The Ultimate Fighter Season 24, Elliot found his wife and best friend in an affair, his wife is UFC Bantamweight Gina Mazano and UFC Lightweight and BKFC Lightweight Kevin Croom aka Crash but Tim Elliot will get a better girl maybe he should date MMA Fighters in Bellator or One, maybe Professional Wrestlers or Martial

Artists, I am happy that Elliot or Tim Elliot is doing okay.

Imagine Tim Elliot, Jeff Hardy and Matt Hardy attacking Edge, Christian Cage and Kevin Croom in a 3 vs 3 Hardcore Bar Brawl, Matt would have killed both Lita and Edge, Lita was wrong too in many ways, love is sensitive and cheating or gold digging hurts people, imagine finding out your girlfriend loves you and cares but all your friends want that money not you, or the other way around, both of them hurt not going to lie with you here, and a large bust had happened and we needed to catch up and now, Fresno Bulldogs attempted to rape the sister of Blackwood, she and her boyfriend and their Golden Labrador Retriever escaped Fresno Bulldogs when of course a Red Feather MC Member Harley with many more took the dog and the couple into their van, Bulldogs attempted to molest Harley's daughter, Harley has many biological and adopted children, Harley killed all 6 of them, like he brought in their friends and using their tools killed all of them, and now, Fresno Bulldogs greenlighted Blackwood's sister and we decided to make 18 Street, Yakuza and Russians go to War with them, this is an offense to it, and now, the sister mentioned to Blackwood, the Fresno Bulldog is spotted in LA and we went there, bringing a golden Labrador and he attacked us, we kidnapped and brought him to our warehouse and beat the crap out of him, Fresno Bulldogs killed many innocent people for having a Labrador or Pitbull, Bulldogs should learn some manners too, and now, we killed him after an interrogation, we got to other Fresno Bulldogs and LAPD Raided them, and arrested all of them down too, and now, we gained a lot of money, buying houses and businesses, EME got their taxes too, and now with that, we started our own shops and all, and atop that, we still were looking for people who survived down.

Franklin Jones
Xavier Jones
Brendon Janes
Kabil Rodriguez
Patley Lopez
Kyomi San

Crew members –

Crew Members –
Leticia 'Lil Feather' Johnson
Michael 'Bailey' Perry
Jack Rollins 'Red Wolf'
Jesse 'Taylor' Calsada
Jose 'Sniffer' Daniels
Angel 'Blue' Lopez
Jey 'Joker' Raul Martinez
Tom 'Tommy-San' Soto
Arman Ivanov 'Neville'
David Lopez 'Bullet'
Gabriella 'Gabby' Reyes
Leticia 'Lil Feather/Letty' Johnson
Breonna Lopez 'Typhoon'
Christopher Guzman 'Skipper'
Demetrius Goldstien 'Dementus'
James Maxwell 'Ashton'

And now, we decided to go head hunting, killing members of Latin Kings and Queens Nation one by one and now, LK and FB are down, they don't have leadership, agendas, allies or enemies, they are wild people and hated by everyone in Fresno, no gang is as hated as Fresno Bulldogs or Tiny Rascalz Gangsters, most gangsters have respect there too like not attacking anyone and Bulldogs man, stealing another man's dog because he had a Labrador to kill the dog, rapes of so many women and children, drug dealing rings, attacking their own friends, attacking and killing Police Officers who were minding their business, they are unlikeable at all aspects now, and with that, we got the last of them and now, and we got a call from Black Dragons.

Black Dragons –
Chan Chong
Zhang Li Chong
Zee Ling Chong
Xiang Chong
Asure13 –
Scally Calsada
Acalan Pineda
Javier Lopez
Atzi Soto

And now, we got them all in there, and began watching Saturday Night Live or SNL Show and began laughing together and having a good time, when Bullets came in flying, Atzi and Javier got shot and killed, and Scally took a bullet too, and now, the outside voice claimed to have killed their families, and now, heating my advice they sent them all away, Javier and Atzi mentioned their grandmothers returned, maybe they were the first kill, it was Jones Family aka Vice Lords, and Bailey, Lil Feather, Blackwood, Red Wolf and Sniffer began sniping their gunman out, as two grandmothers or old ladies laid down in puddles of blood on the door of my house and now, Blue fired a Machine Gun, and wounding one of the brother, Jack sniped the tires and now, Scally phone popped up, and it mentioned pictures of his own dead family and now, more gun shots came in, and The Black Dragons mentioned how a member of MS killed their sisters and brothers in law as well as mother, their father died many years ago, he sold drugs and killed people too.

And now, Zee got shot and killed too, and now with Dragons and Azure 13, and we started a shootout, the LAPD and Vice Lords, sniping down everyone, including the LAPD Officers who bribed us down, we killed everyone down, in a shootout and went down, it was the final shootout happening in here and now, I went down, we cleaned the room too, Gabby began cleaning the room as well, Tigres and Latin Kings as well as Bulldogs joined the collision and attacked SWAT, LAPD, OCSD & CRASH Teams and now, Ultra-Violent Shootouts and I made the families vacate, a family dog got stuck and Jack Rollins took him to his house and killed

3 LAPD Officers, and Blue saved his life, killing the 4th Cop, and they had no Body Cameras too, and now, I spotted the snipers Brendon Jones and Xavier Jones, and we sniped down their 2 snipers and spotted the building, Irish Mob and Armenians killed both brothers and their accomplice down for us, and now, Aryan Brotherhood Members got jumped when Greek Mob Nikos joined them and attacked and killed some Vice Lords Members down too, and now, the Vice Lords got killed, all of them are dead now, a Mayhem Shootout happened, everyone wore a mask to avoid identification and I got the Peckerwoods (Aryans, Irish, Greek and Armenians) to lay low in Texas for a while if they can, and now Kyomi was running around when Tommy-San killed him down and avenged his friends, Dante his uncle lead The Yakuza into the Warzone too, and Tigres and Officers killed each other too.

James Family was killed in a Car Crash by Blue and Sniffer, and he wants revenge, and last second he found out it was MS-13 and now, James died due to wounds of his own, his Native American friend got shot in the head twice and the Chinese Cop was stabbed by Kabil and Patley, the remaining cop, killed Kabil and Patley and another member Steve stabbed him down too, and with there, a lot of blood was spilled down, and I spotted Patley and Steve, shooting Steve down and Patley escaped, Kabil tripped me down and punched me, I took him into a triangle and Gabby shot and killed him down there only.

EME Members got shot down by Fresno Bulldogs and CRASH Teams and now another shootout happened, EME Mercenaries also clashed with Tigres Cartel Members and now, all of Los Angeles was Loose, all hells broke loose as you can say, and now, with that Ashton helped me kill down Patley and Steve too, Dementus was saving wounded members and innocent bystanders down too, and now, with that there, the misunderstanding was cleared down and all bribers dead and now with that, we lost many friends too, Kyomi with Patley, Kabil, Xavier and Bredon are dead, Franklin survived and killed more people, and now, we chased him and his goons outside LA, and now, in a Motel Room, and we entered, and one by one, killed many Bounty Hunters, Bodyguards, Snipers and whatnot, and we reached to Franklin Jones, and he had many of his own goons, we took over the turf down, and sent in Surenos, they killed Black Families, under EME orders, no attention and we killed them all like one by one, and now Tommy-San followed Filthy Frank aka Joji, Afterthoughts with Benee was a great song btw and now, we began cleaning up the mess and funerals for dead friends like Scally, Atzi, Javier, Zee and Xiang, who died in a Car Crash today only and now, Black Dragons and Azure13 voted out of the drug trade too.

And now, we formed a community event and began working on various events together, the LAPD and Other Teams left us finally and now, we began finishing our own projects, Franklin Jones is still out there, he struck again, my son, killed him, attempted, dog mauling.

My Dogs bit Franklin Jones to death as I shot his hands down and beat him to death with it, and now I was so proud of them, Neville too helped us, we hid the guns, they were licensed down and LAPD Officers got rid of the body and left my sons and Neville Sons as well the dogs a treat, all of them at my house and we began living happily ever after, many years later, my kids went to colleges and started working down, Red Wolf moved to Canada with his family and now Gabby died too, and I am having Heart Issues, Blue died from Heart Attack too, and Sniffer died by Drowning, Letty and Bailley are riding with their biker clubs, reunited with their families and shifted to Arizona's best hospitals too.

I have a limited time, and now I end the story, and now Neville has my journal and I passed away, I told my children to not cry, Uncle Dante died peacefully too, and now, the story ends, in another life, I will see you all later.

Thank you for reading Bloodbath, a promised sequel will be coming soon enough and now story of David Lopez aka Bullet has come to an end, and we will be covering a story on their infamous archrivals, Mara Salvatrucha 13 aka MS-13, Assassins Crew in Texas, Bank Robbers Crew in New York, followed by Anton Ivanov – Bulgarian Spy and Contract Killer among more stories, and my answer to Artemis Fowl, Harry Potter & Percy Jackson is also coming soon enough.

And now, David joined his wife and friends and passed away later, his crew disbanded and began their own businesses and the aftermath –

1. *Blue is living a life with his children, married and now living in Bulgarian City of Sofia, where he is the only immigrant of his own area, joining Gypsy Delinquents and working his own scores too.*

2. *Sniffer is also happily married too, and he has shifted to his mother's village, his younger brothers and sisters are now in colleges and offices in Texas, Arizona, Alberta, London and Dublin*

3. *Lil Feather/Letty and Bailey are in Biker Clubs, they formed their own Biker Clubs or Motorcycle Clubs and now ride across The United States, they have their own children and they are born to fight and ride or die energy*

4. *Tommy-San got married to a Dominican who passed away, he later married a Korean and lived happily ever after, he never abused his own children and lived happily with them as well*

5. *Red Wolf aka Jack Rollins continued Submission Grappling, Professional Wrestling and Backpacking now, his children grew up and shifted to Germany with his wife, his dogs got to his father and mother, where Jack lives, he isnt separated or divorced but has a long-distance marriage going on, often visiting his children in Berlin and Munich*

6. *The Yakuza and The Council began owning Nightclubs, Restaurants, Logistics Business and many more, exiting Mercenary Business as well*

7. *Neville shifted to New Jersey and later on Ohio, continuing his life in peace, adopting Hinduism and Buddhism with Catholicism and living a peaceful life, he is now a Vegetarianism*

8. *Asthon is now living his life working in an airport as a security guard, got a flying license and is now a pilot too, flying and with his children especially his son Jason only*

9. *Dementus is now a Video Game Streamer and Councilor for Frustrated Youth like Incels, Angry Skinheads, Communists, Activists, Criminals and Many More, helping people from suicide as well, using his money and funding cancer and many more diseases down*

10. *Black Dragons and Azure13 are now inactive, no drug bust has ever happened, many of them are now free of drugs and illegal activities now.*

And now Russians moved back to Miami, Irish moved into San Bernadino, Armenians are in Arizona, Aryan Brotherhood Chapter Members are living life away from Prison Politics and Kkangpae are living a life, often sporting and organizing down charities and more.

And in another part of Los Angeles, another 18th Street Gang Branch began rising for power and forming their own alliances and now a new player emerged named Rocky or Rosario Rodruguez – Navarro.

The End.

About the Author

Tribhuvan Singh Shekhawat came up with Creative Ideas long ago and never had the courage of implementation, but now in college, he has decided to become what he was destined to be, and he brought to us Yuri Ivanov, an MMA Story in here

About the Publisher

Tribhuvan Singh Shekhawat is the one behind this new book, a product of Manipal University Jaipur and St Xaviers School Jaipur, he is a fan of Professional Wrestling, Mixed Martial Arts and Submission Grappling.

Tribhuvan came up with the story ideas being an imagining person and as claimed, being stuck in fantasy land, after graduating from Xavier's, he decided to become an author while getting a degree in Computer Application, searching colleges and taking a break, using chat gpt discovered Drafts2digital and finally all the stories and hard work came to light, and Shekhawat's career had a start